TO T

Accidental
Arrangements

Alexandra Warren

Thank you for _all_
your support!

Alexandra Warren

Jules

"I swear I have the fakest best friend in the world."

I sealed the last box I was responsible for packing before stacking it on top of the others that lined the wall, all waiting to be picked up the next day. I still couldn't believe my best friend and roommate of the past four years was ditching me to go live the dream, leaving me to find someone new to girl talk with, to get wine drunk on a Tuesday with, not to mention the extra rent I'd paying until I could find someone to fill her room.

But of course that wasn't Elizabeth's concern when she said, "Jules, will you stop it? I mean, you act like I'm just moving away for the hell of it. There's a great job and an incredible man waiting for me on the other side of the country. I'd be a fool not to go."

While I knew she was right, I still rolled my eyes as I muttered, "Sisterhood... what a joke..."

"Jules!"

"*What*? Just because Marcus is the sweetest guy ever *and* you have a six-figure check with your name on it waiting to be cashed doesn't mean I have to be happy about it," I told her as I plopped down on the couch she was thankfully leaving me and refilled my glass of wine with the last bottle we'd be sharing, though it wasn't exactly a share situation considering I had pretty much drank it all by myself.

Elizabeth settled in next to me, turning my way to say, "Well you *should* be happy about it. A win for me is a win for us, Jules."

I quickly finished my sip of wine just so I could smack my teeth when I replied, "Not when the win means me having to find a new roommate."

She finally joined in on the wine, only to bypass the glass and take a swig straight from the bottle. "Who knows? You may find a new best friend to replace me."

"I mean, you're fake as fuck. I probably *should* replace you."

"Jules! Shut up," she screeched as she shoved me in the arm, laughing as she sat the bottle down on the coffee table she was leaving as well. Then she stood up and added, "Anyway, the moving company will be here first thing in the morning to get these so make sure your ass is awake. I need to get to the airport before I miss my flight."

I joined her, standing up with my wine glass in my hand when I asked, "Why are you taking an Uber anyway? You know I would've given you a ride, Liz."

"Yeah, and detoured to that slow ass Taco Bell on purpose just to make me miss my flight," she replied so correctly that it almost annoyed me. But in reality, it only made me a little sadder as I thought about how many of our fondest memories together consisted of drunken drive-thru nights at Taco Bell. And how many more we'd be missing out on now that she was leaving me.

I leaned against the arm of the couch, propping my leg up as I pouted, "Is it really that bad that I want you to miss your flight? So you can stay another night?"

Elizabeth sighed as she grabbed the two suitcases she was taking with her while the rest of her clothes would be getting shipped. "Awww, girl. Don't do this to me right now. The last thing I need is Marcus picking me up from the airport with makeup running down my face."

"I'm gonna miss you though," I whined, knowing *I'd* be the one with makeup running down my face the second she left.

And she didn't make it any better when she pulled

me into a hug and said, "I'll miss you too, Jules. But I'll be back to visit you. And you can come see me. And we can always FaceTime or whatever, though I'm sure you'll be keeping plenty busy."

"Yeah, busy finding a roommate who isn't a disgusting serial killer. You know, stab somebody in the gut *and* leave the bloody knife in the sink like their mama didn't raise them right."

Elizabeth burst with laughter, brushing me off before she grabbed her suitcases and headed to the door. "Girl, shut up. I'm sure you'll find someone completely normal in no time."

"Nobody like you though."

"Awww Juliaaaa," she gushed, forcing me to roll my eyes as I yanked the door open for her.

"*Ugh*, don't do that. I paid way too much to get rid of that dreadful name to ever be called it again."

It wasn't that I hated the name Julia, I just hated it for me. It didn't fit my vibe, my energy, not to mention my deceased mother shared the same name, for whatever reason thinking it was cool to make me her junior.

"I'm sorry. *Jules*," Elizabeth said with extra inflection to please me.

And I gave her a short nod as I replied, "Thank you. Now get out of here before I start crying."

This time, it was Elizabeth rolling her eyes as she stepped out of the doorway. "Jules, you are *not* going to cry," she said before she turned around to actually see my face and..., "*Oh my God*. You really *are* going to cry! I don't think I've ever seen you cry before."

I swiped at the first tear that had managed to slip as I told her, "Yes you have. Remember that time I stubbed my toe on the edge of the bed. And when I hit my knee on the coffee table that one day playing drunk charades. And when I broke up with Charlie. *Whew*, that was

—

3

ugly."

Elizabeth only laughed when she said, "Bitch, those were tears of joy. You were so happy to be single again."

"They were still tears!" I defended before quickly adding, "But anyway, you make sure you shoot me a text when you're getting ready to board the plane, and when you land, and right after Marcus fucks your weave up for the first time in your new place together."

She giggled again. "You know I will, Jules. I love you, girl," she said, dropping her bags to pull me into another, tighter hug.

I tried my best not to spill my wine as I squeezed her just as tight before releasing to tell her, "I love you too, Liz. Now get going for real. I don't want you to see me like this. It's about to go down like the Titanic. *Oh my God*. Who am I supposed to watch all three hours and fifteen minutes of *Titanic* with now?!"

By the time I finished my question, Elizabeth was already halfway down the hall as she tossed over her shoulder, "Just FaceTime me, boo. We can watch it together like old times."

"I'm holding you to that!" I shouted after her before she disappeared around the corner. And for a second I just stood there as if she was going to reappear with a change of plans. But once I heard the heavy steel door close behind her, I knew everything was real.

Now what?

I slipped back into our… *my* apartment, shutting the door behind me as I took a good look at the space. There was still a solid six months left on the lease and my bartending job certainly wouldn't be enough to cover both halves of the rent no matter how much I would've loved to have the whole place to myself, mainly for the opportunity to be able to walk around naked.

At least you'll be able to until you find someone to

4

take Liz's place.

I finished off my glass of wine, dropping it off in the kitchen before I plopped back down on the couch to grab my laptop. It only took a simple Google search for me to figure out how common the "need-a-roommate" thing was. In fact, there were at least a dozen different sites I could use to find one.

"Let's try this one," I coached to myself as I clicked the first link, filling out the short questionnaire that reminded me of an online dating site.

"Are you a drinker? *Definitely.* Are you a smoker? Eh… *experimentally.* Do you have pets? *Only when I need a pedicure really badly.* Do you have a gender preference? *No. As long as they pay their share of the rent on time and don't eat people…*"

In no time at all, I was pressing submit on my information which guaranteed I'd be matched with the perfect roommate within a week. And while the claim of *perfect* seemed impossible, I knew next month's rent was due way too soon to call them a liar now.

"Yo, Jules! They're waiting for a restock in VIP three!"

I peeked up and rolled my eyes at Kelvin, my boss, as I balanced on my stilettos while I finished filling the latest order of drinks for one of the waitresses. It wasn't that I had an actual attitude with Kelvin. In all honesty, him and his brother Maxwell were some of the easiest people to work for, part of the reason why I loved my job at *The Max* so much. But I *did* have an attitude with

5

being responsible for a VIP section I had no interest in tending to.

Most girls at *The Max* loved working VIP because it usually warranted better tips, not to mention being able to rub shoulders with some of the stars. But to me, the people who frequented VIP were some of the most annoying customers. They usually weren't even in the lounge to have fun; only to show off for each other and their various social media accounts. And even though my visit was only going to last long enough to change out the old bottles for new ones, I was already dreading it as I made my way over.

I tried to be as discreet as possible when I slipped through the crowd of people overflowing from the section. But apparently I hadn't been slick enough once I heard someone call out to me, "Yo, pour me another drink. Bet?"

"Not my job. Ask your waitress," I replied sternly, keeping my eyes focused on the table as I reorganized things to make room for the new bottles.

But of course, my obvious disinterest didn't stop the guy from adding, "You know you're too pretty to have such a stank ass attitude, right?"

I shrugged, hardly bothered as I told him, "My beauty and my attitude have nothing to do with this."

"Yeah, but your tip does," he insisted in only a way a lame could as if the sudden reminder of his money would somehow change my stance.

In fact, his comment only made me smirk as I finally peeked up to meet his eyes. Even under the brim of his hat in the mostly darkened lounge, I could tell they were a perfect shade of brown, hooded with unfairly long eyelashes that I knew I could only achieve with the temporary extensions I planned on getting with my next check.

—

6

So of course that fact made me have even more of an attitude when I finally replied, "Actually, I'm not technically working your section so… *nah*. Nice try though."

"What's your name, mean ass?" he asked as he leaned into the table to pour himself the drink he had just now realized I was serious about not making for him.

I was already busy grabbing the emptied bottles as I told him, "My name is Mean Ass. Just like you said. How'd you know? You must be a psychic."

"Sarcastic too, huh?" he asked with a grin, showing off every last one of his pearly whites.

But before I could get a little lost in his smile, I heard Hope shout from behind me, "*Jules! We need you back at the bar ASAP.*"

Somehow the guy's smile managed to get even fuller as he said my name with extra, completely unnecessary inflection. "*Jules*. That's your name. Mean Ass Jules. It's a pleasure to meet you, pretty girl."

I quickly corrected him, "We're not meeting. I'm just dropping these off so you can show your cornball ass homeboys and the girls who are willing to use them to get to you how much money you have."

I could tell he was truly offended as he snapped his head back to say, "*Damn*. I can't have a good time with my friends without you thinkin' I'm on that?"

Sure, it was probably a little unfair for me to jump to conclusions. But that certainly wasn't enough to stop me from firing back, "You really shouldn't care what I think. Enjoy your night."

"*But I didn't even…*"

I didn't stick around long enough to hear the end of his sentence, slipping through the crowd to get back to the bar where I belonged. And it didn't take long for me to fall back into my groove, going back and forth

7

between fulfilling orders for the waitresses and tending to the patrons at the bar top.

When things finally slowed down a bit, I couldn't help myself in peeking back over to VIP just to see if the stranger was still doing exactly what I expected him to be; showing off for his audience of hanger-on's. But he wasn't, instead sitting on one of the couches looking at the tab Hope must've recently delivered to his section now that the night was winding down.

He looked… *troubled* - worried, even - as he flipped through his wallet before pulling out two different credit cards to shove into the check holder.

"Uh oh… ol' boy must've went over budget…" I thought to myself with a laugh as I wiped down the bar top.

It wasn't unusual for people to go all out for their audience and be stuck with some unruly bill they couldn't afford at the end of the night. And it honestly wasn't fair; people posing as friends just to drink for free and sneak out before the check showed up.

But then again, his problems were none of my business.

He had clearly made his bed, and now it was time for him to lay in it.

Levi

"What the fuck?"

I approached the door of my apartment and found a crowd of people carrying boxes of my belongings out as if I had called them to do so myself. But since that was far from the case, I was all but ready to go off until I saw my agent, fresh suit and all, standing near the doorway.

"Yo, Damien. What the fuck is going on?"

Damien had the nerve to offer me some half-hearted ass smile as he peeked up from his phone to say, "Sorry, man. I tried to warn you, but you haven't been picking up the phone."

"Yeah, cause I've been busy bustin' my ass in the gym trying to get back on the court next season," I fired back as if he didn't already know it as the truth.

In fact, Damien knew all of my moves, from my morning ritual to the balance in my checking account after a crazy night out with the homies. There hadn't been a secret between us until now where he had a whole ass moving company packing my shit. And I could tell things were really as bad as they looked when he sighed before he said, "Levi, I know how bad you want to get back in the league, but I already explained how slim the chances were months ago."

"You said slim. Not non-existent," I reminded him as I dropped my duffle bag on the floor, quickly picking it back up once I saw one of the movers reach for it.

"Well unfortunately, time is proving otherwise," he replied as he turned to walk away, though I quickly caught him by the arm to stop him.

"But this is my crib, man. Where are they taking

my shit? Where am I supposed to go?" I asked in a panic, already thinking about how much of it I could fit in my car.

Most of it was shit I really didn't need, had just splurged on when I got my first real check from the league right before my first knee injury. But after spending three quarters of the year rehabbing only to tear the ACL in my other knee during the first game of the preseason, I had been demoted to the D-League which eventually panned out to be no league at all once they decided not to resign me, claiming I was too much of a liability.

"Look. I did more than my due diligence as your agent and set you up with a storage unit until you can get back on your feet. But as for a roof over your head, I suggest you start looking at extended-stay rates around here," he finally replied dismissively as he turned to walk away once more.

But again, I caught him by the arm to ask, "*Extended-stay rates*? Come on, man. You know my pockets. I would've paid the rent on this bitch if I had that kind of money."

"You sure found that kind of money to go out last night."

I shrugged as I told him, "Yeah, and I'll be making payments on my credit card for the rest of the year because of it."

"Well maybe you should be looking for employment at the extended-stay instead," he offered in another attempt to dismiss me.

"Yo, fuck you, man. How about that?" I asked, though my anger really wasn't at him. I mean, I should've been mad at myself for getting in this predicament in the first place. But going from no money at all to more money than I knew what to do with had turned out to be way more of a curse than a gift.

Growing up, nobody around me really had money so none of us learned what to do with it when we actually got it. And it certainly didn't help that people were coming out of every corner once I got on, expecting me to save the whole hood with my miniscule rookie contract. Sure I had gotten some people the help they needed, had gotten a couple bills up to date for a few others. But now that I was out of the league with no money to my name, it was like everybody had somehow managed to disappear.

Well, everybody except for Damien as he easily brushed off my insult to say, "That's not going to change your situation. Now I might be able to get your ungrateful ass a job down at the car dealership with my brother to hold you over, but that's the best I can do."

"*At the dealership*? What I look like selling cars? I'm fuckin' Levi Graham, man."

"Correction. You *used* to be Levi Graham. Now you're just another has-been athlete who got plagued by injuries before their talent could actually be seen. Is it unfortunate? *Yes*. But that's the reality of the situation. I told you when I first signed you to the agency that this professional sports world is brutal. You have to eat or get ate. And *you*… you got devoured."

"So now what? I'm supposed to go sell cars and sleep in the back room until I make enough for a new spot to lay my head? How am I supposed to focus on getting back on the court when I can't even get a good night's rest?"

Damien only sighed, his lips in a tight line when he said, "I'm sorry, Levi. But I've already done all I can do for you right now."

"Come on, man. Just loan me a couple hundred. I'll pay you back as soon as I make it."

While I wasn't sure how I was going to actually make it back, or when I was going to make it back, I knew getting money from Damien was the only way I'd be able to keep my ass from being homeless.

From the NBA to fuckin' homeless in a matter of a couple years.

What a life.

I watched as Damien pulled his checkbook from the inside pocket of his suit jacket, opening it to drop a few scribbles with his signature black ink pen before ripping it off and handing it to me. "Here's $1500. That should be enough to cover two months' worth of rent."

"*$1500 for two months?* This place costs double that for one!"

"Well it sounds to me like you're going to have to lower your standards drastically. Hell, maybe you can even get a roommate. But the life of luxury is over, Levi. It's time to get back to reality."

He offered me a little sympathetic pat on the shoulder just as his phone began to ring, surely with the client who'd be replacing me on his roster. And while I couldn't blame him for moving on, as I watched him excuse himself to take the call, it only infuriated me to the point of screaming, "This is some bullshit!"

And as if the devil was really trying to stunt on me, I heard a little voice behind me ask, "Excuse me? You think I can… get a selfie with you? Maybe an autograph or somethin'? Not every day I get to help evict an ex-NBA player."

"How about I autograph my foot and shove it up your ass?" I threatened though I knew the little dude was no match.

But to my surprise, he didn't back down, instead suggesting, "As long as I get to keep the shoe."

"*Unbelievable.*"

&

"I don't know, Levi. I mean, a roommate might not be the worst idea in the world. At least until you can get back on your own feet."

There was no use in hiding my frustrations as I plopped down on the couch in my sister Lily's two-bedroom apartment while she rocked her youngest to sleep. It was the same apartment building we had grown up in as kids, though it was clear Lily had outgrown the space as the living room was currently doubling as a playroom for her seven-year-old twins and a resting spot for the almost two-year-old in her arms.

"You only say that because you have a house full of roommates. *Lifemates.* And they don't even pay any rent," I teased as she passed the little one to me to give her arms a break.

Then she rolled her eyes as she adjusted Anastasia's head while insisting, "You know I would take you in if I had the room."

"And you know your crib is far from a long term option regardless, sis. Can't even take a nap around here without somebody checking my pockets, or crawling on my head, or asking if I have games on my phone."

"Hey! That's your nephews and niece you're talking about," Lily said with a laugh as she straightened up the toys scattered amongst the living room floor.

"Yeah, the niece and nephews I'm glad I put money away for before all of this shit went down. They're lucky none of us can touch it until they turn eighteen," I admitted as I watched baby girl's eyes flutter closed. But the second I thought I was in the clear, they

—

cracked right back open.

Damnit.

"Well you know they appreciate you, Uncle Levi."

"Yeah they better," I replied as I watched Anastasia's eyes slowly drift closed once again.

But this time, they actually stayed closed, even when her mother shouted, "Anyway! I know your long ass isn't gonna survive too many days on this couch, so what are you going to do?"

"I guess I'll... *I don't know.* What should I do?"

Lily and Damien had both given me some reasonable options, but none of it sounded like anything I actually wanted to do. Then again, I didn't really have much of a choice. And it was obvious Lily felt the same way when she finally answered, "Swallow your pride and find something around here for a reasonable price. You know the landlord loves your game. I'm sure he'll be willing to cut you a deal."

"Yeah, but he's a crook just like the rest of these niggas. You know how they are. Probably would be using his master key to snoop all up and through my shit, not to mention I'd practically be walking around here with a target on my back. I'm sorry I couldn't get you out of here before I fucked shit up, Lily."

While I had taken care of a lot of people while I was on, my ultimate goal had always been to get my sister and her kids out of the hood. But somehow, the fast life had managed to chew me up and spit me out long before I could actually make it happen. And while that was easily at the top of my list of regrets, Lily didn't exactly agree when she brushed off my apology to say, "I am not your responsibility, Levi. Never have been and I never will be. I'm doing what I have to do just like everybody else in this world. And now it's your turn to do the same."

"How much does rent cost around here anyway?" I

asked, more out of curiosity than anything.

Lily shrugged, finally joining me on the couch when she answered, "About a thousand a month once you include utilities."

"*A thousand a month for this piece of shit*? No offense, sis. But that's outrageous."

"Let's not forget you were also raised in this piece of shit."

"And you see how I turned out," I muttered, once again faced with the reality of the situation I had managed to get myself in.

But my personal pity party did nothing to stop Lily from firing back, "Get over yourself, Levi. You fucked up your money and now your back is against the wall. I know basketball has sheltered you from this thing called life for a long time, but it's time to wake up from that dream. It's time to start a new chapter."

She was right.

Basketball had afforded me a number of opportunities beyond just a paycheck; from being a standout in high school which meant teachers wouldn't dare give me a bad grade just to make sure I kept my eligibility to play, to college where I had people lined up wanting to write my papers for me, and even now where I could still walk into plenty of the local restaurants and eat for free. While I hadn't thought much of it at the time - *expected it in fact* - there was certainly a lot I hadn't learned along the way.

"You really think I can find a little roommate or whatever? I don't even know where to start, where to look…"

Lily smacked her teeth in annoyance. "My God, don't you have any life skills? Or did you leave them all in the halls of that bougie ass college you went to?"

"Duke is one of the top basketball programs in the nation," I defended, though it was hardly any use once I heard her spot on response.

"Duke also coddled you to the point where you forgot where you came from. And let's not even get on the league. I mean, what's the point of having all of that money just for them to give you everything for free?"

"For me to trick it off obviously," I muttered as my eyes fell on Anastasia who was still sound asleep.

"Enough of the self-sabotaging, Levi. Go grab the laptop from the twins and I'll... help you get this figured out," Lily said as she stuck her hands out for her daughter.

I was slow to hand her over, making sure I didn't wake her as I deposited her onto her mom's lap. And then I took the short trip down the hallway to the twins' room, only to find them laying on their bellies face deep in the computer.

"Aye, knuckleheads. Me and your moms need the computer for a minute."

"But we watchin' Netflix!" the youngest by three minutes shouted, easy to identify by the short dreads he wore compared to his brother who rocked a curly taper fade like me.

"This is important, Andre," I told him as he looked to his big brother for confirmation of what to do.

And while Andre was a little easier to persuade, Adrian had no problem firing back, "So is Netflix!"

"Adrian... don't make me body slam you. Hand it over."

They both grunted as they unplugged the charger cord before handing the computer to me with a pair of matching attitudes that I found way too amusing to leave as is. So instead, I dug in my pocket and pulled out a few stray dollar bills from the night before and stuck it out to them.

"Here. Run across the street and grab a snack or

somethin'. We'll be done by the time ya'll get back."

I fully expected them both to light up and snatch the money from my hand. But to my surprise, they both just… looked at it, forcing to me insist, "Here. Take it."

Andre completely avoided my eyes while Adrian confessed, "Mama said don't ask you for no money cause you ain't got none no more."

Wait, what?

"That's what your mama said, huh?" I asked to which they both nodded in unison. "Well it can be a secret between the three of us. Deal?"

This time, my question warranted the lit up faces that I originally expected as Adrian snatched the money from my hand before handing some of it to Andre.

"Thank you, Uncle Levi!" they shouted as they slipped out of the room in front of me.

And I was right on their heels as I told them both, "You're welcome. And remember, it's a secret."

"Hold it. Where are ya'll going?" Lily asked just as the twins made it to the front door.

It was clear Adrian was working hard to hold up his end of the bargain, choosing silence as opposed to an actual response. Andre on the other hand was quick to spill, "Uncle Levi gave us some money to get some snacks from across the street."

Damn, so much for that secret.

Lily peeked up at me to confirm and I nodded as I told her, "It was a fair trade. And why did you tell the twins I was broke?"

"Because you are," she answered with a roll of her eyes before turning her attention to the twins to say, "Ya'll better come right back. Don't talk to anybody other than Mr. Johnson at the register. And hold hands when you cross the street."

"Okay!" they shouted in unison as they barged out of

the screen door.

And once they were gone, I was sure to tell Lily, "I ain't that damn broke."

But my words were obviously less than convincing as she quickly replied, "Yet here you are. Sleeping on my couch. Trying to find a place to stay until you can make enough money to get yourself out of this mess you call a life..."

"Are you gonna help me or you just gonna keep talking shit?"

"Being poor sure makes you sensitive," she stated teasingly just as I was cracking the laptop open.

And while the truth to her jokes certainly didn't put me in the best of moods, accepting it as the truth was also the first step in getting this shit figured out.

Jules

"So… how's the roommate search going? Any good prospects?"

I held my phone against my ear with my shoulder as I took a sip of my second glass of wine before I continued scrolling through the latest batch of supposed perfectly-matched inquiries in my email inbox. And while the first five emails worth of options had proved themselves to be everything but perfect, I was hopeful that day six would be the lucky day.

Though that didn't stop me from teasing my best friend when I told her, "Quit pretending like you care, Liz. You and *your* roommate are doing just fine."

"You mean, me and my *fiancé*?"

I almost dropped my phone in shock when I hopped off of the couch and asked, "Bitch, what? Shut up! Marcus proposed?!"

And I could literally hear her smile through the phone when she replied, "It was so beautiful, Jules. He had an orchestra playing in the lobby when I made it back to our building after doing a little sight-seeing. There were rose petals from the elevator leading to our front door. And when I opened it, there he was… down on one knee."

"Where did I go wrong in life?! I *mean*, that's amazing!" I shouted before quickly adding, "And the ring?"

She giggled. "The ring is gorgeous, of course. You would've thought I picked it out myself."

"Well send me a picture or something. And how am I just now finding out about this? No disrespect to Mama, but as your best friend, I definitely should've gotten the first phone call."

Again, Elizabeth only giggled. "It just happened last night, Jules. And we... spent the whole night celebrating."

"Amazing proposal, amazing ring, and amazing dick as the cherry on top? That's like the ultimate trifecta, Liz. I'm so jealous!"

While I definitely wasn't thinking about relationships, or marriages, or new life beginnings anytime soon, I was still a little envious of how quickly things had happened for Elizabeth. Though it was clear she didn't see it that way when she replied, "Jules, you are *not* jealous. You always thought Marcus was boring and lame, and I was ruining my life by moving out here with him."

"Girl, I was just saying that because I didn't want you to leave me. But now that you're already gone and engaged, I've changed my mind," I told her before I took another short sip of my wine.

And I could pretty much assume she was rolling her eyes when she said, "Whatever. All I know is you have some bachelorette party planning to do Maid of Honor."

Another jolt of excitement blasted through me as I repeated, "*Maid of Honor*? Are you serious, Liz? You really trust me with that kind of responsibility?"

"I mean, if you're up for it. I know money might be tight for you with the whole no-roommate thing, but..."

While there was definitely some truth to her statement, I quickly cut her off. "No! I'll figure out a way. I mean, we've been talking about this day since we were teenagers, right?" In fact, I could remember the exact conversations, along with the scribbles in our notebooks of our signatures featuring our new last names.

"Now don't you go gettin' all mushy on me already. We have to save the tears for the wedding, boo," she stated just as I felt them welling up in my eyes at the memories.

But I sucked them up as I sat back on the couch, the phone lodged between my ear and my shoulder as I told her, "You're right. Well let me get you off of the phone so you can get back to your man. I mean, your *fiancé*. Ahh I'm so excited for you!"

I knew the exact bashful smile my best friend was wearing even though I couldn't see her when she replied, "Thank you, Jules. And let me know if I can help with the roommate thing. I know I'm thousands of miles away now, but my internet works all the same."

I pulled the laptop back onto my lap, scrolling through the latest batch of inquiries I had already been sifting through when she called. And suddenly they all seemed like the perfect match I needed to ensure I'd be able to afford the price tag that came with being Maid of Honor.

"You worry about your wedding planning. I'll take care of this. Matter of fact, I think I just found one right now," I told her as I clicked on one of the profile matches that stood out from the rest for reasons I couldn't admit out loud.

Though Elizabeth's questioning wasn't exactly on my side when she asked, "*What*? Just that fast?"

I shrugged as if she could see me while I skimmed the information. "Yeah. I mean, everything seems normal. And it says he'll even pay two month's rent in advance."

"*He'll*? As in he? As in a guy? You're gonna have a guy for a roommate? Come on, Jules. You know better."

I instantly became defensive when I asked,

"What's wrong with that? I mean, the bedroom is clear on the other side of the unit, we'll only share the common spaces, and *hello*... two month's rent in advance. It can't get any better than that."

"Well did you at least see a picture? Make sure he

21

doesn't look like some crazy person?"

Her question prompted me to double-click his profile image to enlarge it as I assured her, "I saw the picture, and... *damn*."

"*What*? What's the matter?" she asked in a panic as I got lost in his eyes that looked strangely familiar even though they were slightly covered by the glasses he wore. His chestnut brown skin was baby's bottom smooth. But there was definitely nothing baby about his strong jawline along with the crisp layer of facial hair that framed his full lips.

"*Jules*? Jules, you still there?"

I flinched at her words, feeling caught red-handed as I quickly clicked out of the picture like it was porn. "*Huh*? Oh, nothing. Everything is fine. He's regular-degular. Not a smoker, not a drinker, not a partier, doesn't like clutter," I read out loud, finding that part of the information more than suitable for my needs.

Or maybe it was his profile picture making me a little more lenient as I heard Elizabeth ask, "So basically everything opposite of you?"

"Perfect match."

While I had never felt more sure of anything, Elizabeth wasn't nearly as convinced when she asked, "Are you sure you want to live with a guy, Jules? I mean, you know how you can get."

"How I can get? What's that supposed to mean?" I asked as I went back to his profile picture to take a better, more objective look.

But my objectivity quickly turned to sensitivity down below, even when Elizabeth said, "You know exactly what I mean."

"But he's not even like... *attractive*," I lied with ease as I imagined the perfect teeth hidden under his closed-mouth smile.

"*Jules…*"

"I mean, maybe he's cute to somebody but…"

"Jules, he's fine, isn't he?" she asked, calling my bluff in only a way she could.

But for whatever reason, I still held on tight to the last thread of my morality when I admitted, "He's not ugly. That's all."

"Girl, don't mess around and have your roommate turn into your bedroom boommate."

I couldn't help but laugh as I defended, "I can control my vagina, thank you very much. And besides, if he's looking for a roommate that means he's probably broke."

If nothing else, that fact would help me draw the line. Though Elizabeth wasn't making anything easier for me when she replied, "Yeah, just as broke as you who's also looking for a roommate. Don't be a bougie bitch."

"Anyway! I'm going to reach out to him and see if he's interested in the room," I told her as I clicked the button to respond to his inquiry.

A new wave of nerves rushed over me as I tried to come up with an appropriate message that didn't sound too desperate. But then again, this wasn't about my shallow, lustful interest. This was about his interest in the room and my interest in his half of the rent.

So I kept it simple as I typed while reading out loud, "Hello. I received your inquiry and would be more than happy to meet your needs…"

"*Meet your needs?* Oh my God, Jules. You definitely wanna fuck."

My hands went still on the keyboard as I screeched, "I do not! I just… don't know what to say."

"Just say you received the inquiry, and you'll be willing to accept his offer for the two-month advance if he's still interested in the room."

I practically typed Elizabeth's words verbatim,

quickly pressing send before my liquid courage rubbed off enough for me to back out. Then I listened in as my best friend told me about all of the dope shit she had already done in her new city, turning my nerves about my own situation into envy of hers. But the nerves quickly returned once my computer chimed signaling I had received a reply.

I double-clicked to open the message, my heart racing as I did a quick scan for the important details before I cut her off to say, "He just responded, Liz. Said he can give me the rent ASAP if he can move in this weekend."

"*This weekend*? That's like, tomorrow. Are you sure he's safe? I mean, the urgency makes him sound a little *too* desperate. Like you'd be harboring a fugitive or something."

"You have to pass a background check before you get approved for the website. And besides, he looks so innocent in his picture. All buttoned up and studious with his little glasses on. I hardly see anything going wrong," I told her as I snuck another peek, already imagining waking up to him half-dressed cooking breakfast in the mornings.

A live-in lust bucket.

How perfect.

"Well… if you feel that confident, I say go for it. What's the worst that could happen?"

The worst was happening.

Maybe not worst in the traditional sense, but worst as far as my brilliantly irresponsible idea was concerned once I did a Google search on the roommate I had already approved the morning before he was set to move-in.

Levi Graham wasn't just some random, around the way guy looking for a roommate. He wasn't some normal computer geek, or lawyer, or teacher.

He was a superstar.

Well… *former* superstar, who had obviously fallen on hard times if he couldn't afford a place of his own.

According to Google, his monthly salary was once equal to all of the money I had made in my lifespan, he had been featured on various magazine covers dating back to his high school days, and he had just recently been cut from his professional basketball team which explained his current circumstances.

Then again, it didn't.

I mean, how was it even possible for someone to blow through that kind of money in such a short period of time?

"Probably poppin' bottles in the club with associates every night," I answered to myself as I finally realized why his eyes had looked so familiar in the first place.

After looking through the Google images associated with his name, I learned the profile picture I had been infatuated with was from his one year spent at Duke which was a solid three and a half years ago. And while it may have been representative of who he was at that time, the more recent tabloid headlines certainly disagreed with that persona. Fights in the club right before the draft that almost tanked his stock - *whatever that meant* -, public disagreements in the media with his coaches that almost got him traded long before he even played a single game, along with a laundry list of petty drug charges that had gotten dropped more than likely thanks to his celebrity privilege.

I couldn't believe I had tricked myself into believing I

was actually doing the right thing by offering the room to someone who appeared to be an everyday Joe. And I was just getting ready to look into the protocol for undoing my approval when there was a knock on the door, startling me to the point of slamming my laptop shut. I moseyed over to the door, peeking through the peephole to find the bad boy himself with a duffle bag in each hand and a backpack on his back. His head was covered in a hood as he waited for me to answer. And while I considered leaving him there to wait a little longer - maybe even long enough for him to change his mind and leave - I also knew I had to accept my responsibility... or lack thereof.

So I pulled the door open, completely avoiding his eyes which was easy to do considering how much taller than me he was, as I said, "Hello. Welcome. Come on in."

He followed my instructions, stepping inside and setting his bags by the door before he pulled his hood off and extended his hand to me. "Hey. How you doin'? I'm Levi."

"Jules," I told him with a nod as I accepted his hand into mine.

It was... large, *exceptionally so*, to the point where my mind was already drifting off until he said, "I think I know you from somewhere."

I yanked my hand away, shaking my head as I told him, "No you don't. I'm a completely random stranger."

"Nah, I'm pretty sure I remember you. I remember your hair. And your lips," he replied just as he licked his own. And I'll be damned if the simple act didn't almost distract me from my original stance until I saw the stereotypical basketball player tattoo on his neck.

"The hair isn't mine and my lips literally change color every day. Sometimes twice a day," I told him as I finally closed the front door behind him before adding, "Your room is over there. You're more than welcome to use the couch and stuff out here, but I assume you have bedroom furniture coming?"

Instead of answering my question, he said, "*The Max*. You work at *The Max*, don't you?"

"Never heard of it," I replied as I attempted to change the subject once again when I continued my tour. "Since I have my own bathroom in my room, feel free to make this one your own. But that's usually the one guests use when they come over since its closest to the living room."

"My sister mentioned something about you being a bartender," he said as he peeked into the bathroom that was mostly bare since Elizabeth had taken all of the decorations with her.

And while I wasn't sure what his sister had to do with anything, I had no problem telling him, "I am a bartender."

"And I remember the girl at *The Max* said your name was Jules. Your name *is* Jules, isn't it?" he asked, right on my heels as I led us towards the kitchen.

"Must've been my doppelgänger," I answered with a shrug as I dug into the fridge before offering, "Would you like something to drink? My stuff is usually off-limits, but I'll let it slide this one time."

Again, he ignored my question to ask his own.

"Are you playing with my head on purpose?"

"Look. I needed a roommate. You needed a room. You have your space and I have mine. Now if you have any questions about the place, the area, whatever, I can help you with that. But as for my personal life? That's really none of your business," I told him firmly, serving him the same attitude he had gotten the first night I informally met him.

And it was clear he remembered that night as well as

I now did as he smiled when he replied, "Mean Ass Jules. It really *is* you. What a small world."

"Too small," I muttered as I took a sip from my bottled water.

"Hey, you ain't gotta be like that. I promise I'm not a bad person," he said with the innocence of the profile picture that had tricked me into making this dumb ass decision in the first place.

And while it was honestly even more convincing now that I was seeing it live, remembering the details of his profile allowed me to fire back, "You're not a bad person yet you *clearly* lied on your application."

His face scrunched. "What are you talking about? I didn't lie about anything."

Now my attitude could really develop as I listed, "Not a partier? Not a drinker? I saw you do both."

"Well considering you just tried to lie to my face about who you were, I'd say we're even," he countered, shutting me up with ease.

Since there was hardly any use in continuing down the combative route, I sighed before I insisted, "How about we try this again? Get off to a better start? I'm Jules."

"Levi. Levi Graham," he replied with the same smile he had given me back at *The Max*. The one I had almost gotten lost in the same way I was doing now.

Snap out of it, Jules!

"Nice to meet you," I said as I turned away, making myself busy putting away the dishes that were leftover in the dish rack.

But instead of just leaving me alone, going to his room, or at least checking out the rest of the place, he challenged, "Is it really?"

"I'm trying *really* hard to stay pleasant right now. Don't mess it up," I replied, opening the cabinet and standing on my tippytoes in an effort to put the stack of plates away without using the step stool that for whatever reason felt embarrassing to use under his watch. But my struggle didn't last long as Levi stepped in to take the plates from my hand and placed them with ease, his height giving him a clear advantage as he closed the cabinet door behind him.

"Alright, my bad. It's nice to meet you too. And I appreciate you taking me up on my offer with such short notice."

"You're welcome. Now if you don't need anything else, I'm gonna go… mind my business," I told him as I tried to escape his aura.

But he stopped me dead in my tracks when he insisted, "Actually I *do* need something else." *Oh God, here we go.* "I need to give you this money before it gets lost. *Oh*, and one of my boys is gonna be helping me move the rest of my shit in a little bit. We'll try to keep it down," he said as he handed over an envelope straight from the bank according to the logo printed on top.

I was tempted to pull out the money and count it right in front of him. But since I was trying hard at the whole, "*Don't be rude*" thing, I simply told him, "I appreciate the heads up."

"No problem, pretty girl."

While my right mind said don't do it, I couldn't help myself in challenging, "Is that what you call all of your women? *Pretty girl?*"

"Why do you assume I have a bunch of women? Or assume that you're one of them?" he countered, causing me to stumble over my words.

"I… *I mean…*"

The full smile was back as he saved me from making a fool of myself. "I'm kidding, Jules. I called you pretty girl because you *are* a pretty girl. I don't mean any harm.

Just stating an observation."

"Well… good," I told him as I crossed my arms, gnawing at my lip while I tried to figure out my next move.

And Levi only made things even more uncomfortable when he repeated, "Good."

"I'm… gonna get out of your way. Let you get all settled in. Let me know if you need anything or whatever," I said as I slipped past him and all but darted straight to my bedroom.

But I wasn't far enough to miss the amusement in his tone when he replied, "Will do."

Levi

"You could've warned me my bartender roommate was going to be a girl, Lily." - Levi

I pressed send on the text and shoved my phone in my pocket before I climbed onto the moving truck to grab one end of the mattress while my boy Wes grabbed the other. We had been moving things all afternoon and into the evening; first from the storage unit into the moving truck and then from the truck into the apartment. And while it would've been much easier to just call somebody to have it handled for me, my pockets didn't exactly speak the same language. So I was happy that Wes actually agreed to it, even though it was clear he was over it now that we were close to finished.

We squeezed the mattress through the front door, guiding it past Jules's collection of furniture and eclectic decor before placing it against the wall in the bedroom I'd be calling home for at least the next five months. Then I pulled my phone from my pocket to check for my sister's response.

"Sorry! She was the first one to respond. How's the place?" - Lily

While I should've known putting my sister in charge of finding me a crib would equate to some sort of catch, there was no denying that she had at least picked a more than decent place for me to lay my head.

"Its dope. Definitely a steal for the price." - Levi

"Yo, can a nigga get a glass of lemonade for his hard work or what?" Wes asked as he plopped down on the floor in my new room, resting on his back as he put his hands over his face in exhaustion.

"I got you, bro," I told him with a laugh as I left the room for the kitchen.

Even though Jules had the door of her bedroom closed, I could still hear her singing as she got dressed according to the smell of burnt hair permeating the air; something I'd have to get used to again in living with a woman. I opened the fridge, peeking over to the closed door once again before grabbing two of her bottles of water that I'd have to replace. Then I headed back to my room while I checked my phone for Lily's reply.

"And the roommate?" - Lily

I laughed to myself, knowing the roommate was definitely a topic deserving of a full blown conversation. But since I didn't have the energy for it after moving all day, I sent my sister a basic response.

"She's got a little attitude, but she'll work for now." - Levi

"Here you go, Wes." I told him as I tossed one of the waters his way before cracking open my own. I took a long swig and then a second, finishing it off with ease before I checked my phone for Lily's response.

"Exactly what you need. Somebody who doesn't care who the hell you are and will treat you accordingly." – Lily

I shook my head as I sent her reply.

"Thanks for nothing, sis. Love you." - Levi

"Love you too, stupid." - Lily

I smiled at my phone, knowing Lily had definitely came through in the clutch regardless of the awkward situation she had put me in with Mean Ass Jules, though I really should've been calling her Fine Ass Jules. While my first time meeting her - *if I could even call it that* - wasn't exactly pleasant, I definitely wasn't complaining about being able to wake up to her pretty ass every day. Even with all of her attitude and feistiness, there was no

32

denying how sexy she was, her full lips kissable as hell no matter what color they were. The hair she argued wasn't hers was a shade of honey blonde that looked good against her golden brown skin. And while she had answered the door in jeans and a t-shirt, there was no forgetting the way both landed against her full breasts and hips.

Jules was a woman - *all woman* - no matter how much our height difference might've said otherwise. What she missed in inches, she surely made up for in personality.

I offered Wes a hand to help him off of the floor before I led us to the living room to watch TV since I hadn't hooked up the one in my bedroom quite yet. But we hadn't even made it to the couch when I heard Wes whisper, *"Gotdamnnnnnnn...."*

I peeked up to see what had caught his attention, and... *"Shit.* Jules, where are you going lookin' like that?"

She rolled her eyes, checking herself out in the mirror near the front door as she answered, "Uh… to work? To earn money? To keep the lights on around this place, perhaps?"

I felt silly asking her, "You really go to work in… *that*? All night?"

And she had no problem rubbing it in when she answered, "The higher the hem, the better the tips. I mean, you've seen it for yourself, right?"

Of course I had seen it. Hell, I'm pretty sure I had even commented on the shit the night I first saw her. But now that I actually knew her, something about it all felt… *weird.* I mean, I knew for a fact if Jules would've been serving my section in the barely-covering-her-ass skin tight black dress she was wearing, not to mention the sky high red bottoms she had on, I'd be trying to throw her more than just a good tip. But regardless of how I felt

33

about it, Jules had no problem challenging, "Now are you finished with your evaluation so I can go, Dad?"

"*More like daddy...*" Wes muttered, causing me to push him in the shoulder.

"Shut the fuck up, man," I whispered to him before turning my attention back to Jules to say, "I'll um... see you later then."

"He means, *we'll* see you later. I think you look amazing, Jules," Wes commented as he stepped to her.

And while the sight had me feeling some type of way once again, everything settled when I heard Jules fire back, "Who the hell are you?"

"*Me?* I'm Wes. Levi and I played in the league together," he answered with the arrogance and charm that usually worked on any woman we came across.

But clearly not with Jules as her face scrunched when she replied, "*Ew.* Goodbye." Before she left the apartment for good.

And I couldn't help but laugh at the defeated look on Wes's face as he turned back my way to say, "Damn. She's rough. Bad as hell though. What are you gonna do with that?"

I plopped down on the couch that smelled like it had just been sprayed with Febreze, as if Jules already knew I was going to be a little funky after moving all day. But no matter how intrigued she might've had me, even from something as simple as a little spray, I knew my situation – living with her as my roommate – was temporary. So I had no problem telling Wes, "I ain't doin' shit. Jules is... *I mean...* you see how she is. I'm just tryna get this money and get back into the league so I can get up out of here."

Of course, that didn't stop Wes from insisting, "But since you *are* in here, you might as well get *all the way* in here. If you know what I mean."

"I'm cool on that, bruh. Real talk," I told him as I turned on the TV, hardly surprised to find it on the Lifetime channel.

"Yeah, you say that now until you see all that ass strollin' out of here a few more times. Once she starts being nice to you, it's a wrap. I'm calling it now," Wes replied as he finally joined me on the couch.

"Well how about you call your own shit with Chloe? Ya'll still kickin' it, right?"

The question seemed to make him uncomfortable as he shrugged before answering, "Yeah, somethin' like that. Why? You heard somethin'?"

"What you mean, did I hear something? What would I have heard?" I asked, having a strong feeling his sudden tenseness had something to do with the answer to my question.

And it certainly made sense once he said, "She's... pregnant."

"With your baby?"

He turned my way, his face scrunched as he replied, "Yeah, nigga. Why you say it like that?"

"I mean, I'm just sayin'," I told him as I brought my eyes back to the TV, mainly to avoid his.

It wasn't that I had any dirt on Chloe or anything like that. I had just always questioned her intentions from the jump when it came to Wes. But I guess if they were still hanging on after all of this time, and now had a baby on the way, there was nothing left for me to say. And clearly Wes felt the same way as he said, "Well don't *just say*. I ain't tryna hear all that."

"I'm happy for you, man. Real shit. Congratulations," I told him, giving him a little pat on the shoulder.

And this time he actually looked excited about it all when he replied, "Thank you. Now let me get up out of here before she starts blowing up my phone.

Pregnancy got her hormones on a thousand."

I laughed as I stood up from the couch to walk him to the door. "I'm sure it does. And I appreciate your help today, man. Couldn't have done it without you."

He pulled me into a brohug as he replied, "You know I got you, Levi. And I know you'd do the same for me."

"Just say the word and I'm there," I assured him as I pulled the door open.

Regardless of what type of person he seemed to be to most people, I knew deep down Wes was good at heart. And that was exactly the type of energy I needed around me if I wanted to get my life back on track.

After sending Wes on his way, I came back to the couch and surprisingly got a little caught up in the stupid ass movie on Lifetime. Well… caught up in it enough to doze off to it. And I could feel the light from the screen flickering against my eyelids as I heard the door unlock behind me. But when I sat up to see what was going on - to confirm what I figured was going on - I only caused a ruckus as Jules all but jumped out of her heels the second she saw me.

"*Shit*! Don't you have a room to sleep in? A bed?" she asked with a hand to her chest as she tried to calm herself down.

I ran a hand across the short curls on top of my head as I told her, "My bad. I fell asleep on accident. But uh… how was work?"

I figured the least I could do was make a little small talk now that I had already scared her half to death. But when she pulled her shoes off, picking them up by the backs with her fingertips, she only replied, "It was work. Goodnight."

"But wait, I…" didn't even get to finish my sentence before she had already ducked off into her room.

"Damn, she's tough," I muttered to myself as I went

to the fridge to grab something to drink, settling on one of the fruit-flavored beers Jules had in stock. It wasn't my usual thing, but it would at least be enough to chill me back out until I could fall asleep for the night.

I made my way back to the couch, flipping through the channels with one hand and sipping my drink with the other. And to my surprise, Jules actually reemerged from her room, this time wearing an oversized pajama shirt with a silk scarf tied around her head.

"You're still out here? I thought you'd be gone by now," she said as she went to the kitchen and grabbed the same thing I was already sipping on.

"Nah, I'm wide awake. What you still doin' up?" I asked as she joined me in the living room, choosing to sit on the loveseat opposite of the couch I was sitting on.

And while I thought her hanging out with me was some sort of truce, she quickly reminded me that I had it all wrong when she replied, "Minding my business the same way you should."

"Having an attitude twenty-four hours a day must be draining as hell," I teased as I took another sip of my drink.

And she matched my sip, swiping the back of her hand across her mouth to catch the excess before replying, "When it includes dealing with niggas like you? *Definitely.*"

"*Niggas like me?* What's that supposed to mean?" I asked, feeling offended by whatever imaginary group she was putting me in without really knowing shit about me.

But instead of answering with words, she grabbed her phone, typing in her passcode and scrolling through before tossing it to me.

"What's this for?"

She took another sip of her drink, her lips looking a little too good against the rim of the bottle, before she

—

insisted, "Just read it."

"Can I come through?" - Don't Answer

"You were lookin' good as hell tonight, J. Can I see you later?" - Don't Reply

"You up?" - Boy Bye #3

"And that's not even including the ones I've already deleted," she added as she tucked her legs under her, making the hem of her t-shirt rise a little higher. Though the new length was nothing compared to the hem of her work dress.

"So you really think I'm that guy? The annoying booty call after the club nigga?" I asked, more amused than anything as I tossed the phone back her way.

And she actually looked convinced of her little theory when she replied, "I'm almost sure of it. For all of those pretty girls of yours."

"Jules, you really don't know me," I told her as I finished off my drink, setting the empty bottle on the coffee table as I watched her face slowly twist in disgust.

"First of all, use a coaster next time. Second of all, I Googled you and saw plenty. I mean, is there a socialite you haven't dated? Or did they all leave you once they found out you were flat broke?" she asked teasingly, though the shit really wasn't funny at all.

In fact, her little comment actually fucked with me enough for me to defend, "Shit ain't always been this way. I was on for a minute."

"More like a second or two..." she muttered as she took her bottle to the head with a few long gulps.

"You sure talk a lot of shit. You know that?"

She shrugged. "I'm just stating the facts."

"So how about you state some facts about yourself then? Where you from? What's your story?" I asked, desperate to take the spotlight off of my situation and put it on hers.

And I could tell she was a little uncomfortable by my questioning as she readjusted in her seat, gnawing at her lip before eventually answering, "I'm... from the Lou. St. Louis, that is. I moved out here to get into acting and modeling only to find out I wasn't as good as I needed to be to book anything serious, not to mention I'm short as fuck. Lucky for me, my best friend already lived here and had a room for me to stay until I could provide for myself with the money I make bartending. But now she's gone, and..."

"You're stuck with me? The broke ass baller?"

"Precisely," she replied with a smirk.

"Well you shouldn't give up on your dreams just because someone told you you weren't any good, Jules. You just have to... work harder, get better, keep going. You know, push through."

"Is that what you're doing? Working harder? Getting better? So you can get back to your old life?"

"Precisely," I answered with a smirk of my own.

I watched intently as she climbed off of the couch, stopping by my seat to pat me on the shoulder and say, "Well... best of luck to you, Levi. I'm going to bed."

"Wait a minute... you're being nice? Am I dreaming?" I teased as I watched her hips switch on the way to her bedroom.

But instead of answering my question, she simply tossed over her shoulder, "Goodnight, Levi."

"Goodnight, Jules."

Jules

Sunday mornings were always the worst.

After being on my feet all night at the lounge two weekend nights in a row, practically doing double the amount of work I did on any given weekday, I wanted nothing more than to lay on the couch, eat foods that didn't align with my summer body goals, and catch up on all of the shows I missed out on during the week.

But first? Breakfast.

I dragged myself from my bedroom to the kitchen, scrubbing at my eyes until they felt a little less groggy. But the clarity only allowed me to see the *last* thing I needed to be looking at first thing in the morning, no matter how much of a treat it felt like in the moment.

"*Holy shit…*" I whispered to myself as I watched Levi, a towel wrapped around his waist and his skin still covered in beads of water, as he dug in the fridge and pulled out… "Hey! That's my last yogurt, asshole."

He jumped from the sound of my voice, turning around with a ridiculously perfect smile as he said, "My bad, Jules. A nigga's stomach was growling all morning and I had to do something ASAP. I'll go pick some more up before I go workout."

"Yeah? Well what if I want some right now?" I asked as I leaned against the countertop, crossing my arms in a pout while I watched him indulge.

"Here. Have a bite," he insisted as he dug into the carton with his spoon for a second time and stuck it out to me like a baby.

And of course I blocked it, dodging his attempts to feed me as I screeched, "Ew! I don't know where your mouth has been."

"I just brushed my teeth," he admitted as he took another, fuller bite, being super extra when he licked the spoon clean, though I was sure he knew exactly what he was doing to me.

Still, I held firm, snatching an apple from the fruit basket as I told him, "Toothpaste doesn't kill Mono-germs."

"Ahh. You got jokes," he said with a laugh as he took another bite of *my* yogurt. But instead of getting even more upset, I made myself busy rinsing the apple which also helped me to avoid watching the way his tattoo-covered chest flexed when he talked.

At least he used some of that money to invest in good, quality ink...

"Actually, I'm dead serious. For all I know, you could've had some girl in your room before I got back from work," I told him, though I hardly believed myself considering he was in the same exact spot that I left him in when I got back.

"*Could've*. But I didn't. I mean, we haven't even set the house rules yet," he replied as he tossed the now-empty yogurt container in the trash before setting his used spoon in the sink.

I rolled my eyes, taking an oversized bite of my apple to alleviate the stress while I came up with what I considered most important. "Rule #1: Don't eat my shit. Rule #2: Don't drink my shit. Rule #3: If you dirty the dish, you clean the dish. Rule #4: Wear clothes."

"Uh… those little boy shorts you have on don't exactly align with the code of conduct," he said as he took a not-so-secret peek at my ass that was one dropped apple away from being completely out.

But once again, I held firm, sticking my chin up as I reasoned, "This is my apartment. I can wear what I want."

He took a step forward and my face only met his chest, forcing me to tilt my head back to find his eyes. "Correction, this is *our* apartment according to that rent money I just gave you yesterday. But for the record, I don't mind making a little amendment to the rule if that's what you're going to wear."

"Stop while you're ahead, Levi," I told him with another roll of my eyes as I slipped past him to discard the rest of the apple that was hardly meeting my appetite now that I had been exposed to the tempting milk chocolate dessert of his existence.

And he certainly didn't make it any easier as he ran a hand across his facial hair and insisted, "I'm just sayin'. But you know what? I'll respect the rules since you can't handle all of this body I got goin' on."

I quickly brushed off his arrogance. "Oh please. I've seen better…"

"Better what? My abs are on point and you know it," he said as he ran a hand down his… *twelve-pack? What the fuck?*

But while his abs were definitely envy-worthy, they hardly rivaled the thing stealing my attention from under his towel, making it easy for me to tell him, "Abs aren't everything."

"Abs *are* everything. So admit it, mine are on point, huh?" he asked with a cocky grin, obviously desperate for my stamp of approval.

The stamp of approval I traded for a shrug when I told him, "If that's what you're into."

"Man, you're a hater."

Again, I shrugged. "I don't have it in me to hate something I don't care about."

"Mean Ass Jules. Back at it again with the slick mouth," he teased as he turned to leave the kitchen.

And I made sure to remind him, "Don't forget the yogurt."

"I got you, pretty girl. You need anything else?" he asked, stopping right in the threshold of transition from the tiles of the kitchen to the carpet of the living room.

While I could think of a number of things to ask him for, starting with dropping that towel of his, somehow I found it in me to ruffle his feathers and answer, "Uh… tampons."

His face scrunched instantly as expected. "*Tampons*? I'm not buying you tampons, Jules."

Of course I knew my request was ridiculous, but officially having a one-up on Levi was way too fun to not challenge him even further. "So why'd you ask if you weren't going to follow through with my request?"

"I thought you'd say like… more apples, some bread, maybe a gallon of milk. You know, something normal," he insisted as he waited for me to agree.

But since agreeing meant our little game would be over early, I crossed my arms over my chest, resting all of my weight on one leg as I reasoned, "Tampons are completely normal. But… if you're afraid of losing your little man-card, I understand."

He sighed, obviously taken aback by my attack of his manhood. And while I was convinced he was just about ready to give up talking to me and end the conversation for good, he surprisingly came through with some logic of his own. "It would be different if you were my girl or somethin'. What am I supposed to tell the cashier when I roll up?"

This time, it was me stepping to him, reaching to pat him on the shoulder as I suggested, "Just tell her you're on your period." Then I slipped past him to head back to my bedroom, being sure to close the door behind me.

I waited until I heard the front door close with Levi's

exit before reemerging in the living room to watch TV the way I originally planned to do for the rest of the day. And somehow I ended up getting caught up in a movie I had seen a million and one times with Elizabeth, not to mention the fact that we also had it in our DVD collection. But my solo chill session didn't last long as the door jingled with Levi's return just as I was in the middle of reciting one of my favorite lines.

I purposely didn't acknowledge his presence until I felt a plastic sack land on top of the blanket I was snuggled under. "Here," was all he said as he continued towards the kitchen.

"What the hell are these?" I asked, sitting up a little straighter to grab the sack and find...

"Tampons. Like you asked for," he answered as he made himself busy putting away my replacement yogurt, a small case of bottled water, and a fresh 6-pack of fruit-flavored beers.

"I… I was just joking, Levi. I didn't really need these," I admitted, feeling flattered by his actions but also childish now that he had actually gone through it.

And my positive reaction was completely opposite of his as he slammed the refrigerator shut and said, "*What*? You had me in that bitch sweatin' tryna figure out if your ass had a heavy flow, workers asking me twenty-one questions and calling me the perfect guy just for you to be making jokes, Jules?"

"I mean, thank you. Seriously. I'll be sure to use them when my period really does come."

Levi only rolled his eyes as he headed straight for his room, prompting me to leave my perfectly-cozy spot on the couch to right my wrong.

I caught him just gently by the forearm to say, "I'm serious, Levi. Thank you for getting those. That was really sweet. Maybe you aren't some basketball asswipe after all."

He turned back my way, his face far from amused as the hard lines of his jaw tightened. "I already told you. You don't know me, Jules. You think you do, but you don't. And maybe we should keep it that way."

"*What*? Why? I mean… we have to live together for at least five more months. We might as well get along, right?" I asked in a weak attempt to mask the interest I still hadn't fully accepted.

And I had obviously done a damn good job as Levi pulled away from my hold to say, "Nah, we don't have to. I'll stay out of your way and you'll stay out of mine. Just like you wanted."

"But…"

The slamming of his bedroom door in my face caused a rush of mixed emotions, from anger to annoyance to… *damn, maybe I really am that wrong.*

"Levi! Levi, I'm sorry! *Damn*," I yelled through the door.

And I was just getting ready to give up when it finally cracked back open. "What was that?" he asked, his face pulled into a smirk as he waited for me to repeat myself.

It was clear he was fucking with me the same way I had fucked with him. But it was still only right for me to tell him, "I said I'm sorry. I shouldn't have… done whatever I did to you."

"Half-assed apology…" he muttered as he started to shut the door once again.

But this time I caught it with the palm of my hand, leaving just the slightest crack for me to admit, "I'm serious, Levi. I really am sorry. And I'm… *grateful*. For you going through with it even if I was only joking."

He sighed, shaking his head as he pulled the door all the way open to unveil the duffle bag hanging from his shoulder. Then he stepped out, shutting it behind him as

---

46

he said, "Fine, Jules. We're good. Enjoy your little tampons and yogurt, and I'll see you later, alright?"

"Okay," I answered with a nod as I watched him intently while he strolled to the front door.

I hated the way it made me feel to see him leave, as if he wasn't going to come back or something crazy like that. I mean, I shouldn't have even cared. Our lives were completely separate. We had nothing in common but an address. Yet here I was, pouting as he stopped just short of the door to ask, "Uh… is there something else you need, Jules?"

"*Huh*? N-no. I… have a good day," I told him with a wave of my hand as I returned to my rightful place on the couch.

And while I was still trying to sort through all of my nonsense, somehow Levi seemed to have it all figured out when he replied, "You too, pretty girl. You too."

Keys jingling in the door forced me to wake up from what was easily my fourth nap of the day, each one more fulfilling than the last since none of them were planned. But I wished I would've woken up a few minutes earlier as the boisterous ruckus of kid-noise nearby forced me to sit up and see the absolute last thing I expected to see strolling into my apartment.

"Sorry, Jules. I told them to be quiet, but… you know how kids can be," Levi said with a half-hearted smile as two little boys argued about what they were going to watch on Netflix below him.

I sat up a little straighter, being sure to cover my

thighs with the blanket as I asked, "Levi, what is going on? Who are they?"

He smiled proudly, adjusting the smallest one in his arms when he answered, "Jules, meet the gang. This is Andre, Adrian, and baby girl Anastasia."

"*The gang?* Whose gang?" I questioned, my heart pounding as I waited for his response.

Of all the things I had read about Levi, him being a father had certainly never been mentioned. And considering how old the boys looked, it hardly seemed possible for him to be responsible for creating them. Then again, Levi had spent quite a bit of time in the limelight meaning he could've easily gotten a head start on things of that nature.

But my thoughts were thankfully trumped when he replied "Oh! *Shit.* These aren't *my* kids. They're my sisters. She got called into work and needed a babysitter last minute so I volunteered. I hope you don't mind."

I shook my head, keeping myself wrapped in the blanket as I stood up. "Uh… nah. Not at all. I'll just go to my room."

"You don't have to. I mean, I can keep them all in mine," he insisted as little Anastasia wrapped her arms around his neck, obviously a big fan of her uncle. In fact, they all seemed to hold Levi in high regard as they waited nearby for instructions on where to go.

So once again I assured him, "No, no. It's fine. They need to be able to spread out. I'll go."

"Uncle Levi, she's so pretty," one of the boys gushed from behind me the second I made my way passed them on the way to my room.

And I heard the amusement in Levi's voice when he teased, "Hey man. What do you know about girls being pretty?"

"I like girls! They're my friends," the other one

shouted proudly.

And again, Levi teased, "That better be the only thing they are. But you're right, Adrian. She is pretty. *Very* pretty."

For whatever reason, my heart fluttered at his agreement. Of course I knew Levi found me at least a little attractive, but hearing him outwardly express it to two obviously important people in his life made me feel even more… *giddy.*

Still, that didn't mean I was about to suddenly turn into his fan. So instead, I simply tossed over my shoulder, "Uh… thank you. Both of you. Have fun."

The boys went back to their discussion of Netflix options, but I could still feel Levi's eyes on me until I shut the door. And instead of going to the bed, I rested against the back of the door, trying to figure out my next move.

It wasn't supposed to happen this way. I was supposed to stay out of his way and he was supposed to do the same. I mean, I still didn't know much about him. And the things that I did know didn't exactly paint him in the best light. But somehow his natural, genuine energy managed to overrule all of my preconceived notions, allowing the part of me that had no business getting involved to make its way to the forefront of my thoughts. Or maybe it was just the fact that I was in a dick drought and he was fine as hell.

Either way, I knew I had to nip my little crush right in the bud before it turned into a major disaster. Though it sounded like another disaster was already brewing as I heard a crash from the living room, followed by a, "He did it!"

"I turn my back for two seconds to put this pizza in the oven and ya'll are already breaking stuff?!" I heard Levi shout through the door, followed by the sounds of his heavy footsteps.

"We're sorry, Uncle Levi! We didn't mean to," the boys spoke in unison, obviously tapping into their twindom.

And I found the situation completely amusing until I heard Levi say, "Go tell Jules what you did. Now!"

Wait what?

A few seconds later there was a small knock on the door, forcing me to lift myself away from it so that I could grab a pair of shorts to put on. Then I pulled it open to the sight of both boys wearing a matching set of trembling bottom lips.

While one, Andre, already looked on the verge of tears, Adrian straightened up enough to stammer, "Uh... *J...J...* Jules. *We...* We broke your thing."

"What thing?" I asked in a panic, stepping out to assess whatever damage they had caused.

And I could hear the nerves in the spokesman-twin's voice when he pointed and answered, "The elephant. We was just playin' with it and the tail came off."

I released a heavy sigh, grateful that the thing they thought they were responsible for breaking had actually occurred long before I even knew they existed. In fact, the broken tail only reminded me of the night it occurred when Elizabeth got a little too live celebrating her very first sorority anniversary.

But the delay in my response only caused little Andre's tears to breakthrough, urging me to assure him, "Aww, it's okay. You don't have to cry. I can fix it."

I was just getting ready to pull him into a hug when Levi chimed in, "Nah, let him cry. They shouldn't have been messing with stuff that wasn't theirs to begin with."

"Well maybe if you had been watching them a little more closely like you were supposed to, this wouldn't

50

have happened," I fired back, serving him a side eye as I comforted Andre.

And I was hardly surprised when Levi shrugged me off to say, "Man, they ain't my damn kids."

"That doesn't make you any less responsible," I told him before turning my attention back to the kids to ask, "Now how about we sit down and find something to watch altogether? I think Netflix just added some new movies."

While I hadn't intended to take over Levi's little babysitting gig, it felt like the only thing I could do if I expected to keep the rest of my things intact, especially as I watched baby girl go reaching for one of the candles that I thankfully hadn't lit recently.

But Adrian didn't exactly make things any easier for me when he smacked his teeth and replied, "We already saw all those baby movies."

"*Baby movies*? Well what kind of movies do you watch then?" I asked, a little afraid of what he would answer. If my estimates were right, they couldn't have been any older than eight, though I had a strong feeling they might've inherited the height gene from the same person Levi did giving them an extra boost.

But regardless of my guess, I still wasn't expecting Adrian to reply, "Tyler Perry."

"*Tyler Perry*? Like, Madea?"

"That old lady is so funny!" Andre added, wiping at the leftover tears as he made his way to the couch with Adrian in tow.

I peeked over to Levi for approval, not exactly sure if Madea was age-appropriate. But Levi only shrugged, leaving me to make the call on my own. And since they obviously must've known plenty about her from previous experience, I decided, "Well… alright. Madea it is."

I was already busy loading the Netflix app on the TV

when Levi announced, "The pizza should be done in a minute." Before asking, "Yo Jules, you think you can do something with Ana's hair?"

"Excuse me?" I asked, turning around in my seat to meet his eyes.

And he only nodded in baby girl's direction to say, "Her hair. I tried to do some pigtails, but you see how that turned out."

I followed the direction of his nod over to Anastasia who was now minding her own business as she sat on the floor playing with her small collection of toys. And regardless of how content she was being in her own little world, there was no missing the fact that the ponytail on one side of her head was way high while the other was way low.

"Oh wow. That poor baby," I said with a laugh.

"You got me? Please?" he begged, his palms together as if he was praying.

And while I had already done plenty, and had now signed up for at least an hour and a half longer of a shift, Levi's puppy dog eyes managed to force an answer out of me when I replied, "Yeah. I got you."

Levi

The kids had already dozed off by the time Lily texted me to say she was on her way. And while I usually would've been complaining about her being a whole two hours later than she said she would be, for whatever reason I didn't mind as much today.

Actually, I knew the exact reason I didn't mind.

Jules had managed to swoop in and save the day, keeping the kids busy and wearing them out in ways I wouldn't have even been remotely capable of doing.

Naturally, I wondered where her skills came from, or was it all instinct. And as if she could read my mind, she blurted, "They remind me so much of my little brothers. Or how they used to be. They're almost grown men now."

"You have brothers?"

She shrugged, peeling herself from between the sleeping twins as she answered, "Yeah. Three of them actually. They're technically my half-brothers, but… same difference."

"Do you get back to see them often?" I asked, assuming they, along with the rest of her family, were back in her hometown of St. Louis.

But I could tell the question made her uncomfortable when she released a heavy sigh, making herself busy gathering the leftover paper plates from the pizza as she answered, "I… can't. My father doesn't let me." Then she made her way to the kitchen while I sat there processing her response.

I could pretty much assume her actions were intended to dead the conversation. But I couldn't help myself in joining her in the kitchen so that I could ask, "Doesn't let you? What do you mean, he doesn't let you?"

I watched as she stuck the plates in the trashcan, pushing them down with extra force to ensure the top would close before she answered, "He... banned me. From seeing them. Said if they talk to me, they'll go to hell on the same train I'm supposedly riding on by being out here."

"*What*? That doesn't make any sense."

"He's one of those guys, Levi. A hyper-religious prick who uses his supposed love for the bible to mask his hate for any and everything as if he was ever perfect," she replied, obviously annoyed as she used a wet washrag to wipe the countertops that were already spotless.

"But why would he hate you for following your dreams?" I asked in an attempt to piece together the information she was giving me. And my question prompted her to at least stop what she was doing to lean against the countertop with her feet crossed at the ankles and her arms over her chest as she stared at the ground, gnawing at her lip in deep thought.

The silence was thick as I waited for the response that eventually came in a softened tone. "*Because he...* he associates following my dreams with... exploiting myself."

"*Exploiting yourself*? Acting and modeling are both pretty honorable professions. He should be proud," I told her, more confused than anything by her explanation.

But a couple of things suddenly made sense when she replied, "Proud of me for doing the devil's work? Nah, that's not how it goes. But you know what? It doesn't matter cause I'm not doing that shit anymore anyway."

She started back into her cleaning frenzy, grabbing the broom to sweep the imaginary crumbs from the floor. And while I shouldn't have even cared, shouldn't have been so invested in her backstory, another question sat way too heavy on my tongue to hold it in.

So I didn't.

"Is that why you stopped? You continuously got rejected for the big roles, and thought... maybe he was right?" I asked causing Jules to freeze in place as she turned to meet my eyes. And I could tell hers were troubled as her gaze became heavier and heavier until the few short knocks on the door interrupted.

Jules darted from the kitchen while I made my way to answer the door. And when I pulled it open, Lily stormed in as if she had been to my place a thousand times, quick to rattle off, "I am so, so sorry, baby brother. The third shift manager didn't show up, so I got stuck at the restaurant until they could find somebody else to come in and... *Oh.* I'm sorry. Hi, I'm Lily. Levi's sister."

I hadn't even noticed Jules was still in sight until she accepted the hand Lily had extended her way. "Jules. Levi's roommate."

Lily flashed a smile my way before turning back to Jules to say, "I really appreciate you letting him take over that room. He was getting on my last nerves back at my place, emptying my refrigerator on a daily like I didn't have three hungry kids to feed."

"Yours too?"

"Hey! I replaced everything I ate, plus extra," I defended before telling Lily, "Your kids are knocked out. You want me to help you get them to the car?"

"How else are they gonna get there?" she replied teasingly before turning to Jules to ask, "You think you can grab the little one?"

Jules perked up as if the request surprised her. "Oh! Um... of course. Let me go find some shoes," she said before heading for her bedroom.

And she was hardly out of earshot when Lily was

55

already gushing, "I like her. And she's even cuter in person than she was in her profile picture. I mean, what's a filter when you look like that naturally?"

While I hadn't even seen the picture of Jules Lily was referring to to make such a call, there was no doubt in my mind that she was right. But since that was the last thing I needed to be admitting to my sister, I simply replied, "Yeah, that's what your son said too."

"My son? *Oh God.* Which one?" she asked as she gathered all of Anastasia's toys that were scattered across the floor and put them in a backpack.

"Andre the little loverboy," I answered as I shook him on the shoulder to wake him before moving onto his brother, both of them slow to move regardless of my actions.

"You leave my baby alone. He's gonna make a great husband someday," Lily said with a laugh as she zipped the backpack shut.

And just as she finished her sentence, Jules emerged from her bedroom wearing a pair of sweatpants and... *Jules wears Jordans?*

Lord, help me.

"Alright, little missy. Help me out here," Jules said as she went to lift the deadweight of Anastasia's sleeping body from the loveseat while I helped the half-sleep twins get their shoes on and their mom worked on their jackets.

But when Lily peeked over to her baby girl, she gushed, "Wow, Levi. You actually did a pretty good job on her hair for a change."

"Actually, that's all Jules. She was kind enough to handle it for me."

Lily smacked her teeth, pushing the tiny backpack over her shoulder as she advised, "Girl, don't you fall into the same trap we're all stuck in."

"*Trap*? What trap?" Jules asked as she patted Ana's back in an attempt to keep her asleep.

And while I wasn't exactly sure what Lily was talking about myself, I certainly wasn't expecting her to reply, "Doing all of Levi's dirty work while he continues to coast through life without a real care in the world. He didn't even know how to find a place to live. I ended up doing all of the work."

While Jules immediately looked surprised, she quickly masked it to say, "Oh wow. That's… interesting."

And of course Lily was quick to agree. "Right? I can't wait until he starts this new job tomorrow. Maybe it'll knock some common sense into him."

"*New job*? I thought basketball was your job..."

I ran a hand along the back of my neck, the embarrassing truth sitting like a lump in my throat though it hardly rivaled how embarrassing my first day of work was sure to be. But now wasn't the time to be ashamed or concerned about the opinions of others. I had to do what I had to do, starting with being honest in replying, "It is, but… it isn't exactly going to keep the bills paid right now. So my agent got me a job at his brother's car dealership."

The shock on Jules's face was clear as day as she stopped just short of the door to say, "Wait a minute… you're going to be a car salesman? Do you even know anything about cars?"

"Can't possibly be that hard," I answered confidently as I wrapped an arm around Adrian's shoulder to help guide his zombie ass to the car while Lily took care of Andre.

The silence between us all was thick, the only sounds being the click of the car doors unlocking and being opened. And while Jules put Anastasia into her car seat on one side, Lily and I helped the twins get into the other before she side-eyed me, communicating whatever she thought she couldn't say out loud.

"*What I do?*" I asked with my eyes.

But again, Lily only looked annoyed until Jules joined us to say, "It was a pleasure to meet you, Lily."

"Likewise, Jules. I'm sure we'll be seeing more of each other soon. And thanks for helping with the kids. I know they can be a handful."

Jules brushed Lily off with a smile as she insisted, "They were a treat. They're welcome to come by any time."

"Girl, don't say that if you don't mean it. Their little clothes are way too easy to pack," Lily replied with a laugh that Jules joined in on before thankfully amending her offer.

"Well maybe not *any* time. Just… *again*. When absolutely necessary."

Lily nodded. "I can appreciate that."

And while it was good to see them hitting it off, I couldn't help myself in jumping in to say, "Hey, what about me? I'm the one that fed them."

"Let me guess… frozen pizza?" Lily asked as she opened the driver's seat door and slid inside.

And I held onto it as I corrected, "Nourishment."

"Right. I'll see you guys later."

I closed the door for her, giving her hood a pat before heading back towards the apartment only to find Jules a solid twenty feet ahead of me.

"Yo, Jules. Wait up," I called after her, doing a little jog to catch up.

But my words did nothing to stop her surprisingly long strides as she tossed over her shoulder, "What do you want, Levi?"

"I'm… sorry. For pressing you like that about your

dad and stuff. It's not my place to be all in your business this early in the game."

She finally acknowledged my pursuit, stopping in the frame of her bedroom door to say, "Correction; It's *never* your place to be in my business. The quicker you learn that, the better off you'll be."

"Jules, wait…"

My sentence was cut short by her slamming the door in my face similarly to the way I had done to her just that morning. And while I had only done it to get back at her for her little tampon stunt, I could tell her version was a response to something much deeper.

Cars were hard.

Selling cars was even harder.

I thought my "celebrity" status would be my best marketing tool as far as my commission was concerned. And while people were definitely thrilled to meet me, take pictures with me, and even ask for my autograph, when it came to actually making a sale, they all managed to back out before I could get them to sign on the dotted line.

I was already yanking at the stupid tie I was forced to wear at the dealership as I strolled into the apartment that was eerily dark and quiet, the only signs of Jules being the lingering perfume and burnt hair smell in the air. I could pretty much assume she was still pissed from the night before, purposely avoiding me even if that meant her going into work early just to ensure she wouldn't run into me.

But then again, maybe I was giving myself too much credit. Maybe the perfume and burnt hair was in preparation for a date with one of the annoying booty call niggas; a little meet-up for a quickie to get her through the work night.

"Damn, you sound jealous," I thought to myself as I flipped on the light switch for the kitchen only to find a bouquet of flowers on the counter. My curiosity got the best of me, forcing me to take a peek at the card tucked in a holder between the lilies.

"I know these are your favorite. Miss you, Julia. XOXO Charlie."

"Julia? Who the hell is Julia?" I said out loud as I struggled to stuff the card back into its rightful place just as I heard the resounding sound of keys jingling at the front door.

And the second Jules noticed me, her face pulled into a tight scowl. "Exactly why are you going through my shit?"

"I… I thought maybe they were for me," I lied, earning me a stiff eye roll as she slipped past me to the fridge.

She made herself busy moving around some of the groceries I had bought, quickly getting annoyed as she replied, "You know good and well those weren't yours, Levi. Why haven't you learned how to mind your own business yet? I mean, you obviously have plenty of shit of your own to worry about. *Oh wait.* No you don't. Everybody does it for you."

"Wow. That's a cheap shot," I told her just as she slammed the refrigerator door shut, leaving empty-handed.

"It's a *true* shot. A game winner. You know all about that, don't you?" she asked as she headed for her bedroom.

60

And I was right on her heels, even following her inside so that I could question, "Who's Charlie?"

"Who's Levi?" she fired back as she left me to head for her closet that I was seeing for the first time. It was almost double the size of mine.

"He your ex?" I asked as I leaned against the frame of the door while she blew through the hangers trying to find something to wear.

And it was obvious she was a talented multi-tasker, looking for clothes while also finding the wit to challenge, "Is he yours? I mean, you thought the flowers were for you, right?"

"Jules, come on. I'm just asking you a simple question," I reasoned, trying to bring things back to a neutral playing field.

But I was hardly surprised when Jules didn't comply as she yanked a dress from the rack and replied, "So am I." Then she slipped past me and headed for her bathroom, closing the door behind her in attempt to end the conversation as usual.

I stood outside of the door, leaning against the wall as I tried to figure out my next move. I could let her win, leave it alone, and mind my business as she asked me to. Or I could... keep going, work harder, and get my question answered.

Since it was clear my current approach wasn't working, I tried a better, more passive one when I yelled through the door. "Look. I shouldn't have been looking at your stuff. You're right, that was wrong of me."

"Glad you noticed," she shouted back.

"So is he your ex? Somebody I need to worry about showing up here?" I asked, attempting to turn the issue into something different as a way to get her to spill the beans.

But once again, Jules didn't budge as she yanked the

door open and breezed past me when she answered, "Maybe he is. Maybe he isn't."

"Jules, I'm serious. I'm not tryna get into a fight with a stranger cause he thinks I'm here tryna get at his girl," I told her as I watched her dig through the pile of heels in the corner of her room, deciding on a pair that easily gave her an extra five and a half inches.

And she was already busy shoving her feet inside when she stiffly replied, "I'm not his girl."

"So he's…"

"He's a person who sent *Julia* flowers," she answered as if that helped to clear up anything, though the response did prompt another equally important question.

"Well who the hell is Julia?"

"My mother," she tossed over her shoulder as she turned off the light in her bedroom, leaving me in the dark as she headed for the front door.

And again I was forced to catch up with her so that I could ask, "Why is someone sending your mother flowers to your apartment?"

Her hand was already on the doorknob when she turned back my way wearing the same scowl she had on when she first saw me. "Why do you care? This shit was never any of your business to begin with." Then she turned the knob and added, "I gotta get to work."

"But I'm not done talking to you," I told her as she stepped out, attempting to close the door behind her.

And she only rolled her eyes when I caught it, continuing to follow her tracks even when she insisted, "Well I'm done talking to you."

"Jules, you can't keep shutting me out like this for no reason."

"I can and I will until you get the damn picture. Or do you need somebody to decode that for you too?" she asked as she used her key to unlock her car door before climbing inside.

And this time I was catching the car door instead of the front door as I told her, "Man, you can chill with all that. For real."

"And you can grow the hell up. For real," she fired back as she tried to yank the door from my hold.

"Grow up? The only one being childish is you."

"*Childish*? Really, Levi? I'm being childish because you can't seem to get it through your thick ass head that my business, my life, doesn't concern you? Contrary to popular belief, I'm not your fan. Hell, I'm not even your friend. We're roommates. Sharing a space. That's it. So stay in your fuckin' lane and quit trying to barge into mine before I run your ass over."

Jules

"You know this is exactly what your ass gets, right? Trying to go for the eye candy only to end up with an annoyingly nosey roommate. I mean, I was just sure you'd be throwing that ass back by now."

While Elizabeth was laughing at my pain over the phone, I could only roll my eyes as I made the drive to *The Max*. I still couldn't believe how much Levi had managed to get under my skin in such a short period of time, going from the lusty eye candy that Liz had already mentioned to a complete pain in my ass.

What a waste of talent.

"I really wish this was as funny as you're trying to make it. I mean, you know it takes a lot for me to really be mad at something these days. And let me tell you, my knuckles are turning red as we speak," I admitted as I gripped the steering wheel even tighter to help alleviate the stress.

But apparently my best friend had a better alternative as she suggested, "So maybe you *should* be throwing that ass back. Fuck out all of that frustration you have built up and get a fresh start."

I shook my head at her nonsense, cracking the slightest smile even when I told her, "You're not helping, Liz. It's like the more he runs his mouth, the more unattractive he gets. I'm just waiting for him to say something for me to officially draw a line of fire."

Elizabeth sounded less than convinced as she repeated, "A line of fire? What could he possibly say for that to really happen, Jules?"

I shrugged as if she could see me. "I don't know. He

thinks women only belong in the kitchen. Or he… supported Trump."

That made her laugh. "So you're going to write him off for his political views?"

"That shit has nothing to do with politics. That's a vote of conscience. Or lack thereof. Hell, I may just have to kill him off for that. Like Nat Turner said, if you're not down with the cause, you gotta go."

"I thought you said you didn't see that movie?" she asked just as I was pulling into the employee lot, taking note of the fact that the regular lot was already packed meaning it was bound to be a long Monday night.

I turned off the car, unbuckling my seatbelt as I replied, "I didn't. I just saw somebody say something about it on Twitter. But anyway, let me get into work before I get all riled up again and end up cussing out a customer for no reason."

Again, Elizabeth laughed as she insisted, "Jules, it'll be fine. I mean, he can't possibly be stupid enough to keep trying you, right?"

I sighed as I used one hand to keep my phone close while I climbed out of the car, giving a silent wave to Hope who was also just showing up for our shift. "I sure hope not. But after talking to his sister, I'm not so sure. I mean, if anybody, she would know. And she didn't exactly seem confident in his basic life skills."

It was honestly amusing to see the interactions between him and his sister; their closeness obvious, though it almost seemed like Lily was more of a mother to him than a sibling. And that was another thing that hadn't come up in my Levi-research; information about his parents.

Naturally, I wondered if his family dynamics were anywhere near as hectic as mine.

"He's survived twenty plus years in this world as a

black man. That means he's gotta have some kind of skills, right?" Elizabeth asked as I stopped just short of the employee entrance to finish our conversation.

And even though she had definitely made a solid point, I pretended to be less than enthused when I told her, "Girl... if you say so. I'll hit you up later though. Oh, and tell Marcus I said hey and congratulations on the baby you've probably already made."

"Bitch! Don't jinx me!"

I cracked a real smile as I quickly replied, "Love you. Bye!" Before hanging up and strolling into work.

As expected, the place was packed, forcing me to squeeze through the crowd to get to my station at the bar. And once I got there, the drink orders started pouring in to the point where I could hardly remember what I was mad about to begin with.

Until he showed up.

And not only did he show up, he showed up looking so damn good that I automatically began to hate the mother and father who I had yet to learn anything about for creating him. I hated the doctor who delivered him. I hated his barber for the last minute shape-up he must've gotten after I left for work. I hated his jeweler for selling him the diamond in his ear. I hated his... *dentist* for the pearly white smile I could see even from the opposite end of the bar.

That was exactly where I planned to stay until he disappeared, though I could feel him watching my every move. It was... *unnerving*, and annoying, not to mention the multiple comments I got from some of my usual customers about it, all checking to make sure I was okay.

But the tip of the iceberg was when Hope came my way to gush, "Levi Graham wants to talk to youuu."

Levi Graham as if he was some... mythical gift from God instead of my headass roommate.

—

I rolled my eyes as I wiped my hands on a towel before heading his way, licking my chops in preparation for the fire I planned to unleash. And of course, while I was fueled by the negative, he was on the complete opposite end of the spectrum as his smile grew with every step I took.

"Why are you here?"

His arrogant smirk was also annoyingly handsome as he shrugged. "Had a long day at work. Got into a fight with my roommate. So I figured I come get a drink. Now what do you recommend, pretty girl?"

"Devil's piss."

His face twisted when he asked, "You're joking, right?"

And I was already busy gathering the materials to make it as I told him, "Actually I'm not. I mean, if you really need to get the edge off, it's the perfect drink."

"How about a beer instead? I have workouts in the morning. Can't be too fucked up."

I completely ignored his request, continuing to concoct my suggestion as I told him, "There are beers at home. You know, where you belong."

"Nah, I don't feel very welcome there right now."

While I knew the angle he was taking, trying to guilt trip me into feeling bad for telling his ass off, I was sure to hold strong when I nonchalantly replied, "You've already paid a full two months' worth of rent to live there. If that doesn't make you feel like you belong, I truly don't know what will."

"Maybe if my roommate wasn't such a…"

"A, what?" I asked, cutting him off and fully ready to toss the drink I had just finished making in his face.

But I couldn't do it once I saw the adorable smile he wore when he answered, "A little monster."

"That'll be twelve dollars," I replied as I slid the glass

his way.

And again his face was twisted when he asked, "*Twelve dollars*? How are you gonna charge me for a drink I didn't even want?"

I shrugged. "You never said you didn't want it."

Before he could reply, a little voice nearby interrupted to say, "Don't worry. It's on me. I'm Layna."

My eyes were rolling harder than a PBA bowling ball on the last frame as I watched it all unfold; watched Levi get so easily sucked into the *real* mythical creature that was Layna of the infamous blog Layna's Logic.

While I never really had anything against her, had never knocked her game even after watching her go for one of my bosses who was *deep* in love at the time, seeing the way she preyed on Levi literally made me sick to my stomach. Though it was obvious he didn't care nearly as much as he replied, "Levi. Levi Graham," serving her the same smile he had been serving me all night and managing to piss me off all over again.

There was no way I was going to admit why I felt the way I did, but I was more than tempted to once I watched Layna gush, "I know who you are, silly. I've been following your career since Duke. How are your knees?"

He shrugged, taking a sip of the drink his little sponsor had yet to pay for before he answered, "They work like a charm."

"Mine do too."

"Twelve dollars, Layna," I interjected, smiling with my mouth but scowling with my eyes.

And the bitch had the nerve to give me a dismissive wave, keeping her eyes on my roommate as she said, "Just put it on my tab."

I could feel my blood boiling as I watched her and Levi share dreamy looks, her leaning in to whisper in his ear and him giving an obviously impressed nod at whatever hoe ass shit she was surely sharing. Probably the same hoe ass shit she shared on her wack ass blog.

I released a heavy sigh, trying to calm myself down as I turned away to plug the drink order into her tab at the register. And when I finally turned back around, they were gone.

Where the fuck did they go?

I stepped onto the bottom rail of the bar, looking down both ends before I peeked out to the crowd and thankfully found them on the dance floor. Well… not exactly thankfully considering they were basically dry humping each other. But I suppose that was better than actual penetration.

Why do you even care, Jules?

I wasn't interested in Levi. I didn't even… *like* him. He was annoying, and arrogant, and irresponsible, and immature, and he pissed me off every chance he got. That was almost the exact recipe for, "*Stay the fuck away from me before I cut you.*"

But the other deeper, darker side felt jealous as I watched him whisper something in Layna's ear that made her giggle. The other deeper, darker side envied the way he wrapped an arm low against her waist as if they had known each other for months instead of minutes. The other deeper, darker side was getting red knuckles all over again as I squeezed his glass of half-drank Devil's Piss in my hand and…

"*Shit!*" I screamed as the glass cracked, shards falling all around me with a few small pieces lodged in my hand.

While I knew it was impossible for all of the eyes in the lounge to be on me, that was exactly what it felt like as Hope screeched, "Jules! What happened?! Oh my God! You're bleeding so much!"

I looked down to my hand that was growing bloodier by the second, grabbing it at the wrist as I turned towards the back of the bar to the sink designed specifically for handwashing. I tried to stay cool as I watched the red flow of water rush down the drain, turning back to Hope to ask, "Can you sweep that glass up for me? I don't want anybody to get hurt."

Her eyes were panicky as she nodded her head just as Kelvin swooped in to find out what was going on. "Damn, Jules. What the hell happened to you?"

I turned the faucet off, grabbing a paper towel to hopefully stop some of the bleeding as I answered, "I... dropped the glass. And it broke."

"On your hand?" he asked, more confused than anything by my explanation.

And even though I knew it was a lie, I told him, "It was fragile. Really fragile."

"*Damn.* Maybe we should get them replaced then. I'll talk to Maxwell about it," he said as he grabbed another paper towel for me to trade out the blood-stained one with.

I pressed it against my wounds as hard as I could, though it didn't seem to matter as the second paper towel filled with blood just as fast as the one before it. Still, I couldn't help myself in insisting, "No, no. It's fine. They're fine. It was just an accident."

"Do you see that paper towel? That doesn't look like just an accident. I'm not tryna have you sue our asses over this shit."

I was almost offended that he'd even think I would do such a thing, though I really shouldn't have been considering I was his employee. Still, I had no problem telling him, "I wouldn't dare. It was just an accident. *Really.* I'll be okay."

"Are you sure? You may need to go to the emergency room. Get that all stitched up. Or glued together. Or something."

"No, seriously. I'm fine. I promise."

He pulled out another paper towel, handing it to me just as the blood was beginning to drip from the last one. "Jules, this is the third paper towel you've bled through. That's not normal."

"So maybe it's the cheap paper towels we need to talk about getting replaced," I told him as I pressed down on my wound once again.

"How about you just take the rest of the night off?" Kelvin suggested as I pulled the paper towel away, grateful to see it no longer looked like a crime scene.

And that fact allowed me to argue, "What?! No! I mean, I don't want to. *I*…. I really need the money, Kelvin."

"Don't worry about the money. We'll pay you for the full shift."

"But what about my tips?" I whined, knowing that was *really* where I made my coins.

Still, my whining wasn't quite enough to convince Kelvin as he said, "Jules, I hardly doubt that will make much of a difference. I mean, it's well into your shift anyway, and the bar closes in an hour."

"Do you know how much I make in tips in an hour? That's the difference between my lights being on or off," I reasoned no matter how true it actually was.

And it was clear Kelvin knew I was storytelling as well when he teased, "You mean, the difference between your weave being Malaysian or Peruvian?"

I brushed him off with a wave of my good hand. "Nah, those are both about the same price and already worked into my monthly budget. But seriously. Can I stay? *Please?*"

Kelvin sighed, obviously more exhausted from the night than I was as he replied, "Fine, Jules. Get bandaged up and we'll work you back in when you're ready."

My smile was full blown when I told him, "Thank you, boss man. You're the best. You and Tiana will be getting an *amazing* baby gift from me once junior gets here. Oh, and Ellie too. You know that's my homegirl."

It was truly fascinating to see the way Kelvin had grown from a playboy college graduate, to a family man and soon to be husband. But after meeting his fiancé Tiana on several occasions and then meeting her daughter at *The Max*'s quarterly family outing, it was easy to understand why she was able to turn him out for good.

"Let me guess. You're gonna buy gifts for the kids with all these extra tips you were supposedly going to miss out on if you left? Yeah, alright Jules," Kelvin joked as he grabbed the First Aid Kit and handed it to me to get myself back in one piece.

I stayed at the back of the bar while I worked to get the couple of Band-Aids I needed in a comfortable position on my hand. And I was just about done when I heard Levi and Layna make their grand return.

"*Yoo-hoo*, can you bring me my check please? We're ready to leave."

While her use of *we're* felt like a blow to the chest, something about Layna in general suddenly had me on edge. So I turned their way, choosing not to hide my scowl this time as I told her, "You can wait."

I watched closely as she smirked, blushing Levi's way before turning back to me to say, "Little Jules-y. That's not very good customer service, now is it?"

Her question had me flexing my hand, the wounds throbbing with each squeeze though the sharp pains felt like nothing compared to the damage I wanted to do to Layna's face when I told her, "I'm not exactly interested in being *good* right now. So like I said, you can wait."

It was clear her pleasant little demeanor was over, her tone dropping from a peppy pitch to a more serious one when she challenged, "I don't think Maxwell or Kelvin would appreciate all of this hostility."

I shrugged. "Maybe not. But they appreciate my skills way too much to be worried about your complaints."

"I was in Maxwell's wedding. You really think my complaints don't hold weight around here?" she fired back as if that fact was suddenly supposed to change my mind.

But I wasn't afraid - not of her or of losing my job - when I answered, "I really don't. Like, not even a little bit."

"We'll see about that," she muttered as she started to climb off of the bar stool to make good on her threat.

But to my surprise, Levi caught her by the wrist to stop her. "Yo, chill. You ain't gotta do all that, Layna. Jules is cool."

"Well her attitude isn't, and it needs to be dealt with," she replied, her non-existent panties somehow managing to be in a bunch.

And of course I couldn't help myself in pulling the wedgie just a little more when I added, "Your knack for giving shitty relationship advice on that blog of yours should probably also be dealt with, but I don't see anybody running to the internet Gods to save the day."

"You know what…"

"Layna, just get your check so we can go. It's not that deep."

"Yeah, Layna. It's not that deep," I mocked, feeling like I was in charge now that Levi had given me a little leverage to show out.

Layna rolled her eyes, digging in her clutch for a couple twenties before tossing them at me over the bar like I was a damn stripper. And while I should've been ready to deck her ass, I couldn't help but smile as I teased, "Wow. And I didn't even have to dance for it.

How kind of you."

Instead of responding with words, she only grunted before taking Levi by the hand and dragging him towards the exit. I would've been lying if I didn't acknowledge how watching them leave together left a small stain on my ego. And even though I felt like I had won the battle in the moment, it was clear Layna was going for the war.

Levi

I was prepared for the worst when I walked through the front door of the apartment only to find it as empty and dark as the first time when I arrived after work. I fully expected Jules to be home, and not just be home, but be ready to kill my ass for leaving *The Max* with who she obviously thought of as an enemy considering the way she had served Layna so much attitude. And while it was clear Layna was down for whatever, my conscience wouldn't allow me to follow through and betray Jules no matter how clear she had made her disdain for me.

It was like somehow, regardless of the way she tried to box me into the stranger-roommate category, I refused to conform. I refused to be trapped, or be the trap that Lily had already amounted me to. I refused to... *give up.*

It didn't make any sense. I wasn't desperate for her friendship, we didn't work the same hours so it was easy to avoid her, and she obviously didn't share my same interests. But it felt like I had no control over the situation, even when she strolled into the apartment a few short moments after me.

Her attitude was obvious as she made sure not to acknowledge me when she headed straight for her room without saying a word. And while I probably should've taken the hint, I decided to wait on the couch for her to reemerge in new clothes the way she always seemed to do.

I heard clear as day when she opened her door, letting out an annoyed sigh as she made a beeline for the kitchen. And I was quick to hop over the couch to join her, though I could immediately tell my presence wasn't appreciated.

She didn't even give me her eyes when she asked, "Can I help you with something? Or are you just here to rub it in my face?"

"Rub it in your face? Rub *what* in your face?"

This time she looked up, a Gatorade - *my Gatorade* - in her bandaged-covered hand as she replied, "You and Layna. I'm just sure she gave you the ride of your life."

Her assumption instantly grinded my gears as my face scrunched with irritation. "Man, I didn't even do anything with her. We walked out together, but that was it."

Jules looked less than convinced, brushing me off to say, "I really don't care if you fucked her, Levi. That's your business. I mind my own. Trying to be a role model around here, you know?"

"I'm serious, Jules. I didn't do anything with her. Yeah, we got our little flirt on but I left it at that," I told her honestly, though she didn't seem to care either way.

In fact, she decided to be sarcastic when she replied, "So... you... want a cookie, or...?"

"Gotdamn, Jules. Why do you hate me so much? I didn't even do anything to you."

She crossed her arms over her chest, getting in a defensive stance so she could fire back, "I don't hate you. Why would I hate you? I don't even know you."

"You sure knew me well enough to call me out on my lifestyle, on my past. Hell, even on my present like I'm some damn child," I told her, feeling myself growing hotter by the second as the pent up anger finally began to boil over.

And Jules certainly didn't help to calm anything when she replied, "A child. *Wow*. Never thought of that one. But now that you mention it..."

I cut her off. "Will you quit with that sarcastic shit? I'm tired of you treating me like I'm some scrub or somethin' just cause I don't do everything your way."

Jules put a hand to her chest, cocking her head to the side to repeat, "*My way*? I never asked you to do anything my way."

"Oh yeah? *Don't drink my shit, Levi. Don't eat my shit, Levi. Don't leave your basketball there, Levi. Wash your dishes, Levi. Do something for yourself, Levi*," I mocked in my best her-impression.

But instead of actually listening to what I was saying, she only shrugged. "Sounds pretty adult-like to me. But back to this child theory…"

"You know what? Fuck you, Jules."

"Fuck me? *Wow*. Fuck me, huh? Because *I'm* the one causing us to butt heads, right? *I'm* the one not holding up my end of the bargain and abiding by the house rules? *I'm* the one… *mmmm*…."

I wasn't sure what came over me, but it didn't matter as I slid my tongue between the threshold of her lips, lifting her from her feet and setting her on the kitchen counter so we were eye-to-eye. And while mine were wide the hell open out of pure determination, hers were closed as she embraced the feel of our mouths smashed together, her lips being just as cushiony as I imagined them to be when she wrapped her arms around my neck and her legs around my waist to pull me closer.

I could feel my dick growing harder by the second as she moaned into my mouth, yanking at the hem of my shirt to pull it over my head and giving me a quick second to breathe before I went back for more. And somehow more turned into me pushing the seat of her tiny pajama shorts to the side so that I could reach her… *Oh shit, she's waxed.*

My heart started beating even faster as I ran a fingertip along her swollen pearl, already imagining what she felt like, what she tasted like, and what kind of sounds she would make whenever I got the chance to fuck her good. And it was clear Jules wasn't interested in making me wait as she pushed me away just enough to get rid of her shirt before moving onto her bra.

I licked my lips as I watched her reach back to undo the clasp, freeing the perfectly-round breasts that felt especially weighty in my hand once I finally got the chance to cup them. I teased her nipple between my fingertips as I went back to her mouth that was still coated with the cherry-flavored lip gloss she wore in exchange for real lipstick. But it really didn't matter what she had on considering I was going to devour her regardless.

I moved my hand from her breasts to her hair, pulling her closer and deepening the kiss I had been longing to give her, though I hadn't truly realized it until this moment. In fact, I had never realized how bad I wanted Jules until I was having her now, until I was between her legs ready to make good on whatever she wanted to happen.

And she definitely wanted it to happen as she put her hands between us to undo the button on my jeans followed by my zipper before pushing them down with ease. I stepped back so that I could free her of the shorts that had already been a tease, leaving her completely bare as she waited for me to make my move.

So I did, dropping to my knees and diving face first into what I already knew would be my kryptonite. It almost didn't seem fair for her to have such a sour ass attitude towards me, but taste so sweet. But then again, it made all the sense in the world once I heard her hiss, "*Shitttt Levi.*"

Her little whimpers of pleasure sounded like heaven as I kissed, and nibbled, and teased her with my tongue, sliding a finger inside while I continued to lick her clean.

80

It was as if in that moment, nothing else mattered besides releasing whatever sexual tension lied between us. I was going to give her everything she deserved, and she was obviously ready to do the same when she demanded, "Come fuck me."

I stood up from my kneeled position, ready to wipe my face free of her juices. But before I could, Jules pulled me closer, desperate to taste herself on my tongue as she tied hers with mine, turning me on even more than I already was.

While she held onto my neck, I stepped out of my boxers, my dick springing towards her heat like a dart searching for a bullseye. And at the very last minute, she stopped me to ask, "Wait. You don't... have anything, do you?"

"Have anything? What do you mean?" I asked, confused not to mention anxious as I stood there ass out ready to go.

But it felt like a wave of air hit my fire similar to someone trying to blow out a birthday candle when she clarified, "Like a... STI or something?"

I tried to hide my annoyance as I told her, "Jules, come on. I'm clean."

And her face scrunched as she released her hold around my neck before asking, "How am I supposed to know?"

"Jules... you're killin' me right now," I told her, once again trying to hide my irritation to save the moment.

But to no surprise, Jules wasn't nearly as interested as she quickly fired back, "Yeah and your STI could kill me, or trounce my ability to have kids, or increase my chances of cervical cancer."

I couldn't help but be offended when I asked, "You think I would lie to you? I take this shit seriously too you know."

She shrugged as if she didn't believe me, brushing me off to say, "Yeah, you might now. But that doesn't mean you always did. When's the last time you got checked?"

"During my health screening with the league."

"Like... the first league or the second league?"

I sighed, my dick still at full attention when I answered, "The first one."

"That's a while ago!" she screeched, snapping her legs shut and pushing me away so she could hop down from the counter.

She was already busy gathering her discarded clothes in an attempt to cover herself, but clothes were the last thing on my mind as I told her, "I haven't even fucked with anybody like that since then."

"*Lies.* I read at least three articles about three different women you were linked to," she replied as she yanked her shirt over her head.

"Linked to. Not dating, not kissing, and definitely not fucking," I told her honestly as I finally decided to gather my clothes now that the moment was completely lost.

It truly wasn't even fair that the media got to do whatever they wanted to when it came to my life, giving people who didn't even know me - like Jules - the opportunity to make false assumptions. But it was clear her idea of assumptions was even more abstract than I imagined as she slipped into her shorts and fired back, "So that's what this is about? You just wanted to fuck me?"

"Jules, you're being ridiculous. I mean, did you forget you just kissed me back? You locked me between your legs? You *literally* just told me to come fuck you?"

"Yeah, but that was before I came to my senses. And I'm *so* glad I did," she said as she stomped towards her room like a damn baby.

"Man, you're even crazier than I thought," I muttered

as I stepped into my boxers.

And Jules almost caused me to tip over as I balanced on one leg while she got in my face to say, "Crazy? I'm not crazy!"

"Is screaming it supposed to convince me, or…?"

"Ugh! I can't stand you!" she shouted just as loud as she headed towards her bedroom once again.

But the second she hit the door frame, I was sure to catch her with my words when I replied, "Yet you just wanted to have sex with me five minutes ago? Yeah, okay Jules. Whatever you say."

Instead of replying, she only grunted as she used her usual defense mechanism and slammed the door behind her. And while I would've found the action a little offensive any other time, in that moment, I decided I was better off not caring at all.

Jules

So maybe I was a little crazy. But it wasn't exactly the same kind of crazy I assumed Levi had in mind.

My "crazy" didn't come out as a result of being unsure about what we were doing, but the fact that I was *so* sure until I found a loophole in the system, saving myself and my emotions in the process. I mean, there was no way in hell I could just… engage in hot kitchen sex with my annoying ass roommate and go back to normal. Seeing his dick - in all of its chocolate, veiny glory - was already enough to knock me off of my rocker. I couldn't even imagine what would've happened if I would've actually indulged.

Or maybe I should've indulged.

It was already a whole morning later and I was still throbbing between the thighs waiting for Levi to finish what he started. And boy had he started, that mouth of his surprisingly being good for more than just getting on my nerves. But you would've thought he had already met my body in another lifetime, knowing exactly where to kiss and lick with precision to make me come alive. In fact, the only thing he hadn't done was make me *come* alive.

But since that was my responsible decision - to stop while I still had a functioning brain - it was simply something I would have to live with until further notice. Because that was the thing… I wasn't sure I could even lay eyes on Levi without thinking about fucking him. I couldn't go into the kitchen without thinking of his face lodged between my thighs. So even if I had saved myself for now, it was practically inevitable that I'd find myself in a similar situation later.

Or maybe not.

Maybe Levi was completely turned off enough to never go there with me again. Maybe he would stay in his room, or stay late at the dealership, or hell, even stay late at his basketball workouts all to avoid me the same way I wanted to avoid him. I had already stayed in bed long enough to hear the front door close and lock with his departure to work. And since I pretty much knew his daily routine at this point, it wasn't impossible for me to be able to keep it up.

If you want to keep it up, Jules...

I was just getting ready to pull myself from the bed when my phone began to ring on the nightstand. And while the number wasn't one that I had saved in my contacts, I recognized the area code from my hometown which was enough for me to actually accept it thinking maybe it was just an old friend.

But once I said, "Hello?", I immediately realized the mistake I had made in answering the second I heard his voice.

"*Julia*. Julia, is this really you?"

"Dad?" I asked, as if I didn't know the answer to my own question. But then again, I didn't understand. I mean, he was the one who had written me off. I was no longer apart of the family, no longer welcome. So how was it even possible for him to have not only found me, but willingly reach out?

A chill ran down my spine as I heard the smile in his voice when he said, "You still remember my voice. That's good to know."

"Can I... help you with something?" I asked, growing more and more uneasy with every second that ticked by.

And my heart just about stopped when he finally answered, "We... *me and the boys*... we miss you down here."

Wait, what?

Again, none of it made sense. While I couldn't help but notice how the name of the woman he expected me to call stepmom was missing from his admission, I was also hung up on the fact that he claimed to miss me as if he wasn't the one who had pushed me away; as if he wasn't the one who had ousted me for my choice. And not only that, how could my brothers miss someone they hardly knew? They were older now; wiser, more mature, and probably even more like their father which meant they surely hated me just as much as he did no matter how much his phone call seemed to contradict that.

But since he *was* still on the phone, I somehow found it in me to reply, "That's... interesting. I mean, I'm surprised they even remember me considering the way you and Laura practically erased me from every family photo."

This time he sighed, and I could only vaguely remember the face he more than likely paired with it. "Julia, I've been praying day and night, asking God to help me figure out how to get my eldest daughter back and you know what he told me? He said, reach out to her and I'll do the rest. He said, let me work. So here I am, reaching out to you and letting God work."

"What do you mean, eldest daughter? Do you have another one I don't know about?"

He sighed again. "Laura is pregnant."

"Jesus Christ, Dad. You're almost sixty-years old! What are you going to do with a newborn?!" I yelled as I stood up from the bed, pacing back and forth in the confines of my room while I digested the new information.

I have a little sister on the way?
Is she even my little sister?

I suppose she was just as much of my sibling as my

half-brothers were. But then again, it wasn't like I'd ever have the opportunity to see her, or meet her, or influence her the way I had been able to do for them before I left. Though I was sure they had erased all of my teachings from their memory the same way they had been forced to erase my existence no matter how much my father insisted otherwise.

"I never question God's blessings, Julia," he finally replied as if that somehow justified having the child who really could've been his granddaughter.

And I could only shake my head as I told him, "I'm just sure you don't, Dad."

"Now tell me, are you done following the devil's lead? Are you ready to come back home? Where you belong?"

I should've known this was coming...

This time, it was me sighing as I clarified, "I'm exactly where I belong. God told me so."

"God did no such thing."

"And you know that because you're God, right? That's how this works?" I challenged, rolling my eyes that for whatever reason felt on the verge of tears.

"*Julia...*"

"My name isn't Julia anymore. My name is Jules," I corrected.

But of course my will - not to mention my legal papers - didn't matter to my father as he replied, "God blessed me with a daughter named Julia. Your name is Julia."

"Well you know who else's name is Julia? Your deceased wife! You know, the one you refused to help even though you knew how miserable she was. The one you literally controlled to death. The one you did away with the same way you did me, leaving her to die alone. You didn't even let me go see her! *You...* she was on her deathbed and you just wrote her off like some damn animal."

My chest was heaving up and down as I held the phone to my ear with one hand while I used the other to swipe at the tears that had finally been freed; the tears I hadn't shed over my mother in a long time. In fact, I wasn't sure if I had ever properly mourned my mother's suicide. And it certainly didn't help that my father forced me to believe her actions were aligned with the devil which meant it wasn't for us to even acknowledge.

"Julia, you and I both know your mother was under terrible influences when she did what she did to herself. The people she wanted to hang around, the life she wanted to live, that wasn't God's plan. And you know what happens to people who don't follow God's plan."

Again I corrected, "Actually I *don't* know. But I bet I'm going to find out by being out here, huh?"

"Loving the devil's work will send you straight to his home."

"I remind you of her, don't I?"

He coughed, clearing his throat before he asked, "What are you talking about?"

"She wanted to be free, but you didn't let her. And now that I'm doing what she always wanted to do, following the footsteps she never got the chance to create, you can't stand it. You can't take that I've survived all of this time without your Gung-ho for Jesus ass."

His voice was dangerously low when he said, "Julia, don't you speak that way to your father."

And I could only laugh as I repeated, "My father. *Wow.* The father who pops up all of these years later to do what exactly? Because if you're looking for some sort of reconciliation, this ain't it. I mean, maybe you aren't as in tune with your God as you think you are. Might want to check the connection, give those wires a jiggle..."

"Julia, that's enough!" he shouted, making me jump as if he was actually in the room with me.

But he wasn't. I was alone. And I planned to keep it that way when I told him, "You're right. That *is* enough. Goodbye, Dad."

"Julia!" he shouted again, only to be met with me hanging up the phone. And even though he was gone, I could somehow still feel his wrath as I plopped down on the bed and burst into tears.

I should've called in.

Being at work - being around people in general - had my blood boiling as I replayed the conversation with my father over and over again in my head. I wasn't sure what he expected me to say, what he expected me to do. But if coming home and dropping to my knees to praise him was what he had in mind, he had clearly dialed the wrong number.

I used a washrag to wipe circles against the already spotless bar top, doing just about anything to keep myself sane until I could make it home. Though it was clear I wasn't the only one who was aware of my frustration as I peeked up to a set of curious eyes.

"Yo, Jules. What's going on with you? First it was the glass, and now you're about to scrub a hole into my damn laminate?"

I sighed, continuing my cleaning as I insisted, "I'm fine, Kelvin. Just... stressed."

"*Stressed*? It's not like you to be stressed. I mean,

you're usually one of the bubbliest people I know."

While I had definitely shed more tears in the last few weeks than I had in my adult life as a whole, this time I was able to at least crack a half-hearted smile as I told him, "Well everybody isn't happily celebrating new engagements and babies like you, boss man. Some of us have real world problems."

He sat down at the bar, crossing his arms on the counter to ask, "What happened? You didn't get a part in a show? Missed out on a modeling gig?"

I laughed as I turned around to grab his usual beer, cracking it open and setting it in front of him as I admitted, "I haven't auditioned in a long time. A *really* long time."

"Then maybe you should. I mean, that's when you're the happiest, right? When you can get in front of the camera?"

I shrugged. "I wouldn't know. It's been so long."

Kelvin took a quick swig of his beer, then a second before advising, "You gotta do what you love, Jules. Go after what you want. I mean, I know you ain't tryna serve and clean up after these greasy ass niggas around here for the rest of your life."

I laughed a little harder, tossing my towel his way as I told him, "Maybe I am. I mean, the gig pays pretty well. And I even get to drink for free when I'm not on the clock."

He shook his head as he took another sip. "Those are both terrible excuses. But seriously, Jules. Maxwell and I both want you to succeed. We want all of ya'll to succeed in whatever you're after. I mean, you see Mia just landed the gig of her dreams. Hope is almost done with law school. That means you're up to bat, homie."

He was right.

Bartending was never supposed to be a full-time

thing, and it definitely wasn't a career no matter how much I had my eye on the new manager position the guys had just opened up. But I wasn't out here to serve drinks, to rely on tips for my livelihood. I was out here to chase the career of my dreams, to do what I loved, to make my mother proud.

So instead of avoiding the topic any longer, I simply told him, "I'll think about it."

"Time is going to pass regardless," he added as I turned around to the register to cash out my tips.

And once I was done, I slipped from behind the bar, stopping to pat him on the shoulder. "Thanks for the pep talk, boss. I'll see you tomorrow."

He gave me a little nod as I peeled my feet from the floor with each step across the sticky bar floor. And to my surprise, I actually felt like I had gained a little energy from our conversation. But once I made it home, all of that new found energy was drained from the sight waiting for me on the couch.

Levi was the first to turn around from the sound of my arrival, his expression neutral as he offered, "Jules… what's up? You remember Layna."

I suppose his announcement was enough to make Layna turn around to peer at me before turning back towards him to ask, "Am I missing something?"

He shook his head. "Nah. We're just roommates. Ain't that right, Jules?"

I couldn't believe that his words actually stung, forcing me to swallow hard as I answered, "Yup. Just roommates."

Layna stood up from the couch, smoothing her hands down the dress that was way too fancy for just hanging out before she announced, "I'm… gonna go. Maybe we should try my place next time?"

"Yeah. You should," I answered for him, crossing

my arms over my chest as I watched her stroll to the door in the stiletto heels I had been eying for months now.

Of course that annoyed me even more than I already was.

"Let me walk you to your car," Levi said as he hopped up from the couch to follow her.

But she was quick to turn around, putting a hand to his chest to stop him and say, "I'm fine. I'll be fine. I'll text you when I make it home, okay?"

"Or nah," I chimed in from behind, earning a sigh from Levi and an eye roll from Layna, both equally satisfying as far as my ego was concerned. But watching her give him a little kiss on the cheek was enough to bring the tension back even though it was followed by her leaving like I wanted her to.

"Jules, what the hell was that all about?" Levi fired my way the second the door shut behind her.

And I remained in my defensive stance when I asked, "*Just roommates*? Your face was between my thighs last night and now we're just roommates?"

"Yeah. Actually we are," he replied nonchalantly, blowing past me to head into the kitchen that really should've been cut off with caution tape considering the scene that had occurred during the aforementioned night.

In fact, the details of that night were just enough for me to toss back, "*Wow*. Did you kiss her? Please tell me you kissed her. I'd love to hear how much she enjoyed my flavor on your lips."

Levi didn't even turn my way, instead keeping himself busy yanking open the fridge as he replied, "That's none of your business. I mean, why do you even care? You don't want shit to do with me no way."

"And obviously that's for good reason. *Good grief.* First I had to deal with my father and now I'm dealing with this shit. Can my day get any worse?" I asked more to myself than him.

But it was clear he had picked up on my words as he inquired, "*Your father?* What does your father have to do with this?"

I sighed, feeling like I had nothing to lose by telling him, "He called. He asked me to come home. And he… reopened just about every wound he left."

"*Shit, maybe I do have something to lose…*" I thought to myself as I felt the tears welling up in my eyes yet again.

But there was no way in hell I was going to cry in front of Levi, even when he offered a genuine, "Damn, for real? *I'm…* I'm sorry to hear that."

Of course I brushed him off. "No you're not. Save your bullshit ass apology. I don't need it."

"I'm serious, Jules. I mean, I'm sure that fucked with your head. And to answer your question, no I didn't kiss her. She hadn't even been here for that long before you came home."

While he appeared to be telling the truth, I couldn't help myself in spewing, "Well thanks for that warm ass welcome. It's so greatly appreciated."

Then I yanked at the fridge door he had just closed, pissed when it wouldn't open thanks to the extra suction no matter how hard I pulled. And Levi only made the moment more embarrassing when he stepped in and opened it with ease.

I rolled my eyes, sidestepping him to reach inside for the street tacos I had leftover from lunch. Then I slammed the door shut before tossing them in the microwave.

"Jules, are you alright?" Levi asked as I pressed the numbers to add a few seconds to the clock.

And as I pressed the button for the time to start, I asked, "Why wouldn't I be?"

"Jules, you just put foil in the microwave."

"Shit!" I screeched just as the foil began to spark. And I was already going for the door when I asked, "Why didn't you stop me?!"

Instead of being as frantic as I was, he only shrugged. "I don't exactly know my place around here anymore."

"*Your place*? You wanna know your place? Let's start with out of my damn way," I replied as I got on my tippy toes to grab a real plate from the cabinet.

And of course he couldn't help but to offer assistance even though his reply completely contradicted his actions. "Only if you vow to do the same."

"*Me*? I never get in your way," I told him as I accepted the plate he grabbed for me with an attitude.

But it was clear I was the only one upset as he plastered on a smirk to ask, "Oh yeah? Well what was that with Layna then?"

Now it was me shrugging as I told him, "Consider it a favor, dumbass. If you knew anything about her, you'd know she's a notorious ho. The VIP section at *The Max* is her favorite preying grounds. Hell, she's probably just fuckin' with you so she can write about it on her blog when she's done with you. It certainly wouldn't be the first time."

"Layna is cool peoples. You're just a hater," he insisted as if he suddenly knew more than me. As if I was just… making it all up.

But instead of being offended, I focused on getting my taco plate in the microwave. If nothing else, they'd ease the extra stress that was sure to come from me challenging, "A hater? What is there to hate on? I don't want you."

Levi's smirk remained as he said, "Yeah alright, Jules. Keep telling yourself that lie."

Was it a lie? I wasn't even sure.

—

But none of that seemed to matter as I released a heavy sigh, the hot plate making my fingertips tingle as I told him, "You know what? I'm drained. All around drained. So if you really believe Layna is cool peoples, then go for it. Have your fun. Live your life. I have a hard enough time keeping my own shit together. The last thing I need to be doing is adding yours to the agenda."

Levi

"You know you fucked up, right? I mean, it's one thing to flirt with the girl. Hell, I would've even taken you going to her spot to blow her back out one good time. But to bring her to your crib? The crib you share with her arch-nemesis at that? What'd you think was going to happen?"

I sipped from my water bottle, trying to make sense of Wes's logic as I worked to catch my breath. While he was only working out to keep in shape during the last remnants of the offseason, I was working harder than ever to ensure this would be my last time off. I wanted to get back in the league so bad that I was doing just about everything in my power to make it happen.

But considering the current conversation we were having, it was clear my off-the-court situation was occupying a little too much of my headspace as I reasoned, "We were just kicking it, Wes."

Instead of agreeing, Wes smacked me on the calf with the tip of his towel. "Doesn't matter. Women see all of that shit the same way. You could've been getting your dick sucked and I'm sure Jules would've been equally upset."

"Well damn. Maybe I should've been," I told him as I thought about how many times Layna had offered, one of my top reasons for turning her down being out of respect for the household; out of respect for Jules.

But Wes only shook his head, his face not as readable as I would've liked when he said, "Nah, bruh. Keep your dick to yourself. Don't ask why, just... keep it to yourself."

"Jules already told me she's a ho," I offered, figuring his words had something to do with that same concept.

But this time Wes laughed as he said, "Nah, she's not a ho. I mean, we'd all be hoes if that was the qualifier. But she's just... manipulative as hell. Go back in the archives of that blog of hers and you'll see what I mean."

"Don't tell me you got a story on that shit," I asked, thinking back on Jules's assumption for Layna's involvement with me.

And again Wes laughed as he answered, "We *all* got stories on that shit, bro. I'm talkin' exposés out the ass. But anyway, back to your continuous fuck ups."

Even though Jules was obviously upset with me, I still managed to defend, "I didn't fuck up."

And while I felt sincere in my stance, Wes was far from convinced as he said, "Nigga… you had her pretty ass spread eagle in the kitchen and couldn't even come correct. Then you had another chick in the crib the next day? Yeah, you fucked up."

"Well what about her? Why is all of this on me?" I asked as I took another swig from my water bottle.

"Cause you're the man. It's always our fault," he answered as he stood up from the bleachers, patting me on the shoulder before making his way back down to the court. And I was right behind him, feeling even more lost than when I came in.

"So what should I do? Should I apologize? I mean, I already apologized about the shit with her dad and that didn't even have anything to do with me."

"Wait. Jules got daddy issues? Aww man. *Now it all makes sense*," he said more to himself than to me.

Though I heard him clear enough to correct, "Jules just has issues, period. And her holier-than-thou daddy just happens to be on the list."

While I still hadn't gotten the full background on the

situation with her dad, I had enough evidence to recognize he was far from father of the year. And if yesterday's attitude served as any update to what she had already shared, Jules was just as affected by his actions now as she probably was when it was all still fresh.

"So start there. Get her some flowers or somethin', on behalf of her shitty ass pops," Wes advised as he picked up the basketball and started spinning it on his middle finger.

And I was quick to snatch it from him, dribbling it from side to side as I asked, "*Flowers*? What do flowers have to do with her dad?"

"Flowers work for everything, bruh. You just gotta get a little creative with the name. Like, *fuck-your-dad* flowers or somethin'."

Now it was me laughing as I repeated, "*Fuck-your-dad* flowers? You're kidding, right?"

"Hell nah I'm not. I mean, you see how it made you laugh? She'll do the same. Then she'll be happy. Then you can make some progress with her instead of fuckin' up your in-house… opportunity."

While I could pretty much assume what he really meant by opportunity, I shook my head, tossing up a shot as I told him, "Man, you're crazy."

"Just listen to me, Levi. Have I ever steered you wrong?" Wes asked as he grabbed the rebound and tossed the ball back to me for another shot.

"Not recently," I answered as I put up the shot; all net just like the one before it.

And this time he didn't pass the ball back, instead putting it to his hip to correct, "Not *ever*. So get the flowers, maybe even a little treat to go with it. You said she likes sea-salted caramels, right?"

"Nigga, why do you even remember that?"

"It's all in the details, my man. The quicker you learn

that, the more prosperous you'll be. Now get your black ass back on the baseline so we can run these drills again. The league will be calling any day now and I'll be damned if you're not ready when they do."

I had my flowers, I had my sea-salted caramels, and now it was showtime as I took a deep breath before using my keys to enter the apartment. At least, that's what I tried to do, only to find the door locked no matter how hard I pushed and quickly realizing Jules must've locked the top lock.

"*Why in the hell did she do that?*" I thought to myself as I decided on knocking since that was really my only option. And it took a second round of knocks for her to actually come to the door. Though she only pulled the door partially open, sticking her head through the small crack she had created.

"Um... Levi. *Hey.* You're home. *Early.*"

"Jules, what's the matter with you? Let me in," I told her as I tried to keep the flowers out of her immediate sight.

But she didn't budge, instead choosing to whisper back, "I... can't. You can't come in right now. It's not a good time."

I rolled my eyes, trying not to get annoyed as I reminded her, "This is my apartment too, Jules. I can come in when I want."

"But..." she trailed just as I gave the door a little push that forced her to move out of the way. And once I stepped inside, I immediately realized why she was acting so weird.

"Julia, who the hell is that?" the random nigga asked as he stood up from the couch.

I looked over to Jules who seemed a little panicky when she answered, "Uh… this is Levi. My roommate. Levi, this is my ex."

"Not for long, Julia. You and I both know that," the dude said with an arrogant smirk as he stepped to her side, close enough for me to take a good look at him.

No wonder he's her ex.

I wasn't usually one to hate on another dude's looks, but… Jules could definitely do much better. And just thinking her name reminded me to ask, "*Julia*? Why does he keep calling you Julia?"

Again, Jules looked panicky, completely out of character as she stammered, "Um… see… well… Julia *used* to be my name. Before I got it changed. Legally. To Jules. He's having a hard time with the transition."

Instead of paying him any mind, I kept my attention on Jules - *or Julia* - to clarify, "So this is Charlie, right? The one who sent you flowers that day? The flowers you said were for your mom?"

"*Your mom*? Julia, what is he talking about?"

This time Jules snapped, turning his way to correct, "My name is Jules. *Jules*. We've went over this way too many times for you to still fuck it up, Charlie."

Ol' boy had the nerve to shrug, his smug little smirk plastered on once again as he said, "You'll always be my Julia."

"No I won't! I'm not even your Julia right now. Or your Jules. Or anything. I don't even know why I let you in in the first place," Jules replied as she headed for the door.

And Charlie Brown was right on her heels as he said, "Aww come on, babe. Don't be that way. We were perfectly fine before *he* showed up."

"Yo, she said she's cool on you. Now get outta here with that shit," I reinforced, crossing my arms and daring him to try something. And no matter how much of a tough guy he might've thought he was, he took one look at me and knew better than to cut up.

So instead, he focused on Jules to ask, "Julia, you're just gonna let him talk to me this way? After all we've been through?"

Jules rolled her eyes, her face pulled into a smirk of her own as she said, "Charlie... come on now. It was never that deep between us. You just caught me at a very... vulnerable time."

"So now what? You're gonna be with this clown?" he asked, tossing a hand my way without making eye contact.

Again, he knew better.

And it was clear Jules was over it as well as she pulled the door open and answered, "No. I'm just not going to be with you. It's really not that complicated."

Ol' boy had the nerve to groan as if that was going to change anyone's mind before he stepped out, ready to offer some parting words. But before he could say anything, Jules and I took one look at each other and decided on slamming the door in his face.

"Thank you, Levi. For running interference. I really appreciate it," Jules said, still laughing as she locked both locks, reminding me of where this whole situation had begun.

"Why'd you lock the top lock?"

The question made her a little uncomfortable as she gnawed at her lip and looked down at her feet to answer, "I was... I don't know. I guess I didn't want you walking in on anything weird."

"Anything weird? Like what? The two of ya'll

fuckin'?"

Her usual jolt of energy returned as her face scrunched when she replied, "What? No! I wasn't gonna fuck him. That's not even worth the trouble. But anyway, what's with the flowers?"

"They're for you," I told her as I handed them over.

She was already smiling as she sat them on the counter, pulling at the card to read, "*Wow*. Fuck-your-dad flowers. How fitting. Thank you, Levi."

"That's not all," I added as I dug in my duffle bag and pulled out the overpriced box of sea-salted caramels.

And while the flowers had brought a smile and a laugh, the caramels were the ones to bring full on joy as she shouted, "Oh my God! I swear I just finished off my last box before Charlie showed up! These are *right* on time."

Her excitement had me excited, though I tried to remain neutral as I told her, "Just wanted to brighten your day a little bit, I guess."

Jules was already ripping at the packaging of the box of caramels as she said, "Look, Levi. I know I've kind of been a bitch to you lately. And while you deserved the majority of it, I don't want you to think I'm just some hateful person. I really *don't* hate you."

Her words were definitely believable, but I knew the only way we could make good on them was if we made actual use of them. So instead of taking them at face value, I told her, "Prove it."

"*Prove it*? How?" she asked as she popped a caramel into her mouth which was honestly distracting as hell with the way she closed her eyes and moaned the second it melted.

But I swallowed her, trying to be as clear as possible when I answered, "Let's kick it tonight. Me and you. As friends."

Even though I knew it was a stretch, I wasn't expecting her to be so surprised when she asked, "*You're… you're serious?*"

I nodded. "So serious. It's about time we finally get to know each other, right?"

She smiled, nodding the same way I had as she answered, "Yeah. Yeah, you're right. Let's do it. I'm game. What do you wanna do?"

"Well first things first, we gotta hit the store for some grub. Fridge looking fresh out of BeBe's apartment," I joked as I sat my duffle bag down in the living room.

But it was clear Jules didn't get the joke when her face scrunched with confusion as she stuffed another caramel in her mouth and asked, "*BeBe*? Who's BeBe?"

"You've never seen *BeBe's Kids*?"

She shrugged. "Never even heard of it. Is it a drama? Chick flick?"

I couldn't help but laugh as I explained, "It's an animated comedy. Hood classic. Maybe we should watch it tonight."

She quickly agreed, nodding the same way she had done before. "Cool. Dinner and a movie. Sounds like a…"

"Not a date, Jules. You don't even like me remember?"

"I said I can't stand you. Never said I didn't like you," she replied with her infamous smirk as she went for another caramel. But this time I stopped her, catching her wrist to steal it and pop it into my own mouth.

Damn, no wonder these are so expensive.

Jules nodded as if she could read my mind before allowing me to reply, "Play semantics all you want to, pretty girl. Now what you tryna eat? Spaghetti is my specialty."

Again, she looked surprised when she asked, "What?

You're going to cook too? Like... real food?"

I shrugged. "Shit, we gotta eat something, right?"

"You're right. I'll help you."

"Bet. Now go put on some real clothes so we can jet down the street."

Jules glanced down her petite little frame before peeking back up to say, "*Real clothes*? These are real clothes."

While I could definitely appreciate her choice of clothes for selfish reasons, I knew it wasn't exactly appropriate for public no matter how much she thought otherwise.

Still, I tried to explain it lightly when I asked, "You said you didn't wanna fuck Charlie, right?" And I watched for her little nod before I added, "Well why do you have on dick appointment shorts?"

Jules burst with laughter as she repeated, "Dick appointment shorts? They aren't *that* little!"

"That's not what your ass cheeks said," I replied with a laugh of my own.

An appreciative laugh, that is.

But it was clear Jules had finally caught my drift as she shouted, "Fine! Let me grab some pants and we can get out of here." Offering me the perfect last view on the way to her bedroom.

Jules

"Okay. This is getting more and more weird the longer we stay in here."

I felt on edge, looking around the store as I held onto the basket while Levi grabbed the pasta from the top shelf.

"What are you talking about, Jules?" he asked as he tossed it in the basket before adjusting the hood on his head. The hood that was supposed to be helping disguise him from the public though it obviously wasn't doing its job as we still caught glimpses from just about every person we passed.

At first I thought it might've been our height difference making us look like a meme-worthy circus act. But the more aisles we walked through, the more I realized Levi was *really* the star of the show.

"You don't notice all of these people looking at you? All of these people snapping pictures of you? Pictures of me?"

Instead of being paranoid about it all, Levi had the nerve to joke, "You're so famous."

"I'm not. I mean, I want to be. But not right now," I told him as I caught another person taking a picture, hoping it wouldn't end up in the wrong hands. The last thing I needed was some trash ass picture of me floating around the internet before I could jumpstart my career; the career I still wasn't even sure I wanted to pursue.

And while it was still a toss-up on my end, Levi felt sure of it as he said, "Well get used to it, pretty girl. You're gonna be a star one day."

"What makes you so sure?" I asked thinking maybe

his reasoning would help me be able to figure things out for myself.

But I certainly wasn't expecting him to answer, "Cause if you can put even an inkling of the energy towards your craft that you put towards having an attitude with me, you're bound to succeed."

"Thanks for your vote of confidence, asshole."

His little smirk in response grinded my gears and made my heart smile all at once, making me wonder was this a bad idea. But it was too late to turn back now as he replied, "Anytime. Now we got everything? Cause I'm not walking back over here. My legs are on their last after my workout today."

I scanned the contents of the basket, triple-checking to make sure we had all of the ingredients we needed for our meal before I realized, "Wine! We need wine."

"*Wine*? I'm not drinking wine, Jules. That's for chicks," Levi replied as he took off towards the registers.

And while I followed in his footsteps, I attempted to reason, "Just try it, Levi. I mean, it gives you all the buzz you need without the nasty hangover in the morning. And its heart healthy."

Levi still didn't seem convinced as he said, "Wine and *BeBe's Kids*? That's one hell of a combination."

"Well we're one hell of a combination so it's only right."

While the words felt... *different* now that they were already off of my lips, I was glad to see he hadn't picked up on it, instead replying with a simple, "Good point. Go grab your wine. I'll wait for you up here."

I took off towards the wine section like a kid who had just been told they could get a new toy, knowing exactly where my favorite bottle was and grabbing it from the shelf before I returned to the front to find Levi in a squat position with his arm wrapped around a kid.

My heart swooned from afar as the boy gushed, "Thanks for the picture, Mr. Graham."

And Levi was slow to stand up, his legs obviously exhausted from his training as he told him, "My pleasure, little man." Before turning to his father to say, "Ya'll have a good night, alright?"

The man nodded, thanking him again before leaving the store. And I waited until they were out of sight to join him as if it made a difference, setting the basket on the self-checkout stand so I could ring it all up.

"Well that was nice of you," I told him as I scanned the bottled pasta sauce, way too hungry to make it from scratch.

"Anything for the kids," he answered as he handed me the box of the pasta to scan.

"Is that why you do so much for your niece and nephews?"

Levi picked up the bottle of wine, taking a closer look at the label before handing it to me and answering, "I actually don't think I do enough for them. But that'll all change once I get my shit back on track."

"You've been working hard. I'm sure it'll happen," I assured him as I handed my ID over to the attendant for clearance before continuing to ring up the last couple of items.

"Well thanks for your vote of confidence, asshole."

"Hey, I was actually being nice this time!" I told him as I clicked the button to pay. But before I could pull out my card, Levi stepped in front of me and stuck his in the chip reader.

"I'm just fuckin' with you, Jules. You're easy to fuck with."

Once the machine chimed with approval, I grabbed the grocery sacks and replied, "I'm usually not. Totally un-fuck-withable."

But instead of taking me seriously, Levi laughed as he challenged, "Oh yeah? Well why are you always so mad at me then?"

"Cause you get on my nerves. And you do stupid shit. And then you act stupid about the stupid shit that you do even though I believe you're actually a smart human being," I answered as we stepped out onto the sidewalk to head back to the apartment.

Again, Levi laughed as he said, "Wow. That might've been the nicest thing you've ever said to me."

"You're welcome, Mr. Graham," I told him with a smirk before turning my attention back out to the street. But before we could get any further, Levi moved me to the inside of the sidewalk and took the bags from my hand.

While I was honestly a little impressed with his gentleman-instincts, I still managed to offer, "I can carry those, Levi."

But he completely ignored that part, instead choosing to ask, "What happened to Mr. Graham? I liked that a lot better."

"Which is exactly why I'll keep calling you Levi," I told him with a laugh of my own, earning myself a roll of his gorgeous eyes.

"You can't even help yourself, can you? Just gotta talk shit."

"You're easy to fuck with," I tossed back, mocking his words.

But instead of just taking the tease, he got back at me when he replied, "So are you, Juliaaa."

"Hey! You don't get to call me that. You're not even supposed to know about that."

"Why'd you change your name anyway?"

I turned his way to ask, "Do I look like a Julia to you?"

And he only observed me for a quick second before answering, "I don't know. I mean… not really."

"Exactly. It never fit me. And it's also my mother's name," I told him, swallowing hard at the lump that grew in my throat from just mentioning her.

"Oh word? Does she live in St. Louis too?" he asked innocently as we turned the corner onto our block.

And again, I swallowed hard. "She uh… she passed away. When I was younger."

"Damn. I'm sorry to hear that. But I can definitely relate. I mean, I used to think Lily was my mom with how much my mother had to work just to keep us afloat. I always told her I'd get us out of that bind so she'd never have to work again, but… she didn't live long enough to see it."

"Well I'm sure she'd be proud," I offered as I keyed in the passcode to enter our building. I mean, regardless of his current circumstances, it was obvious Levi had seen plenty of success.

But he was less than convinced as he replied, "*Right now*? Nah, she'd be all on my neck for fuckin' this up. But in the long run, I'd die trying to make it right."

"You still have time, you know."

"Yeah? Well so do you," he replied as I unlocked the door for us.

I stepped inside, kicking off my shoes at the door as Levi did the same before carrying the groceries to the kitchen. And I met him there to help put things away while also continuing our conversation. "I'm not sure why you're so confident in my abilities as if you've ever seen me in action."

"Jules, I watched you go from almost about to climax face to straight up angry face in the blink of an eye. If that's not skills, I don't know what is."

"That wasn't acting, asshole! That was real," I told

him as we unloaded the bags onto the counter.

And Levi only laughed as he replied, "Oh I know. And even if I didn't know, my dick will never forget."

"That… wouldn't have been smart anyway. I mean, why would we have even done that to each other?" I asked as I gathered the empty plastic sacks and stuck them under the sink.

But as I bent over, I could feel Levi's eyes on my ass even when he said, "I know right? Made… zero sense."

"Right. *I*… I agree," I told him as I stood back up, resting against the countertop next to him with my bottom lip pulled between my teeth trying to figure out why the hell I had goosebumps, why my heart was pounding, why things suddenly felt… different.

But things definitely clicked once Levi replied, "Well I'm glad you agree. Cause that would've been… *damnit, Jules*." Before turning my way and lifting me onto the counter the same way he had done that night.

Except for this time, it wasn't out of anger or rage. It was out of… *interest*, out of lust, out of passion as he slipped his tongue into my mouth and I wrapped my legs around his waist to bring him closer. Levi lodged his hands under my ass to lift me from the counter, carrying me with ease as we traveled down the hallway towards his bedroom.

But the second I actually stopped to breathe, right after he had already tossed me onto his bed, I remembered, "Levi! We can't. You still haven't…"

"I've always been clean and I have condoms," he answered as he pulled his shirt off and stepped out of his sweatpants, his answer and his actions alerting me to do the same.

"Well where the hell were they at last time?!" I asked as he crawled onto the bed.

And with his face hovering right over mine, he

112

smirked before he replied, "Shut up, Jules." Then did the honors of shutting me up with a kiss just as frantic as the ones before it.

I ran my hands along his chest and his stomach, pulling my mouth away from his to groan, "Fuck, I love your abs."

He smirked with appreciation, kissing his way down my body as he replied, "Well I love your boobs. And your ass. And this… *mmm*…. I love this." Before he pushed the thin fabric of my panties to the side, and immediately began to flicker his tongue against my heat.

"*Gotdamnit*, you're so good at that. Why are you so good at that?" I moaned as he took long, full swipes before using the tip of his tongue to do faster, shorter ones; the combination making me weak as I felt myself on the verge of a release.

But instead of letting me get it, he pulled his face away, taking my panties with him as he replied, "You make it so easy, pretty girl. Now turn over."

He was already reaching for the drawer of his nightstand as I told him, "Levi, wait. Just don't like… fuck up my life with this. Give it to me good, but not like… so good that I can't ever recover."

"Jules, I got you. You trust me?" he asked as he ripped the condom open before sliding it over the tip of his dick.

And as I watched it grow even larger in his hand, I shook my head and answered, "Definitely not."

"Good. You shouldn't. Cause I'm definitely about to fuck your life up."

While I should've been intimidated, his arrogance brought me back to the reality of his existence, allowing me to fire back, "You can't possibly be that damn good."

"Oh yeah? Well let me show you, pretty girl," he said as he hovered of me once again.

But I put my hands to his chest to stop him. "Nu uh. Missionary is for love-making. That's not what this is."

"Well turn over like I told you to so I can tear that ass up," he said as he leaned back onto his knees, making room for me to follow orders. "Yo, your arch-game is crazy. I swear your ass looks ten times fatter."

"That's not exactly a compli… *fuckkkk*."

I couldn't even complete my sentence as Levi drove inside of me without any warning, taking my breath away, not to mention my soul as he grabbed my ass and replied, "It's a compliment, pretty girl. So take it. And take this."

"I… I can't… It's too… too much," I stammered as he consistently knocked down my back wall.

And while I was already on my last, he sounded completely energized as he said, "Perfect fit, baby. You feel so damn good."

"*Levi…*" I moaned, my knuckles turning red as I fisted his sheets, and then his pillows, and anything else I could get my hands on.

"Call me Mr. Graham, baby," he coached with a smack of my ass that made me shriek in pleasure.

"*Mr. Grahammmm…*"

He smacked my ass again, somehow managing to reward me by going even deeper. "There you go. You're a good listener."

And I used the last of my breath to reply, "Well you're... a good… *fucker*." Before coming completely undone; though that didn't mean anything to Levi as he continued to let me have it until he got his own. Then he collapsed next to me, finally breathing as hard as I already was while I tried to piece myself back together.

"Your mattress feels so much better than mine. I'm kinda jealous," I told him, though I was sure my words didn't come out very clear considering my face was still smashed against the pillows.

But he had obviously heard just enough to reply, "It was one of my first purchases when I got on."

I turned my face his way, still breathing harder than reasonable as I said, "Let me have it."

And he only smiled, running his fingertips along my spine as he insisted, "Or you can just… borrow it. With me in it."

"I don't like cuddling. I get too hot when I sleep," I admitted just as his fingertips made their way down to the crack of my ass, eliciting a laugh. "Stop. That tickles."

"Only at first. And then it feels good. But wait… who said I wanna cuddle with you? You'd probably try to fight me in your dreams," he replied as he pushed his finger past the threshold to rub against… *damn, that* does *feel good.*

In fact, it felt so good that I couldn't help myself in replying, "Or I'd try to fuck you in my dreams. Add that to the list of possibilities."

Levi laughed, pulling his hand away but not without smacking my ass before he got up from the bed. "You ain't gotta dream that, Jules. Now get up so we can go cook. Your fine ass worked up my appetite."

"I… can't. I can't move," I whined, pushing my face back into the pillows that smelled like him, a scent I truly hadn't appreciated enough until now.

In fact, there was a lot I hadn't appreciated about Levi until now, and not just his dick that was definitely worthy of a celebration of its own. But his persistence, his commitment, his… kindness and generosity were all admirable, making me wonder did I really not know him as much as I thought I did.

And as if he could rub that fact in anymore, he added to his list of admirable attributes when he announced, "Well you can get up when you're ready. I'll go ahead and get dinner started."

Levi

"Jules, you cannot be serious right now."

I sat back against the couch, trying to stifle my laugh as she wiped her face. "I'm sorry. This is stupid. I don't even know why I'm crying," she said, grabbing a tissue to blow her nose.

And this time, I couldn't help myself, a chuckle slipping out as I told her, "Jules… please stop."

"I can't. It was just… it was so sweet," she whined as she dabbed at her eyes once again.

I still couldn't figure out how in the hell *BeBe's Kids* of all things had brought her to tears, but it made good sense once I looked at the almost empty bottle of wine.

"I think you might've had a little too much to drink, pretty girl."

Instead of accepting my observation, she grabbed the bottle and poured the rest into her glass as she suggested, "Well I think I need some more. And I need to go take some food to the food bank for the kids."

"Jules, it was just a movie. An animated movie at that."

"I know! But it felt so real," she whined again, making me laugh as she took a big gulp of her wine.

And once she sat her glass down on the table, I told her, "Man, go take your ass to sleep. You're buggin'."

She shook her head, surely making things worse for her inebriated brain as she replied, "Nah. We gotta watch something else. I can't go to sleep thinking about those poor babies."

"Man, ain't nobody worried about them bad ass kids. And they're in Vegas now, remember?"

"For now! And then they'll go back home to a fridge full of cobwebs. That's so fucked up," she said, the tears welling back up in her eyes as if she was talking about kids she knew in real life.

In fact, she was so invested that I couldn't help but tease, "Maybe we should grab that leftover spaghetti and take it down to the shelter."

"That's a great idea! Let's go!" she said as she popped up from the couch, stumbling before catching herself on the arm of the couch.

"What? No. I was just joking. Sit down," I told her as I pulled her down onto my lap.

"What happened to Mr. *Anything for the Kids*?" she asked as she turned my way, putting a hand to my chest with a legitimate concerned look on her face.

So instead of continuing to tease her, I replied, "Look, Jules. If you're serious about this, we can go volunteer or something over the holidays. But *only* if you're serious."

"I am," she said with a vigorous nod that I was sure would knock her out.

But since it didn't, I pulled her into my chest and offered, "Alright, I'll set us up somewhere; find a soup kitchen or somethin'. But until then, lay off the sauce, pretty girl."

She pulled away, sitting up to say, "I'm not even drunk. Just a little buzz. A little tingly." Emphasizing her point by putting a little space between her thumb and pointer finger.

And while she had her tingles going on through her whole body, the tingles were definitely concentrated in my stomach as I told her, "Well that shit didn't do anything but give me a damn stomachache."

"Or maybe your stomach hurts cause you ate half the damn pot of spaghetti," she suggested as she tried to climb off of my lap.

———

118

But I was quick to wrap my arm against her waist to catch her when I replied, "Shouldn't have worked up my appetite so much. In fact, I'd love some dessert."

"*Yeah*? What you thinkin'? Ice cream? Brownies? Funfetti Cupcakes?"

"You."

Her face scrunched when she asked, "*Me*? I'm off-limits for at least twenty-four hours. I mean, have you seen your dick? It's pretty damn ridiculous."

"Which must be a good thing considering how loud your ass was screaming. You're lucky nobody called the cops on us," I told her with a laugh, though there was definitely nothing funny about the sounds she made when she came.

That shit was sexy as fuck.

This time, she made sure she got off of my lap, though it was almost pointless considering how close she was still sitting to me when she said, "Well I wish they would've. So I could've filed a property damage report on my vagina."

I burst with laughter, starting to wonder had the wine actually gotten to me as I told her, "Yo, go to bed. For real this time. You're wylin'."

And even though I was laughing, Jules was dead ass serious when she said, "No. I can't. I gotta watch something else. Seriously, or I'll have nightmares."

"Let's watch *Friday* then. That'll put you in a good mood."

"*Friday*? What's that?"

"Jules… you're playin' right? Go ahead and hand over that black card," I told her, sticking my hand out.

But instead of handing over the imaginary membership, she smacked my hand away as she defended, "I didn't grow up watching a lot of TV! I mean, we had a TV, but we didn't really get to watch fun stuff. The only time I got fun stuff was when I went to Elizabeth's and I could only cram in so much."

"So how'd you know you wanted to be an actress if you didn't watch TV?" I asked, having a hard time putting two and two together.

But it made sense once Jules explained, "My mother used to show me videos of different plays and films she was in as a child, showed me different magazine spreads she was a part of during her teenage years before she met my father."

"And your father got her into the church?"

She shrugged. "Not exactly. She went on her own. After being a child actor for most of her life, she told me she struggled with the transition into adulthood. And when she found the church, it felt like home. It gave her peace. Until it didn't."

"What do you mean?"

While I could tell the questions were making her a little uncomfortable, she didn't back down, instead taking a deep breath before giving the full spill. "So you know how I told you my father was overly-religious? Well, he wasn't always. It wasn't until my mother showed interest in getting back into acting that he turned it up. Regular Sunday church and Bible study turned into daily church, multiple services, certain books being removed from the house, our limited cable being completely disconnected. And my mother hated it. But for whatever reason she couldn't get away, she couldn't save herself. So she… tried to end it all."

"Damn. That's crazy," was all I could say, though I was sure it wasn't the most appropriate response.

But that didn't stop Jules from continuing on,

"Yeah, it is. And the craziest part about it was, it didn't even work. Well, not fully. Her body was failing from the overdose, but she wasn't dead yet. And I'm almost sure the only reason she didn't live was because we didn't go see about her. My father blamed her actions on the devil and said we had to stay away. So he let her go. I never even got to tell her goodbye, and he moved onto his new wife and a new life like she never even existed."

"So your brothers? They're from the new wife?"

Jules nodded, pulling her legs under her while adding, "Along with the little sister I apparently have on the way."

And this time, it was my face scrunching. "Little sister? Your pops is still puttin' in work like that?"

"*Ugh.* Don't remind me."

"But for real, Jules. If nobody else tells you, let me be the first to say I'm proud of you for chasing your dreams, for trying to honor your mom's legacy. I know she's smiling down on you as we speak," I assured as I wrapped my arm around her shoulder and pulled her against my chest.

"I sure hope so."

"I know it. Now let's watch something funny so we can get your mind back in the right place," I told her as I grabbed the remote and began scrolling through our options.

"You know, I strangely feel a little better now that I could actually tell the whole story to somebody."

"So much better that you're ready to get back into auditioning? This is bigger than just you, Jules. You gotta do right by your moms."

She put her hand to my chest, turning in my hold so she could see my eyes when she said, "Yeah? Well so do you, big shot. I'm pretty sure your mother wasn't too proud of all that drama you had going early on."

Now it was me getting a little uncomfortable as I tried to keep my face neutral when I explained, "That was actually right around the time she died. Right before the draft. That shit fucked with me so bad. Had me doing drugs, fighting people, all types of shit."

While I fully expected Jules to judge me the way she always had, she actually looked a little empathetic as she replied, "Yeah, I read about that. They never gave an explanation though. Just painted you as a… bad guy."

"Which fucked me up even more. That wasn't even in my character, but that's who they turned me into. Made me look all reckless and out of control when I was really just… mourning. I was hurt. I was lost. I was… alone. Had all of those extra people around me and still felt lonely as hell," I told her with an awkward laugh, shaking my head as all the memories began to flood my brain.

It had been awhile since I even spoke on that time of my life, choosing to focus on my future instead. In fact, I wasn't sure if I had ever released as much as I was now to anybody. But something about the moment, along with Jules being so open about her past, had me not only feeling comfortable as hell, but also… *free*.

"What about Lily? You always had her, didn't you?" Jules asked as she sat up a little straighter.

I returned my attention back to the TV screen as I answered, "Yeah, but she had her own shit going on at the time. I mean, it fucked her up too, not to mention she was still pretty young herself raising the twins as a single mom."

"Well where's their father?"

I shrugged. "*Shit*. The same place as mine. No man's land. Nowhere to be found."

"Well… would you rather know him and be spiteful like me because he's not who you think he should be? Or would you rather not know him at all?"

"That's a hell of a perspective, Jules," I replied once I realized I really didn't have an answer. I mean, sure my life wasn't ideal at the moment, but it wasn't all bad. I had made it out of sketchy conditions, and his presence didn't necessarily mean things would be better no matter how much that was the assumption.

But before I could continue down the long winding road of my past, Jules waved her hand to say, "Okay, seriously. Turn on the movie. This is getting way too deep."

"I like it though. I mean, I feel better too. So thank you for listening," I told her as I pulled her back to my chest.

She tilted her head back to meet my eyes and reply, "You already told me I was a good listener."

"And I meant that."

"Well I meant what I said too. Now turn on the movie, Mr. Graham."

"*Not a cuddler my ass…*" I thought to myself as I looked down the couch - and down my body - to find it halfway covered in Jules. Her head was on my chest and her leg was hooked near my waist as she snored softly. And while I was surprised at how comfortable she was, she definitely had a point about her getting too hot in her sleep, her face practically covered in sweat as it stuck to my t-shirt.

I wasn't even sure how we ended up in this position; wasn't sure at what point we went from watching the movie to cuddling to sleep. But having her so close to me felt way too good to complain about. In fact, all I wanted to do was wrap my arms around her little ass to keep her close for good because regardless of how special the moment felt - *regardless of how special the night had been* - I couldn't count on Jules to keep things this way. She was way too unpredictable, way too wishy-washy, which meant I had to chill before I got too ahead of myself. But of course she wasn't making anything easier as she readjusted her leg over my body and somehow sank even deeper in my hold.

I released a content sigh as I stared at the ceiling trying to figure out my next move. I wasn't looking for anything serious. I had way too much to focus on to also be worried about another person's moves. Truth be told, we *both* had plenty to focus on to be worried about or wrapped up in each other. But I also didn't want Jules to mistake that fact for me not being interested in her.

I was *definitely* interested in her, especially after all that had been shared over the course of the night. I wasn't sure if it was the wine that had us so wide open, or the fact that we were both desperate for the physical and emotional release, but it felt like a good start for whatever was to come. Though Jules was quick to remind me we still had a lot of work to do as she shuffled out of her sleep and groaned, "Let go of me. I feel like I'm on fire."

"You are on fire. If you didn't warn me, I would've thought your ass had a fever. But I suppose it was good while it lasted, right?" I asked as I sat up, twisting from side to side to crack my back.

Jules scrubbed at her eyes before stretching out her arms to say, "I feel like I got a full night's rest already. Like I should go ahead and start my day."

"Jules, it's almost three in the morning. Please don't start your day."

"Why not?"

"You're already a monster *with* sleep. I can't imagine you without it," I teased, earning a shove in the arm that barely made me move.

We sat in silence for a moment, Jules concentrated on her feet while I concentrated on her. I could tell she was deep in thought once she started gnawing at her lip, a habit of hers that I had picked up on along with a few other things. But I still knew to brace myself once she began to speak.

"So I know I… dropped a lot on you tonight. And you don't have to remember any of it if you don't want to. In fact, I'd like it if you could just forget it all."

"Why would I forget, Jules? That shit made you who you are. And it definitely made you easier to understand," I told her as I turned off the TV and stood up from the couch.

But regardless of my comment, Jules still insisted, "I'm not *that* complicated." As she stood up to join me.

I bent my head to meet her eyes and explain, "Yeah, to yourself. But for the rest of us, we're steady trying to figure you out."

"Well it's best to keep you on your toes, right?" she asked, getting on her tippy toes to get even closer.

And I couldn't help but smile when I suggested, "Or on my back. Maybe even my knees."

She poked me in the chest, turning away to head towards her room and tossing over her shoulder, "You're terrible. I'm going to bed."

"But you're not even tired," I called after her.

"Well I will be. Once I get in bed," she shouted back from the threshold of her door.

"How about you go get in mine since you like it so much? I'll just sleep out here," I offered, thought I wasn't even sure where it came from. I guess I enjoyed seeing happy go-lucky Jules so much that I would've done just about anything to keep her that way.

And it was clear she was considering my offer when she leaned against her doorframe, crossing her arms over her chest to ask, "Seriously, Levi? I mean, you hardly even fit on this couch."

"So let me join you then. I'll just… turn on the fan, turn down the air conditioning, put some frozen vegetables under your pillow..."

Jules burst with laughter as she headed back my way. "*Or* you can just keep that body of yours to yourself so I can properly self-ventilate."

"I'll try. Can't make any guarantees though. I already warned you about those little ass shorts earlier," I told her as I took another appreciative look at her ass.

"And I already told *you* I need at least twenty-four hours to recover," she reminded me with a silly grin.

"Come on, pretty girl. Let's hit the sack. I got shit to do in the morning."

Jules was already headed towards my bedroom door when she asked, "What kind of shit?"

"Since when are you so interested in what I do?" I teased as I pinched her ass from behind, making her giggle as she jumped away.

"I've always been interested, I've just never actually had to ask," she replied as she climbed onto the bed, being one hell of a tease and she crawled to the other side on her hands and knees.

Still, I kept her wishes for me to keep to myself in mind as I waited for her to get in position. "So, what? You've just been creeping on me? Listening through my door and peeking out the windows?"

Her face twisted instantly as she pulled the cover over her body. "Nah, it's never that deep. I just know your basic routine. The daily stuff."

"Yeah. Cover it up all you want to, Jules. Your mean ass was checkin' for a nigga lowkey," I told her with a smirk as I pulled the other side of the cover back and joined her.

And while I adjusted on my side, she did the same on hers. "I was never checking for you. I just… noticed you. Because you were there."

"Well I noticed you too. And I'm glad to see you aren't as bad as I thought you were."

"Oh, I'm definitely *that* bad. Don't get it twisted," she joked as she snagged one of the pillows that was already under my head. And since she was obviously in the mood to play, I turned her way to take another pinch at her ass, making her giggle once again.

"You tryna show me how bad you are, or you just running that mouth of yours like usual?"

"My mouth is good for more than just running, Levi," she replied as she turned to face me with a sexy little smirk before sliding over to fill the gap between us.

"Jules... go to bed," I told her, though my words completely contradicted my actions as I tilted her chin up for a kiss that she happily accepted.

"I am in bed. In yours."

I kissed her again, and then again before telling her, "Well aware."

Then she slipped her hand between us, pushing it past the waistband of my shorts. "Ooh. You *are* aware. *Really* aware."

"Jules, stop playin'. I gotta go to sleep, for real."

No matter how good her warm palm felt against my skin, I still had to keep my priorities in check. But of course she didn't make things any easier for me as she teased, "You're just so aware, Levi. I'd hate to waste all of this... *awareness*."

I felt myself thrusting to meet the strokes of her hand as I groaned, "Jules, I ain't tryna hurt your little ass. Go to sleep."

"Or you could… put me to sleep," she suggested, licking her lips as she increased the intensity of her strokes before slipping under the cover.

"Jules… *shit*," I moaned as she took me in her mouth, using her hand to continue her strokes as she bobbed her head up and down. And while her head game definitely had me speechless, I was grateful when she took a damn breath, giving me the opportunity to ask, "What happened to your little twenty-four-hour rule, huh?"

"I didn't say we had to fuck," she answered before going back for more, this time massaging my balls in her hand as she used her tongue to tease the head.

And I could feel myself on the verge of a release until she stopped to take another breath, giving me a chance to clarify, "Put you to sleep without fucking you, yet you steady down there startin' shit?"

She climbed from under the covers, straddling my body and grinding her pussy against my waist as she replied, "You just gotta get creative, Levi."

"Man, I'm too tired to get creative. Just come sit on my face or somethin'," I insisted as I latched my hands under her thighs with every intention of picking her up so I could get her exactly where I wanted her.

But before I could lift her, she climbed out of my hold and returned to her side of the bed. "*Nevermind.* I'll just put myself to sleep."

"Hell nah, Jules. You gotta go to your own bed to do that shit. I'm not about to let you play with yourself in my bed while I'm laying right here, perfectly capable of handling the job."

"Fine. I will then," she fired back as she started to climb out of the bed. But I reached over just in time to catch her by the arm.

"Jules, get your fine ass back here."

"Why? So I can sit on your face?" she asked, her face adorably pouty as she waited for an answer.

"You say it like it's a bad thing. I mean, I ain't never

met a girl who acted like she was too good for a little face lift."

Her pouty face turned into one of confusion when she asked, "Face lift?"

"Riding my face. Face lift."

I was grateful to hear her laugh, even if it was paired with, "That is *so* corny, Levi."

"Nah. Corny is you going to your room when you know you wanna stay in here with me. So what do you say, pretty girl? You gonna let me put you to sleep or what?"

"I mean… I guess… if you're still offering face lifts..." she stammered as she climbed back over my way with the sexy smirk back in full affect.

"You asked. I'm just tryna delivery," I told her as she straddled my lap once again.

Then she put her hands to my chest, grinding against me the same way she had done before as she replied, "Well call you the UPS man."

"*UPS man*?"

She nodded. "Yeah. UPS man. Delivery. Get it?"

I burst out laughing as I told her, "Yo, you can never call me corny again. Cause that was *so* damn corny."

"*Ugh*. Fine. Just put me to sleep already."

Jules

I woke up in a pile of drool, though it wasn't covering my own pillows as usual. In fact, nothing around me was the usual as I rolled around on the mattress that felt as if it was double the size of mine, enjoying the feel of what had to be Egyptian cotton sheets against my bare skin before bumping into a note.

I scrubbed at my eyes as I picked it up to take a closer look.

"Went to the gym, though I'm sure I'll be a step slower since you wanted to play so much last night. Feel free to stay in here as long as you need to. But if you stay long enough for me to make it back, just know you're asking for trouble. ;) - Levi."

I smiled as I read it again, clutching the comforter to my chest as I tried not to squeal out loud.

I was… *satisfied*. And happy. Not to mention completely refreshed as I sat up against the headboard and replayed the events of the night in my head. From tag-teaming to get rid of Charlie, to the not-so-regular trip to the grocery store, onto the dinner and a movie. *Oh wait*. Can't forget about Levi turning me to putty after fucking me into a stupor the first *and* the second time.

"A girl could get used to this…" I whispered as I shimmied to the edge of the bed, swinging my legs around towards the floor so I could hop down and keeping the sheet clenched to my chest as I looked around for my clothes.

But the second I bent over to look under the bed, I

heard someone whistle behind me, "Damn girl. What did I do to deserve all of this?"

I turned around wearing a bashful smile as I replied, "Good... almost afternoon, Levi. How was your workout?"

I watched as he sat his duffle bag on the floor before kicking off his shoes while replying, "Nothing like the workout I got last night, but it was straight. How you feelin'?"

"Excellent. Never been better."

"Do I have something to do with that?"

He was already crawling across the bed towards me, so I waited until he got right in front of me to answer, "You might."

"Oh I might, huh? Just a might?" he asked teasingly as he yanked at the sheet I was still holding onto.

But I managed to dodge his attempts as I insisted, "Levi, quit playin'. I couldn't take any more of your dick if I wanted to."

"But you *do* want to?"

"I mean..." I trailed, gnawing at my lip and earning a hard smack on the ass that made me jump.

"Freaky ass. What you got goin' on today?"

I continued my search around his room for my clothes, my first find being my tanktop. And as I pulled it over my head I answered, "I was actually thinking about heading down to this little improv class. Brushing up on my skills."

I suppose I was feeling a little inspired after talking it all through with Levi and being reminded of my purpose for being out here in the first place. And while it had been far too long since I had worked on my craft in any capacity, I figured improv was a good, free place to start.

Still, I wasn't expecting him to respond, "Oh word? Can I come?"

"You really wanna come?" I asked, more surprised than anything that he was so interested.

He nodded as he scooted a little closer towards the edge of the bed. "Yeah. I'd love to see what you're workin' with."

"Oh yeah? You didn't see enough last night?" I asked teasingly as I reached for my bra that had somehow gotten wrapped around his bed post, opting to toss it over my shoulder as I continued my search.

At least that was the plan until Levi wrapped his arm around my waist and pulled me between his legs before nuzzling his face in my neck as he replied, "I saw *plenty* last night. But wait a minute… that's the kind of acting you do?"

I froze in his hold the second I realized what he was really asking. "*What*? No! I'm not a… porn star. Nothing against them. Love their work. But no. Just… *no*."

"We can make a movie if you want to…" he whispered in my ear before pulling it between his teeth.

And regardless of how good it felt, I still managed to pat at his arms as I told him, "Get off of me. I haven't even brushed my teeth yet. And you *clearly* haven't showered."

"See. So we're dirty together," he said as he pulled me even tighter; tight enough for my ass to graze his dick and… *gotdamnit*.

I almost got caught up once again as I practically moaned, "*Off,* Levi. I need to start getting dressed now if I really expect to make it to the 1 o'clock session."

"Well can I at least watch?" he asked as he finally let me go.

"Boy… go get in the shower," I replied with a laugh as I dropped to the ground to look for my shorts and underwear which I assumed must've ended up under the bed.

"So you wanna watch me then?" he asked from above, obviously thrilled to see me on my hands and knees as I reached as far as I could.

And I shook my head as my hand landed on the silk fabric. "You're crazy. I still can't believe I... *Levi*?"

"What's up?"

I stood up from the ground, one hand keeping the sheet clutched to my lower half and the other holding what *weren't* my panties. "Whose are these?"

"Ah... *shit*," was all he replied as he rolled his eyes and shook his head.

I tried my best to keep my composure, tried my best not to jump to conclusions as I dangled them on my fingertip. "Levi. Answer my damn question. Whose are these?"

"That's a long story," was all he answered, practically forcing me to get out of character as I got right in his face which was really only possible since he was still sitting down.

"Well you better get to tellin'!"

He held his hands up in defense as he leaned back and replied, "Alright, alright. So... the other night when you were at work, Wes came through. But he wasn't alone. He had a little breezy with 'em and they needed a place to... do their thang."

I shoved him in the chest. "What the fuck, Levi?! Is that your thing or something? Offering your bed to any and everybody? I mean, why couldn't they just go to a hotel?! Or to his house?"

While I was livid, Levi was completely calm as he answered, "A hotel comes with paparazzi and Wes can't have that kind of attention since... he's got a little somethin' baking in the oven at home. Which is also why he couldn't go to his house."

"*Wait*... so this nigga has a baby on the way and you

let him come over here, use your bed, to fuck another girl? What the fuck is wrong with ya'll?!" I screamed as I stormed out of his room, taking his sheet with me.

And Levi was right on my heels as he continued to defend, "Wes is one of my closest friends. And I know he would've done the same for me."

"Well that's good to know! I'll know *exactly* where to find you when my intuition kicks in!" I shouted over my shoulder as I continued my pursuit of my bedroom.

"Jules, just relax for a minute. I mean, I was just looking out for him."

That flawed reasoning stopped me dead in my tracks as I turned around to challenge, "Looking out for him? What about his girl? What about his baby? You ever think about their feelings?!"

But again, while I was all emotion, Levi hardly showed any as he shrugged when he replied, "Man, they're not my responsibility. That's his problem."

"That you're contributing to by letting him come over here to do his dirty work. I mean, did you at least change the sheets?" I asked, the need to shower feeling even more necessary as I thought about sharing the bed with a for real stranger.

And thankfully, Levi at least had the sense to answer, "Yeah, Jules. I ain't that damn stupid."

"You sure about that?" I asked with a roll of my eyes, though my attitude didn't faze him one bit as I ditched him to head for the bathroom.

"Listen, pretty girl. I know you may not agree with my choice, but it really wasn't your business to begin with," he insisted as he followed me inside.

And I was already busy turning on the water for the shower when I replied, "Yeah, until her nasty ass left her panties laying around for me to find."

"Well your little nasty ass left your panties laying

135

around too," Levi said with a smirk as he dangled the ones I had previously been looking for on his fingertip.

"Give me those," I snarled as I made an attempt to snatch them from his hand, his reflexes being impressively quick as he made me miss. "Levi, I'm not in the mood for this. Give me my damn panties."

"What you need these for? You're about to go put on some new ones anyway. I'll just hold onto these as a keepsake," he suggested as he stuck them in the pocket of his sweatpants.

Instead of continuing to fight him over it, I stripped off the little bit of clothes I did have on before grabbing my shower cap from the back of the door as I told him, "Go ahead. Cause they're the last pair you'll ever get to see."

"You don't mean that," he said as he pulled his socks off, followed by his shirt, pants, and boxers, completely distracting me from how mad I was supposed to be.

It honestly wasn't even fair how easily he could redirect my attention to the point where I literally had to shake my head so that I could reply, "Yes I do." Before stepping into the water.

And as if I had personally invited him to join, Levi followed suit, obviously not as appreciative of the scolding hot water as I was. His little cringe of pain felt like the perfect punishment as I reached in the caddy for my bodywash. But Levi was quick to take it from my hand, using his other to grab my loofah before covering it with the soap. Then he used his hand to create a foam before rubbing it against my skin, managing to annoy me and please me all at once.

"So you still mad at me?" he asked as he scrubbed lazy circles against my back before moving onto my arms.

"Of course I am," I answered just as he was moving

onto my breasts, paying them extra attention as he exchanged the loofah for his bare hand.

"You don't mean that," he replied as he tweaked my nipple between his fingertips.

And right after finishing my short groan of satisfaction, I whipped up just enough energy to tell him, "Actually I do. I can't be late. *We* can't be late."

"Oh, so I'm actually still invited?" he asked, offering me a moment of relief as he pulled his hand away.

I turned around so that I could see his face when I replied, "You are. But don't let me find out those panties actually belong to she who shall not be named around here without somebody getting their ass beat. Somebody meaning both of ya'll."

Instead of taking my threat seriously, Levi only laughed as he asked, "What are you talking about, crazy girl?"

"Oh, I'ma be a crazy girl alright," I muttered as I turned my back towards the water for a rinse.

"You sounding hella possessive, Jules. Tryna tell me somethin'?"

"*What*? I mean… *no*. I'm just sayin'," I answered as I continued rinsing the rest of my body.

Still, Levi was far from convinced as he said, "Mmhmmm. Sounds like somebody done got turned out."

"*Turned out*? Oh please. You aren't *that* cute."

"Oh, I'm not, huh? I bet I'm cute enough to do this," he said as he slipped his hand between my legs.

And I tried my best to hold strong while also giving him better access as I propped my leg up on the edge of the tub.

"Yeah, if I… close my eyes…" I moaned as my eyes decided to roll to the back of my head instead.

And even though I couldn't see his face, I could hear

his smile as he slipped a second finger inside and said, "You're such an asshole. A pretty asshole. But an asshole nonetheless."

"I don't care what you call me as long as you don't... *shit*... stop doing that," I told him as he created the perfect rhythm with his hand.

His voice was husky, clearly enjoying things as much as I was when he said, "I'm not even supposed to be in here."

"So..."

"You're bad news. A bad influence," he whispered as he ran a thumb across my swollen pearl, almost causing me to collapse as he continued, "But I like it. I like *you*."

"*Mmm*... I like you too... but only when you're doing that," I told him as I rested my head against the wall, letting the water cascade down the front of my body right onto his hand that was comfortably lodged between my thighs while also on the verge of making me come.

"What about when I do this?" he asked as he removed his fingers and put them to my lips, giving me the opportunity to taste all of the goodness we had created together.

I sucked his fingers clean before telling him, "*MMM*... that too."

He bent his head for a kiss, twirling his tongue with mine as if he was trying to catch whatever was leftover before pulling away to say, "See. That shit right there, is how you fuck someone's life up."

And since it was clear I was in control, I wrapped my hand around the back of his neck and pulled him even closer so that I could tell him, "Well consider yourself fucked."

"Yo, that was fun as hell."

"I bet it was considering the way you stole the show. *Oh Levi, you're so amazing. Oh Levi, you're so funny. You should really think about getting into acting,*" I mocked, thinking about all of the compliments Levi had gotten on our way out of improv class.

And my annoyance was obviously clear as Levi pulled up to the red light before turning my way to say, "You sound like a hater."

"No, I sound like someone who didn't bring a guest only to get outdone by said individual," I answered, crossing my arms over my chest in a pout as I looked out of the window.

Levi reached across the center console in an attempt to pull apart my crossed arms as he insisted, "Jules, you did your thing. Why are you trippin'?"

This time, it was me turning his way to explain, "I'm not trippin'. I'm just… *jealous.* You're a natural, Levi."

Levi's acting abilities were just another thing I could add to the list of qualities that weren't even fair about him along with his washboard abs, strong dick game, generosity, and… *basketball.*

He was really good at basketball.

"Why are you complaining, pretty girl? You're a natural too."

"No! I was trying. *Really hard.* You, on the other hand, just showed up and, voila. Magic. I'm surprised an agent didn't show up on the spot with a contract," I replied with a roll of my eyes as I turned back to my pouty position.

Instead of trying to unknot me, Levi decided to rest his hand on my thigh as he said, "Well I'm glad you were so impressed because I too was impressed. I mean, I see why it's your calling."

I rolled my eyes again as I sank a little deeper in my seat and muttered, "Yeah, yeah, yeah. Let me down easy why dontcha."

He moved his hand from my thigh to my cheek, giving it a little stroke as he insisted, "I'm for real, Jules. You're dope. And that was all improv so I'm sure you're even better with a little rehearsal."

While I knew there was some truth to his statement, for whatever reason I didn't feel as confident as he seemed to be when I told him, "You never really know until you book the part... *or don't.*"

"Well have you started looking for auditions? Casting calls and shit?"

I shook my head as if he was actually looking at me. "Not yet. But I will. When the time is right."

"So you mean, when we get back to the crib?" he asked, this time peeking over with a hopeful smirk on his face.

Still, I could only shrug. "I don't know. Maybe."

He grabbed my hand, giving it a little squeeze as he said, "You gotta say yes, Jules. Once you say yes, you can't back out. That's the only way you'll be forced to make moves."

"Fine. *Yes.* I will look some things up before I have to go to work tonight," I told him just so he would let me go meaning I could actually regain my composure after falling victim to something as simple as his touch.

"Thank you," he said with a smile that made my heart flutter just as my phone began to buzz in my lap.

I picked it up and saw it was a FaceTime call from Elizabeth which warranted an automatic answer. And once the video connected, I couldn't help myself in gushing, "There she is. The soon to be wifey."

"And there she is. The soon to be getting her back blown out by her roommate."

If there was something in my mouth, it would've surely been all over the dashboard as my eyes went wide with embarrassment, clueing Liz in on the fact that I wasn't alone.

"*Oh shit*. Uh… hi, sir," she said politely though she still couldn't see him on the other side of the car.

"His name is Levi," I told her just as I peeked over to see if he was actually paying us any attention.

And by the smirk on his face, it was clear he was as I turned the screen his way just as Liz shouted, "Hi Levi. I'm Elizabeth. Best friend and ex-roommate to Jules."

"Nice to meet you. And thanks for leaving," he shouted back with a little chuckle, taking a second to peek at her before turning his attention back towards the road.

I turned the phone my way just in time to catch her mouthing, "*Bitch, he is fine*" before she replied, "You're welcome. Uh, Jules… so I should… call you back? Or you can call me back? When you're alone?"

"*Please*," I told her with a short nod before ending the call.

And while I was hoping the car would somehow return to normal silence, I was hardly surprised when Levi teased, "Soon to be getting her back blown out by her roommate, huh? So you been spillin' tea about me to your friends now?"

"No. It was just a… silly joke," I answered, though he and I both knew that was a lie.

"A silly joke. *Right*. I know how ya'll girls talk. And ya'll ain't as innocent as you make yourselves out to be."

"I'm completely innocent. I don't even know why she

141

said that," I told him with a dismissive wave as I turned my attention back out of the window.

But Levi didn't let it stay there when he replied, "You know exactly why she said that. Though for that to be your best friend, it's a shame you haven't updated her on your status."

My face was scrunched when I turned his way to ask, "Updated her on my status?"

"Yeah. From *soon to be getting your back blown out* to *getting your back blown out*," he answered with an arrogant grin that I wished I could knock right off of his face. But it was the truth; I had definitely gotten my back blown out by my roommate.

Still, I was somehow able to work up a weak defense when I asked, "Who said this was a continuous thing?"

Regardless of how much I was enjoying it, that didn't necessarily mean it would last forever. In fact, I knew it was in my best interest if I nipped things in the bud before I became too attached.

But apparently I was a step too late as Levi replied, "You did. I mean, twice in one night and then this afternoon? Shit, probably tonight too if we're being real."

"Actually, *not* tonight. I told you I have to work," I reminded him as if that was somehow the only reason I wouldn't be riding him like a cowgirl.

Truth be told, it probably *was* the only reason. I mean, it almost seemed impossible that I could just hang out around Levi in private without outwardly expressing my attraction; without acting on the impulse to touch him. Even right now, I was struggling to keep my hands to myself which let me know just how much trouble I was already in.

Lucky for me, he felt somewhat the same way as he replied, "Well I'm sure I'll be up when you get back. And even if I'm not, feel free to wake me."

"Whatever. I'm not going to wake you up because we aren't doing that anymore. It's out of our systems and now we can... move forward accordingly," I pushed out against my own will.

And I was taken aback when Levi easily ate the shit up to reply with a nonchalant, "*Bet.* I'm cool with that. Matter of fact, I got this one girl who's been hitting my phone all day. Maybe I'll link up with her tonight."

He was already reaching for his phone as I turned his way and said, "Whoa, whoa, whoa. Wait a minute... what one girl?"

He shrugged. "I don't know her. But I'm sure I'll get to know her."

"Levi, don't make me have to fuck you up," I threatened as my heart raced just thinking about it all. Thinking about Levi in the face of some random girl he met off the damn internet.

And once again, while I was all emotion, Levi was as cool as can be when he asked, "Why are you gonna fuck me up? You're the one who said to move forward, right?"

"Well, yeah. But I didn't think you'd actually take that shit seriously and do it tonight!"

"Time waits for no man. I mean, who knows? She might be my soulmate," he insisted as he reached for his phone once again.

But this time I caught him by the forearm as I shouted, "Levi!"

"*What*? I'm just sayin'. God could've sent an angel straight to my DMs," he replied with a laugh, obviously making a mockery out of the situation as he pulled off from the light.

So as I fell back into my seat, I was sure to tell him, "Don't bring God into your ho ass shenanigans."

"Damn, Jules. Why she gotta be a ho?"

"I'm not talking about her. I'm talking about you."

Again, he laughed as he clarified, "So now I'm a ho because I, a single man, am interested in getting to know her, a single woman?"

I gnawed at my lip, staring at my hands in my lap as I tried to justify my response of yes. But nothing convincing came to mind, forcing me to answer, "I mean... *no*. Not exactly."

"So what is it then?" he asked, peeking over at me as he watched for a reaction. And there was a thick silence before the light bulb clicked on for him and he continued, "Ahh, I see what's happening here. You really *do* like me."

"No I don't," I defended weakly.

So weak that Levi continued to tease, "I fucked your life up, didn't I?"

"No," I answered as sternly as I could.

Still, Levi remained sure of himself as he said, "Aww come on, Jules. You can admit it. I mean, I will if you will."

"You first then," I insisted as I turned his way once again.

And with perfect timing we hit another red light, providing Levi the opportunity to give me his full attention as he ran a hand along my cheek and said, "You... *and all of that*... you got me good, Jules. You got me real good."

"So if I got you so good then why are you still trying to get at the Instagram honey?" I asked, not understanding how the two went together.

But it all made sense once he answered, "I made that up. I just wanted to see your reaction. Make sure I wasn't in this shit completely alone."

"Asshole!" I screeched as I knocked his hand away just as the light turned green.

And as he pulled off, he put a hand to his ear and

said, "Nu uh. It's your turn. Now let me hear it, baby. Mr. Graham fucked your life up. I ruined you. Destroyed that…"

I cut him off. "Alright, alright. You got me good. *Real* good. So damn good..." I practically moaned as the memories of it all began to flood my brain.

He took a short peek my way, licking his lips as he said, "Damn, girl. I said, let me hear it, not make me wanna pull over and do it again."

"We're almost home, Levi."

His eyebrow piqued when he asked, "Is that an offer?"

And this time, it was me licking my lips as I answered, "Actually, it's a request. A wish of sorts."

"Well your wish is my command, baby."

Levi

"I told you it would work. Wes knows best."

I handed my boy a beer before plopping down on the couch next to him and offering a cheers. His idea of getting the flowers for Jules had definitely been the kickstarter to much, much more. In fact, his idea of flowers was what led to a permanent smile on my face for the past week from getting to know Jules inside and out.

But regardless of the role he played, I knew there was still a bone to pick as I told him, "Well Wes almost ruined shit by letting his broad leave her panties in my bedroom for Jules to find."

I still couldn't believe of all the things Jules could've found in my room, those were it. But I was also grateful that she didn't jump to the obvious conclusion before giving me a chance to explain myself, though that didn't seem to matter to Wes either way as he replied, "*Panties*? I don't even remember her wearing any panties."

"That's not the point, man."

I watched as he took a hearty swig of his beer before finally admitting, "You're right. My bad. It won't happen again."

"You damn right it won't happen again cause I'm not letting you do that shit again."

"*What*? Why not?" he asked, legitimately surprised as he took another sip of his beer.

And this time I joined him, swallowing hard before I told him, "That shit is foul, bro. Chloe deserves better."

While I usually just went with the flow when it came to whatever schemes Wes and I had come up with in the past, now that I knew Chloe was expecting, it made me feel double the guilt. But once again, Wes had no problem brushing it off as he replied, "Chloe is just fine. She knows who she's dealing with. She's always known, not to mention she was the one who insisted on following me out here in the first place."

"But that still doesn't make it right."

Instead of considering my words, Wes made an attempt to put the spotlight on me as he said, "Man, you been pillow talkin' too much. Got you all in your feelings and shit."

Sure he might've had a point. After talking through it with Jules, I definitely drew different conclusions than before, starting with... "This ain't about my feelings. This is about Chloe's. And the baby. What are you gonna do when your little girl gets here? Keep running around like you do now?"

He shrugged. "That's for me to figure out when she comes. But until that happens, I'm gonna keep having my fun. And besides, don't act like you're Mr. Perfect now just because Jules doesn't know the real you yet."

"*The real me*? What's that supposed to mean?" I asked as I took another sip of my beer.

And Wes looked completely convinced of whatever theory he had come up with as he leaned in to reply, "Nigga, you're just like me. You ain't really tryna settle down with one broad. You're just letting her think that until you find something new to hit."

"*Oh, so that's what this is? Passing the time until you find something new to hit?*"

Wes and I both flashed our eyes back towards the door to find Jules standing with her arms crossed waiting for a response. I wasn't even sure how much she had heard, didn't even know she was there. But I knew I had some cleaning up to do as I said, "Jules. What's up, pretty girl? I didn't even hear you come in."

She closed the door before stepping behind the couch and looking down on the both of us. "Well here I am. And here… *he is*," she said with a roll of her eyes as she looked at Wes.

"Hey Jules," was all he could offer, trying his best to keep things cordial.

But it was clear Jules wasn't interested as she gave a stiff, "Wes." before slipping off to her room.

Once the bedroom door closed, Wes turned back my way to whisper, "Yo, why she always acting like that towards me?"

I shrugged, taking another sip of my beer. "She doesn't really have a reason to like you. Especially now."

"What you mean, especially now? I haven't even been around her to do anything new."

While he may not have been around Jules physically, I had no problem reminding him, "Bruh, she literally found your side-piece's panties."

"But she didn't even know they were my side-piece's when she found them. They could've been my main's," he said before adding, "Wait... you told her all that? *Gotdamn*, you can't hold water!"

I was just getting ready to reply when Jules's bedroom door cracked back open, the scent of her perfume seeping out before she actually emerged.

But when she did...

"Damn, girl. Where you heading off to? I know you aren't going to work looking like that," I said as I watched her check herself out in the mirror.

While the backless long-sleeved bodysuit and ripped denim jeans she wore probably seemed basic to her, it looked everything but, especially with the little sandal heels she paired it with. And it was clear I wasn't the only one impressed, Wes barely able to keep his jaw up as he ogled her from the couch the same way I was.

But no matter how hard we stared at her, Jules was completely unfazed as she smoothed the edges of her curled high ponytail and answered, "Nope. Going out with the girls."

"Oh, word? We're coming too," I told her as I stood up from the couch to join her.

And once she noticed me, she turned my way wearing a silly little smirk as she said, "You weren't invited."

"Why not? We can't roll with the pretty girl gang?" I asked teasingly as I stepped to her, giving the tip of her ponytail a little tug.

But she only knocked my hand away as she laughed and answered, "We aren't some teenage clique. But ya'll can do what ya'll want. I mean, ya'll are grown, right?"

"So where are ya'll going then?" I asked as she turned back to the mirror to check her hair once again.

And as she teased her ponytail she replied, "I don't know. Probably Downtown somewhere."

"Downtown? There's only like two decent clubs down there. And one of 'em isn't even really for us."

"We're just trying to get as far away from *The Max* as possible. But if that's not your thing, feel free to accept your *non*-invitation."

"We'll meet you down there in a little while."

She gave me a little pat to my chest as she said, "Sure thing, Levi." before peeking around me to add another stiff, "*Wes*."

And this time, Wes matched her vibes as he gave her a solid, "Jules." Before she left the crib.

I was already busy locking the door behind her when Wes asked, "Yo, we're really going out?"

"Hell yeah. I can't be having my girl out there with the wolves," I told him as I headed to my room to find something to where.

And Wes hopped up from the couch to join me,

teasing from behind, "*Your girl*? Since when is she your girl?"

I kept my eyes on my clothes, sifting through the hangers as I tried to come up with a reasonable explanation. "I meant like... *my homegirl*. She's my friend. We're friends now. And I can't have her out here getting fucked over by some lame ass niggas. Gotta watch out for her, you know? Make sure she's good…" I trailed, hoping Wes would fill in the rest for me.

But instead of taking my word, he leaned against the door frame and said, "Mmhm. Your ass ain't slick. I told you, once she started being nice to you, it was game over."

"You also just told me I wasn't trying to settle down which is the truth. Ain't nobody got time to be worried about Jules like that. I just wanna make sure she's straight," I reasoned as I yanked a pair of jeans and a Versace t-shirt down from the rack, finding it suitable for whatever the night would consist of.

Still, Wes was far from convinced of my logic as he teased, "Make sure she's straight aka make sure another nigga ain't sniffing down her back."

I was already picking through my jewelry, trying my best to brush him off though I knew he had a point. While Jules and I weren't anything official by any means, there was still enough there for me to feel some type of way about other guys checking for her even if there was nothing I could really do about it.

But regardless of all of that, I knew the only way I could get Wes off of my back about it was if I changed his perspective. So as I pulled my t-shirt over my head, I said, "Man, I'm just trying to have a good time with my triflin' ass homeboy. Can I do that? Or is that against the law?"

"You know that's never a problem. Now hurry up

and get dressed so we can get up out of here."

This was a bad idea.

I should've known my jealousy would kick in the second I spotted Jules completely in her element as she danced around with some random dude.

Well... he wasn't exactly random. I knew who he was and clearly Jules did to considering how comfortable she looked as he stood behind her with an arm draped over her shoulder before he leaned in to whisper something in her ear that made her laugh.

"Yo, you see your girl?" Wes asked, giving me chance to break my gaze so that I could pull myself together as a small crowd began to form around us.

Over the heavy bass throughout the club and the fans beginning to flock, I yelled, "Yeah, they're over there."

Wes followed the direction of my nod before he whistled, "*Damn.* Is that the pretty girl gang you were talking about? I got my eye on the one in the purple."

"You should've kept your eyes at home where they belong," I told him as we slipped through the crowd, trying to be polite and shake a few hands on the way to our destination.

And while I led the way, I heard Wes ask from behind, "Man, are you gone let me hoop or not? I would've stayed my ass at home if I knew I was going to be on punishment."

I shook my head with a laugh as I tossed over my shoulder, "Go ahead and make that filthy ass bed if you want to. But you damn sure ain't layin' up in mine."

"Yeah, yeah, yeah, and neither is Jules apparently.

You see ol' boy sweatin' the hell out of her?" he asked just as we bypassed the security before continuing up the short set of stairs into higher grounds which also gave me the perfect view of the VIP section Jules was hanging in. While the section was full of women, including a couple of the girls I recognized from *The Max*, Jules was an obvious standout, stealing not only my attention from afar but also the attention of the supposed man of the hour according to the marquee outside of the club.

Is that why she was so pressed to come down here? To see this clown?

I tried to keep my face neutral as I told Wes, "She's grown. She can do what she wants."

But it was clear I hadn't done the best job of masking my emotions as he insisted, "Man, don't have me in here breaking up fights and shit. I know how you can get."

I brushed him off even though my eyes were still glued to Jules as she posed for a picture with the guy. "I'm not gonna fight anybody. I'm just here to have a good time. Hell, maybe I'll even find something to take home."

To no surprise, my words acted as an instant boost for Wes as he smacked a hand against my shoulder. "Now we're talking. Who you thinkin'? Baby girl in pink? She's cute, huh?"

I followed the direction of his eyes and…. "She's alright."

"What about sweetheart in the red? Nah, she's got ass for days. You wouldn't know what to do with all that."

"Nigga, *what*? I can handle that," I insisted just as the girl noticed us watching, even giving a little wave.

She was sexy. There was no doubt about it. But for whatever reason, I didn't feel inclined to go talk to her even when Wes challenged, "Go ahead then. Go say what's up."

And since I knew he would never let me hear the last of it if I didn't take him up on the quest, I told him, "Let's go check up with Jules first and then I will."

"Aww come on, man. You gotta check in with mommy now? Make sure it's alright to go play?" he teased, earning himself a little push to the chest as we headed in Jules's direction.

And even though I knew I was approaching her for more selfish reasons, I tried to make things sound as normal as possible when I told him, "I'm just gonna let her know we made it, man. *Damn*."

"Alright, bro. Let's hurry up before I lose my prospect."

I slipped through the less crowded VIP area, stopping to say what's up to a few familiar faces before we finally made it to our intended destination. And once we did, I felt my muscles flex as I watched ol' boy give Jules a little kiss on the cheek that she didn't seem too enthused about, but didn't exactly fight off either.

Still, regardless of what they had going on, I put a little bass in my voice when I stepped to them. "Yo, Jules. What's good?"

To my surprise, she actually looked happy to see me, her eyes lighting up when she said, "Levi. *Hey*. This is… Jermaine. Jermaine, this is..."

"Levi Graham. The biggest bust in draft history. I know exactly who he is," he said with a laugh, turning back to his boys for more laughs to validate his corny ass joke.

And since he was in the mood for jokes, I had no problem firing back, "You sure talk a lot of shit for a nigga whose album just flopped."

I could tell I struck a nerve as his lip twitched before he turned back to his entourage once again, this time as if he was signaling trouble considering the way they all seemed to buff up in response. But when he turned back my way, his arrogant smirk was full blown as he said, "You know about my album though, right? What's your favorite song? Cause you still listened to my shit. I still got your money, nigga."

Before I could say anything back, Jules turned over her shoulder to serve him an annoyed look. Then she turned back to me to ask, "Will ya'll chill? I'm trying to have a good time. Not watch ya'll two cockfight all night."

I could hear Wes laugh behind us as I took a quick glance around the mostly packed club, quickly deciding it was time for us to go; us meaning *all* of us. And since I wasn't interested in going back and forth with Jermaine's mainstream rapping ass, I kept my attention on Jules when I said, "This shit is dry as fuck. You and your girls tryna roll to another spot?"

I was honestly surprised at how quickly she slipped from under Jermaine's arm as she answered, "Hell yeah. *I mean...* we can. If ya'll really want to."

"Cool. I'll meet ya'll outside," I told her, hitting Jermaine with a checkmate grin before leaving his spot with Wes in tow while Jules gathered her crew. And even though we were already a few steps away, I couldn't help but turn back to see his defeated expression once again, hardly surprised by the scowl on his face as he watched the girls follow our trail.

Once we made it outside to the curb, Jules was quick to introduce, "Levi, this is Mia. And this is Hope."

Hope was the first to extend her hand, giving me a syrupy sweet smile as she said, "I remember you. I served your section at *The Max* a couple of times."

"Yeah, and you did a good job. I should've tipped you more," I told her with a grin of my own, catching Jules roll her eyes out of my peripheral before I moved on to shake Mia's hand.

"Oh, and this is Wes. He has a baby on the way," she added, making me choke with a laugh as Wes's face went pale.

"Damn, Jules. Why you puttin' all of my business out there?" he whispered, though it was pointless considering we all still heard him loud and clear.

And even if we hadn't, Jules had no problem using her full voice to answer, "These are my friends. I'm not about to let them get caught up in your shit show."

There really wasn't much Wes could say to defend himself. So instead, I broke the silence by asking, "Ya'll tryna roll down to the Black Market? I think Shy is performing tonight."

But my suggestion only got another eye roll from Jules when she replied, "She's kinda... *extra*. What about that one spot? *The Drunken Unicorn* or whatever?

"I thought that bar was for white people," Hope asked as she crossed her arms over her chest, shifting all of her weight to one leg.

And I couldn't help but laugh as I answered, "Nah, they got a mixed crowd. Play most of the shit we like. Let's walk down and check it out."

"These heels are *not* for walking," Jules muttered as she leaned against the outer brick wall and lifted one foot from the ground to adjust her straps.

"Your feet hurt? Need me to hook 'em up right quick?" I offered as I stepped up to her, completely ready to give her a little impromptu rub down if that's what she needed.

But it was clear Jules was back in full-on tough girl mode for our audience as she brushed me off to answer, "No. *I'm*... I'm fine." Before putting her foot back on the ground and leading the way down the block.

And while Jules acted uninterested, Hope had no

problem chiming in, "Girl, you should've gotten your dogs rubbed while you had a chance. I know I would've."

"I said I'm fine," Jules repeated, this time with a little more attitude.

I couldn't pinpoint the reason for her change in energy, though Hope didn't care either way as she turned her attention to me and asked, "Well is that offer good for a friend? I mean, my feet are fine but my shoulders are on *fire*. Trent killed me in the gym this week."

"You work out?" I asked casually, knowing a little conversation would at least make the walk go faster.

"Gotta keep this ass from getting droopy somehow, right?"

Jules snapped her head back with a laugh before peeking over her shoulder to say, "Girl, stop lying. The only thing keeping your ass from getting droopy is your yearly appointment for sili…."

Hope was quick to cut her off while Wes and Mia snickered nearby. "Bitch, didn't nobody ask you. And don't hate cause you're too lazy to come to the gym."

This time, Jules turned around completely, stopping to challenge, "*Lazy*? I am *not* lazy. You know I'm not lazy."

And while I could tell Hope was struggling with a response, I had no problem adding my two cents. "You're right. The Energizer Bunny couldn't even keep up with your ass in…"

"Anyway! We're here. And I should've been drunk a long time ago so we got some catching up to do,"

Jules said, cutting me off as we bypassed the line heading straight for the entrance.

Wes and I both dapped up the bouncer before he pulled the rope back to let us in, the girls leading the way as we followed close behind them. I couldn't help noticing the way Hope stayed closer to me than her friends, putting an extra switch in her hips as if she already knew we were watching. And I was definitely watching; more fascinated with how natural the surgeon made her booty look than anything. I mean, if Jules wouldn't have pointed it out, I certainly wouldn't have been able to tell.

Still, Wes didn't seem to care if it was fake or not as he wrapped an arm around my shoulder before leaning over to whisper in my ear, "That's all you tonight, Levi."

I shook my head. "Nah, I'm good, man."

"She's serving all of that ass on a platter and you're good? What is wrong with you?" Wes asked before quickly continuing, "*Nevermind.* I know *exactly* what's wrong with you."

I gave him my eyes to see what he was talking about, but his eyes were already trained on Jules as she slipped through the crowd towards the bar, catching glances from every dude she passed. And while I already knew Wes had a point, I had no problem shoving him in the arm when he started singing T-Pain's *I'm Sprung.*

Jules

I couldn't stop looking at him.

While I always knew Levi was attractive, even before I knew him - even before I lived with him -, something about his energy tonight had my eyes glued to his every move. Or maybe it was the fact that his every move went simultaneously with Hope's as she basically plead her case for why he should fuck with her.

"*You sound jealous…*" I thought to myself as I rolled my eyes and took a hearty sip of my martini, swishing it around the glass before taking another sip to finish it off. But when I went to stand up, it was clear I shouldn't have drank it so fast as I stumbled a little when I stepped down from my bar stool.

"Damn, girl. You're faded already?" Wes asked as he caught me by the arm even though I was already stable. And since I was, I had no problem snatching my arm away from his crusty ass hands.

"It was only one drink. I'm good," I told him as I leaned against the bar top near the stool I had just abandoned.

And for whatever reason, Wes took it upon himself to take over the spot I had just left as he insisted, "I'm just trying to help, but you're too mad at Levi for fuckin' with your girl to even realize that."

"I am *not* mad at him. Why would I be mad at him? It's a free country and he's a free man," I replied, trying to convince myself more than him that it was the truth.

But my attempt obviously wasn't strong enough as Wes answered, "Because ya'll like each other. It's obvious. The same way you're mad right now is the same mad that got us here in the first place. You know he only wanted to get up out of there cause he saw how close you were getting to ol' boy."

While I was more than happy to get from up under Jermaine once he started trying so hard to impress me and then doubled down by trying to stunt on Levi, I was honestly flattered that Levi's efforts were out of the same jealousy I felt right now.

Still, that didn't stop me from defending, "Jermaine is just a friend of mine."

"Well ya'll didn't look like friends. Not to me and definitely not to Levi."

"Good thing it's neither one of ya'll's business, huh?" I asked with a roll of my eyes as I watched Hope try way too hard for Levi's attention.

And my heavy gaze must've been visible as Wes followed it before he said, "Look. Do you need me to run interference or not?"

"*Interference*? What are you talking about, Wes?"

"You know, get your man over here with you. Where he belongs."

I was quick to defend, "He's not my man. He's just my…"

"*Friend*? Yeah, he said the same thing about you. So like I said, you need my help or you just gonna be the salty one all night?" he asked as he leaned in near my ear without saying anything.

"What are you doing? Get away from me," I screeched with a little shove that hardly made him budge. But he was sure to create real separation once Levi approached us.

"Yo, Wes. What's going on over here? Ya'll cool?"

Wes shrugged as he lied, "Jules had... something in her hair. I was just trying to get it out. Ya'll should talk though." Before hopping down from the bar stool and taking the drink that had just been delivered with him.

At that point, I realized what Wes had been doing all along; trying to create this moment that I honestly wasn't prepared for. But I tried my best to keep it together as I turned towards the bar and asked, "So… are you having a good time? I see you and Hope are hitting it off."

Levi followed my lead, leaning against the bar top with all on eyes on me. "She's cool peoples. Not my type, but cool peoples nonetheless."

"Not your type? Hope is gorgeous. How is she not your type?" I asked, peeking up to find his gaze sitting even heavier than I imagined; as if he had been waiting to get me alone the same way I secretly had been.

He served me his infamous smirk as he answered, "I didn't say she wasn't fine. I just… like 'em a little different."

"Oh yeah? And how is that?"

He took a step closer to me, putting me between his body and the bar top as he answered, "Well… if I had to put my dream girl together, she'd probably be just like you."

"Like me?" I asked, peeking up to meet his eyes once again.

And this time, they seemed even darker as he bent his head when he said, "Yeah. Just… like… *you*."

"*Let's*… take a shot," I insisted, turning around out of pure panic from the idea of him almost kissing me in public. Though me turning around did nothing but allow him to step even closer, his body flushed against mine as he wrapped an arm low against my waist.

"Nah, I'm not drinking tonight. Trying to be a more responsible spender these days."

"My treat then. In fact, let's make it a double," I offered as I leaned into the bar top trying to get the bartender's attention, desperate for any distraction.

Still, Levi only laughed as he said, "Damn, Jules. You sure you can handle all that? I mean, I saw you were already over here bobbin' and weavin' just a minute ago."

"*So you were watching me like I was watching you?*" I thought to myself just as the bartender approached us.

But apparently it wasn't just a thought after all as Levi leaned in to whisper in my ear, "Couldn't take my eyes off of you if I wanted to."

"Uh… light or dark liquor?" I asked, trying to keep my breathing steady as I became more and more aware of his closeness. It was almost as if he was doing it on purpose, taunting and teasing me by simply existing, forcing me to add, "You know what? How about one of each?"

Again, Levi laughed. "Hell nah. You're tryna kill us both. Let's go dark."

I shook my head, pretending to be disgusted. "*Yuck.* Dark liquor puts hair on your chest. I'm getting light."

"Well why'd you even ask, crazy girl?" he said with another laugh just as the bartender prepared to take our order. And instead of answering his question, I ordered a double shot of tequila for myself and ordered him a double shot of Hennessy.

"Hennessy and tequila? You tryna start some trouble or somethin'?"

I peeked at him over my shoulder, my martini a little more settled into my bloodstream when I asked, "*What?* That's what I like. And that's what you like.

Well… I think that's what you like. That is what you like, isn't it?"

"Yeah, I like it. But I'm warning you now. Hennessy does some strange shit to me," he insisted just as the bartender sat the drinks in front of us along with a receipt.

I made quick work of grabbing my debit card from

my clutch, setting it on top of the tab for the bartender to take. Then I grabbed Levi's glass, handing it back to him before grabbing my own and telling him, "Well, tequila does some strange shit to me. *Cheers.*"

We clinked glasses then tossed the shots back; me in two big gulps and him in one, though we both bit back at the sting as we sat the emptied glasses on the bar top.

"You want another one?" I asked as I swiped a hand across my lips to catch the excess that had slipped from the corner of my mouth.

"Nah, I'm straight. I appreciate you though, pretty girl," he replied before leaning in and landing a little kiss to my temple. A… strangely comforting, but also incredibly friendly kiss.

At least that's what I told myself as I tried to commit the feel of his lips to memory while telling him, "You're welcome. Just don't go wasting all of that good henny dick on some random chick."

Levi's little chuckle warmed my skin, or maybe it was the alcohol, as he repeated, "*Henny dick*? I don't need Hennessy in my system to give good dick. If anybody knows that, it's you."

"You're the one who said it does some strange shit to you," I reminded him as I signed the receipt, being sure to leave the bartender a hefty tip.

Then I turned around, feeling confident enough to face him straight up when he finally replied, "Yeah. Puts me all in my feelings, gets me runnin' at the mouth, makes me extra aggressive. But wait… *that's* the kind of strange you were talking about?"

"I mean…" I trailed, pulling the corner of my lip between my teeth as I peeked past him out towards the crowd.

But Levi practically forced my gaze to come back his way once he replied, "Nothing strange about that, baby.

163

You see me. You want me. Shits not complicated."

I quickly brushed him off with a wave of my hand. "*Blah, blah, blah*. Get your cocky ass on somewhere. Ain't nobody tryna hear all that."

"You like this cocky ass though," he said with a smirk of confidence that I couldn't combat if I wanted to.

In fact, instead of continuing to fight it, I decided to own it as I crossed my arms over my chest and fired back, "So what? Is that a crime?"

This time, it was him peeking out to the crowd as he ran a hand across his mouth. "No. But it's definitely a pleasant surprise to hear you admit it out loud."

"Aww come on, Levi. You had to know I was interested in more than just your dick, right?"

I mean, sure his dick might've been the prime focus since opening that can of worms. But the more I learned about Levi, the more attracted to him I became. Not because he was perfect, but because he was… *human*, and honest, and charming as hell.

Still, regardless of how I truly felt, Levi wasn't as convinced when he replied, "Considering how much you've used it since you've had access… *uh*… it was hard to tell."

"Well now you know. I like you, Levi. And seeing you with Hope only made me realize it even more," I admitted, the liquid courage neutralizing the embarrassment I would've felt under any other circumstances.

But to my surprise, I wasn't alone in my feelings as Levi asked, "So how'd you think seeing you all hugged up with Jermaine made me feel?"

"I don't know. Probably like a lucky man since you knew you'd be the one taking me home tonight," I answered with a smirk as I adjusted the chain hanging from his neck, estimating in my head how much it was worth. Not because I was a gold digger, but because it surely could've been pawned to pay a year's worth of rent on a one-bedroom apartment.

But if he would've done that, then I would've never met him, and he would've never been able to say things like, "Yeah, taking you home by default."

"That's not the point. Take your wins when you get them. And let me tell you, all of this right here? *A win.*"

"But I'm the cocky one?" he asked, his smirk returning as he looked down at me.

And I couldn't help but mock him when I answered, "You like this cocky ass though."

He licked his lips, wrapping me in another embrace as he replied, "You're damn right I do. Come on. Let's get up out of here."

I giggled as I pulled away. "Nu uh. I'm here with my girls. You're just a tag-along which means you don't get to call the shots."

Instead of pulling me back in, Levi stepped just close enough to whisper in my ear, "*So you don't want me to take you home and fuck you to sleep? Smack that ass and pull on your little ponytail?*"

"*Wow.* You really think throwing me the dick is going to convince me to leave?" I asked teasingly, the words actually coming out of my mouth almost convincing me to change my answer before I could add, "Well… you're wrong. I haven't been out in a minute and I'm not about to rush it on account of that baseball bat in your pants."

"Well come on then. Let's dance. If that's what you're here for," he replied as he reached for my hand.

But I was quick to dodge his attempt as I told him, "If I wanted to dance with you, I would've just stayed my ass at home and turned on some music."

"Is that an offer for later? A private dance? In just those heels?" he asked, somehow managing to get even closer to me than he already was.

And as I ran a hand along the stubble on his chin, I gushed, "It's not even your birthday, Mr. Graham."

"Well if that's my present, I'm about to expedite my shit."

I burst with laughter as I smacked a hand against his chest, grinning from ear-to-ear thanks to the deadly combination of L's - Liquor and Levi. But unfortunately I didn't get to bask in the moment for as long as I would've liked as Hope stepped up to us, pushing her boobs to the forefront of everyone's attention as she asked - *no, not asked; demanded* -, "Come dance with me, Levi."

And as if he was suddenly under some sort of spell, Levi shrugged as he accepted her invitation. "Yeah, aight. Let's do it."

I watched with wide eyes as they slipped through the crowd to open ground before he positioned himself comfortably behind her.

"You motherfucker…" I muttered, peeking down the bar to find Wes in the face of some girl. And since he didn't belong there, I had no problem interrupting when I called out, "Wes! Wes, get over here!"

His frown was tight as he excused himself before making his way down to me. "Damn, Jules. What's the emergency?"

"*That's* the emergency," I answered, pointing towards Hope and Levi just as Hope was dropping it down to the ground in front of him.

But instead of being in a frenzy like me, Wes's face lit up as he said, "Oh shit. Aye! Go 'head then, Levi! That's my dog."

"You're supposed to be helping me!" I shouted, the liquor only intensifying the mix of emotions I felt.

And Wes did absolutely nothing to make things better when he replied, "Helping you? Last time I tried to help your silly ass, you were ready to jawjack me!"

"Yeah, cause you caught me offguard!" I reminded him, my nerves becoming more and more frazzled the longer I watched them. I mean, how was it even possible for him to have been talking all of that sweet shit one second and be snuggling up with Hope the next?

Before I could answer my own question, Wes offered, "Alright, Jules. What you need me to do then? Dance with you or somethin'? Take you out of here by the hand so he's forced to see where we're going?"

"That almost seems *too* obvious."

"Well the longer you stand here and try to come up with a plan, the longer your girl has to steal your man," he insisted as he sipped from the drink I wished was mine.

Though it was clear I didn't need any more alcohol once I snapped, "He's not my man."

"So why are you doing all of this then? It's plenty niggas in here waiting for me to walk away from you so they can shoot their shot. Just let it come to you and show Levi what he'll be missing out on. I can almost guarantee his ass will be hustling back over here once the song changes."

"But what if he doesn't?" I asked, not feeling as sure of it as Wes seemed to be.

Still, he offered a reassuring pat on my shoulder as he said, "If he doesn't then he's really as stupid as he looks which means you can do better."

He was right.

I *could* do better. Levi wasn't some anomaly. *I* was the anomaly. *I* was the catch. And if Levi couldn't recognize that, it was his loss.

I was just getting ready to turn back to the bar to order up a drink I didn't need when I heard someone behind me ask, "If you're here, then who's serving up the free drinks at *The Max*?"

I smiled as I turned around to find…, "*Danny*. Hey! How have you been? How's Shawntel?"

He pulled me into a quick hug as he answered, "She's... not so good, and I'm here. So that should tell you everything you need to know."

"*Damn*. Ya'll stay going through it," I told him as I climbed back onto the bar stool to give my feet a break.

And Danny joined me, taking the one adjacent to mine as he replied, "Wouldn't have it any other way. But who you here with, Jules? Or are you solo-dolo tonight?"

I waved my hand out towards the crowd, trying my best not to sneak a peek to get an update on Levi when I answered, "Nah, I came with Hope and Mia. They're out there somewhere."

"What are ya'll on strike or something? I'ma have to tell T her man Kelvin is trippin'."

I couldn't help but laugh, knowing that was far from the case as I explained, "Kelvin is cool. We just have lives outside of that place, contrary to popular belief."

"Well let me at least buy you a drink or somethin'. It's the least I could do considering the way ya'll take care of me over there," he said as he waved down the bartender.

The offer was definitely tempting, especially since I was desperate for just about any distraction. But since I was also determined to make it out of here on my own two feet, I replied, "I'm good."

"You sure?"

This time I nodded. "Yeah, I'm sure. The last thing I need is ol' girl coming at my neck cause her friends think you're in here buying me drinks and trying to get at me."

While I hadn't exactly met Danny's girlfriend, Shawntel, in person, I knew plenty about her through stories from him and Tiana who was like a sister to him.

Ever since Kelvin had offered him free drinks whenever he came to *The Max*, he had been sure to take full advantage, which also included him pouring his drunken little heart out about the woman he loved who drove him half crazy; not to mention her homegirls who acted like private investigators when it came to Danny's whereabouts.

But of course, he was far from concerned as he brushed me off to say, "Ain't nobody worried about those silly ass girls. And besides, I should be the one worried considering the way ol' buddy been eying me down this whole time. *Wait a minute...* is that Levi Graham? The ball player?"

"Yeah, that's him," I answered with a roll of my eyes, though my heart was giddy now that I knew I had his attention.

"Maybe Wes is actually good for something..." I thought to myself as I listened to Danny go on to say, "That nigga is so cold in hoops. I don't know how he's not in the league right now." Before continuing on to ask, "You know him like that? Or he just sweatin' you?"

This time I shrugged when I nonchalantly answered, "He's my roommate."

And to no surprise, Danny's face scrunched instantly when he repeated, "*Roommate*? Like your roommate-roommate? Or just your ex-nigga who's still on the lease so he's not moving out?"

I laughed again as I explained, "He's really my roommate, Danny. I have one bedroom and he has the other."

"Yo, that's wild. You think you can get his autograph for me?" he asked as I finally decided to peek out towards Levi, catching his eyes along with the scowl he was wearing.

Checkmate.

I leaned in, being sure to brush my hand against Danny's bicep just to stick it to Levi, even though I was only telling him, "I'm sure he wouldn't have a problem if you asked him yourself. He's super regular."

"You should bring him by the shop one time. Tell him I'll shape him up for free," he insisted just as I peeked out to Levi once again and found him a lot closer than he was the first time. A lot closer and completely alone.

And as I watched him approach, I was sure to keep my smile intact as I replied, "Well... here's your chance to tell him yourself."

Danny's face lit up as he extended his hand. "Yo, what's good man? I'm Da..."

But Levi didn't even let him finish, keeping his attention locked on me when he said, "Jules, what the hell is this all about?"

I smirked. "Just your everyday bar chat."

"So that's how you're doing it now?" he asked as if somehow I was the one in the wrong; as if he hadn't just skipped off to the dance floor with my damn friend.

But regardless of the game we called ourselves playing, Danny had clearly missed the memo as he got off of his bar stool, stepping to Levi and completely out of fan-mode when he said, "Aye, man. I don't know what your deal is, but..."

"*Danny*, I'll... be right back," I told him as I stood up, being sure to step between them before things got too out of hand. In fact, I literally had to take Levi by the hand so that I could drag him through the crowd to the only relatively private spot near the bathrooms.

But once we made it there, I had no problem ripping into him. "What the hell do you think you're doing?"

The sweet, charming Levi was long gone as he stepped to me, trapping me between his body and the wall when he looked down at me and snarled, "Don't play with me, Jules. You knew exactly what you were doing."

"Talking to a loyal customer and friend of mine? You're right. I do know what I was doing," I replied with a roll of my eyes as I turned my face away from him.

But he brought it back, his hand against my chin forcing me to look at him when he asked, "You really think your ass is slick, don't you?"

"And you don't? *Come dance with me, Levi. Come fuck with me, Levi. Come rub your dick against my fake ass booty, Levi*," I mocked, snatching my face away from his hold.

Finally, his hardened facial features began to soften when he ran his fingertips along my collarbone, causing my breathing to falter as I listened to him ask, "So you were trying to make me jealous because you were jealous over a little ass dance?"

"That's so elementary. I was literally just talking to a friend. What you took that as is your business," I replied just as his fingertips began to skim my neckline; a weakness he was obviously well aware of as he took complete advantage of the fact that I was practically squirming down the wall in response.

But instead of completely turning me into putty, he locked a gentle hand against my neck to keep me in place as he crashed his lips against mine, our tongues doing a dance of their own while the heavy bass from the club rocked through the wall behind me. It was honestly a shame how much access I gave as if I wasn't still mad at him for… *shit*, what was I mad about again?

It didn't even matter as I groaned into his mouth just as he began to pull away, taking my bottom lip between his teeth as he let me go.

While it was relatively dark in the club, I was

confident I was red in the face as I worked to catch my breath. And since there was no way in hell I was ready to acknowledge what had just happened, I told him, "Go introduce yourself. The right way. And he wants an autograph too."

Levi brushed his lips with the pad of his thumb, his smirk back in full form when he asked, "Will that be enough to get you to come home with me?"

And even though I wanted to be upset at... *something*, I couldn't help but smile back as I replied, "I'm coming home with you by default. Remember?"

Levi

"I must say, I'm surprised you lasted this long."

I reached over to my sister's carton of fries, snagging a handful and stuffing them into my mouth the same way I had always done growing up before I asked, "What are you talking about, Lily?"

While I was ecstatic when Lily offered to bring me lunch to work, I should've known she was coming with an agenda. The agenda I could no longer avoid when she answered, "You around a beautiful woman with enough attitude to ruffle your little feathers and humble you? Yeah, this was bound to happen."

"What was bound to happen?" I asked, playing as dumb as she already thought me to be as I took a full bite of my double cheeseburger, snagging the pickle that had slipped out onto my wrapper and popping it into my mouth.

But instead of matching my bite on her own burger, Lily leaned further into my desk to gush, "You're in deep, little brother. *Real* deep."

Real deep seemed like an understatement as I thought about how quickly my feelings for Jules had grown; how quickly we had fallen into a routine of enjoying each other's company, not to mention sharing a bed more often than not since she really did have an obsession with my mattress.

And since there was no way in hell I could give my sister that kind of ammunition, I was quick to brush her off as I washed the saltiness of the burger and fries down with a swig of soda. "Man, you're trippin'. Ain't nobody checkin' for Jules like that."

This time, Lily sat back in her seat across from me, crossing her arms over her chest as she said, "Keisha told me she saw ya'll lip-locking in the bar the other night. And considering all the used condoms surely hidden under a ball of toilet paper in the trashcan in your bathroom, you guys are obviously getting *well* acquainted."

"Why were you going through my trash anyway?" I asked as I took another bite.

And Lily smacked her teeth, finally going back to her business - *her burger* - though she quickly hopped back into mine when she replied, "I haven't even been at your house recently, stupid. I just know how you operate."

"So we're smashin'. What's the big deal?"

I was going back in for my burger when a fry smacked me dead in the forehead, forcing me to peek up at Lily's face which was pulled into a scowl. "First of all, don't ever tell me you're *smashin'* someone. That's gross. Second of all, my intuition tells me it's a little more than that. You like her, don't you?"

I shrugged. "Maybe I do. Maybe I don't."

Lily's excitement made me flinch when she popped up from her chair and screeched, "Oh my God! You really *do* like her! I knew it!"

I peeked around the dealership, glad to see there weren't too many people around to hear, though I was still sure to whisper, "Lily, chill. I didn't even say that."

She was already busy pacing the little space in front of my desk as she brushed me off with a wave of her hand. "Oh, please. You went from *"ain't nobody checkin' for her"* to *"maybe I do, maybe I don't"* in a matter of minutes. You like that damn girl."

"So what if I do? That don't mean shit," I reasoned, trying to keep my attention on my food so I wouldn't admit too much. I honestly wasn't sure what I even wanted from Jules; wasn't sure what she wanted from me. And since she hadn't exactly made things clear either way, there was no way I was going to force the issue.

Though Lily was clearly already invested as she said, "It means *everything*. You haven't admittedly liked someone in a long time. A *really* long time."

"But it's not like we're about to be in a relationship or somethin'. We're just… doing what adults do."

"*Doing what adults do*. Listen to you try to rationalize your feelings. That's adorable," she gushed as she finally returned to her chair.

I made quick work of finishing off my burger, reaching for another handful of her fries as I told her, "Lily, will you stop? It's not even that serious."

But my words were obviously not as believable as I needed them to be as she quickly fired back, "Oh, this is serious. I might actually get a sister-in-law out of this."

The words damn near made me sick to my stomach - or maybe it was just the food beginning to settle in - as I repeated, "*A sister-in-law*? Now you're really buggin'."

"What? Jules is a sweet girl. A good pick," she stated confidently as if she had even seen her in person more than once.

Sure, she had been the one to vet her before I moved in, knew about her long before I did. But that was nothing in comparison to actually interacting with her. And since I *had* interacted with her plenty, I had no problem telling her, "Jules is a monster. She was just being nice when ya'll were around."

"Oh, whatever. I'm sure if you actually did right by her, she'd do the same."

"You can believe what you want. But I'm not worried about her. I'm focused on this weak ass job and these workouts so I can get back to my good ass job," I told her as I balled up my wrapper and shot it into my trash can nearby.

All net.

"What a privilege to be able to make millions for playing a child's game," Lily muttered with a roll of her eyes as she took a finishing bite of her burger, balling her wrapper the same way I had and shooting it into the trash can.

Air ball.

I laughed as I stood up from my desk, grabbing the rest of the trash along with Lily's air ball before throwing it all away. And as I returned to my chair, I was sure to remind her, "Child's game or not, those millions will have us eating better than McDonald's for lunch."

"I'll believe it when I see it. But in the meantime, I need you to stop playing before you let Jules get away."

Again, I laughed as I asked, "What are you? The captain of Team Jules?"

"Captain, co-captain, president..." she rattled, forcing me to cut her off.

"Anyway! Jules is a busy girl with dreams of her own that she's trying to fulfill. She ain't trying to add me to that equation."

I didn't think much of my admission until I watched Lily's pupils practically turn into hearts. "Awwww! You guys have had the hopes and dreams talk?! How romantic."

"Man, I can't tell you shit," I whined, though I couldn't figure out if I was more annoyed with her reaction or my own honesty.

But my annoyance did nothing to trounce Lily's excitement as she insisted, "Yes you can. So tell me. What are her dreams?"

I released a heavy sigh, leaning back in my chair as I answered, "She wants to act. And she's really good too. We went to this little improv class and..."

"Levi! I can't believe I didn't know any of this. You went to class with the girl? You just might be in love."

My face scrunched as I repeated, "*In love*? Lily, have you been taking drugs?"

I wasn't sure why my sister was so eager to jump to so many unnecessary conclusions, but I knew I had to nip them in the bud before it was too late. Though it already seemed like it was too late as she replied, "Oh, shut up. You're just deflecting because you have real ass feelings for Jules. I'm happy for you though, baby bro. I hope it works out for the best."

"Yeah, we'll see about that. But like I already told you, I'm worried about getting back in the league, and making enough money to keep my head above water until that happens. Whatever comes as a positive bonus, I'll deal with accordingly."

"Maybe you should take her out on a real date. Dinner and a movie. Bowling. You know, something fun and normal," Lily suggested as if anybody had asked her for dating advice. In fact, I had practically done the exact opposite.

But since I knew she wasn't going to let this shit go anytime soon, I tried a different route when I told her, "I don't know why you're under the impression that Jules is trying to be normal with me."

The way her face scrunched in response made me feel like I was looking in the mirror. "Why wouldn't she be? You're… employed, handsome, charming, a hard worker, and my brother. You really couldn't be more qualified."

"I'm not trying to mess up our arrangement by doing too much though," I admitted. Regardless of how sold Lily was on the idea, I was the one who would have to live with Jules regardless of the outcome.

Still, my concerns didn't seem to matter to Lily as she said, "*Your arrangement*? Friends with benefits is so played out. Just look at me. Friends with benefits gave me a baby girl after I had already sworn off having more kids; not to mention I also lost the damn friend."

My fist clenched instantly at the reminder of my sister's situation, thinking about the way ol' boy had dogged her out and the ass beating I never got the chance to give him. But then again, the situation also gave us a wonderful new addition to the family in Anastasia, so I suppose all wasn't bad.

"That's not going to happen, Lily. Jules and I, we're good. We're chillin'. We're…"

"Going to fuck around and end up with broken hearts because one of you is going to be ready to move on from your little arrangement before the other. And it doesn't help that you live together. It'll be thrown in your face day after day after…"

I was forced to cut her off, holding up my hands to say, "Alright, alright. I'll ask her out. But if she says no, I'm not asking again."

"She's not going to say no, Levi. Just lay it on her thick and watch the magic happen."

"You're joking, right?"

I felt stupid as Jules peeked up at me from the couch with a look of disbelief, her legs crossed with an open magazine resting between them and a bucket of nail polishes sitting next to her.

I should've known asking her out on a date was a bad idea, should've never let Lily talk me into doing it. But here I was, attempting to save face when I answered, "I wasn't. Maybe I should be though."

Jules shook her head, closing her magazine as she said, "No. It's… sweet. And I appreciate the offer. I just don't know if it's a good idea."

"Why not? I'm single. You're single. I like you. You like me," I listed as if those facts weren't obvious.

In fact, they were so obvious that it gave Jules the ammunition to challenge, "So because the elements seem right at a surface level, we're supposed to date now?"

"Not date full-time. Just… go out on one… as friends… or whatever," I stammered before quickly adding, "*You know what*? Nevermind." Saving the little bit of dignity I had left as I turned to head to my room. At least that was the plan until I felt Jules's little hand wrap around my forearm to stop me.

And once she had my attention, she stood up from the couch to say, "I'd… love to go out on a date with you, Levi."

I offered her a half-hearted smile, convinced she was only agreeing to be nice to me even though nice wasn't always her thing. Either way I had no problem letting her know, "You ain't gotta show me pity, Jules. It's cool. I can handle a little rejection."

"But I'm serious, Levi. I want to go out with you."

"Yeah?" I asked, my eyebrow piqued as I actually became hopeful.

And her smile seemed to rejuvenate the interest I came in with as she nodded. "Yeah. So where are we going?"

I shrugged as she let me go. "I don't know. Where do you want to go?"

Her hands flew to her hips as she cocked her head to the side and asked, "How are you going to ask me out on a date with no plans, Levi?"

I shoved my hands in my pockets, rocking from side

to side as I explained, "I mean, I got ideas. Just nothing solidified. I didn't want to pick something on my own and have you all bored and shit."

"Well give me your ideas then."

I released a heavy sigh, nerves I didn't even know I was capable of having rushing to the forefront as I answered, "I was thinking we could, *maybe*, go to one of those indoor trampoline spots. Jump around a little bit. Use our energy outside of the bedroom for a change."

Once the words were off of my lips, I was fully prepared for Jules to laugh me off, call me stupid, and turn me down. But to my surprise, her face actually seemed to light up when she said, "I'm down. Let's do it."

"Seriously?"

"Yeah. Why do you sound so surprised?" she asked as she grabbed the bucket of nail polishes and sat them against her hip.

And I could only shrug as I told her, "I don't know. I guess I just assumed you'd rather be wined and dined. Treated to the finer things."

While Jules wasn't overzealous in her need for expensive shit, it was obvious in the stuff she had laying around the house, laying around her bedroom, and sewed into her hair, not to mention how stuffy and rich her ex Charlie looked the one time I saw him. I was just sure he had taken her to all the fancy restaurants in town and on trips to exotic places, all things I could no longer afford.

But once again, Jules managed to surprise me when she replied, "Levi, I didn't have much of a childhood outside of the church. So any opportunity to feel like a kid again is like giving me a chance to experience all the things I might've missed out on growing up."

"Well, damn. Now I feel like this isn't good enough. Like we gotta go to Disneyland or some shit."

She laughed, taking off towards her room with her bucket in front of her as she tossed over her shoulder, "We can save that for another day. This is a perfect start."

"Wear something comfortable. I'll pick you up at eight," I called after her, excited for whatever was to come.

And she stopped just short of her door frame, turning around with a smirk plastered on her face when she asked, "Pick me up? You mean, meet me in the living room?"

"Let a nigga do right by you, girl. *Damn*," I teased, making her blush instantly.

"Alright, alright. I'll see you at eight. And don't be late."

Jules

I stepped out of my room five minutes after eight on purpose, the sound of my door creaking open being enough of a signal for Levi to turn my way from the couch, and then stand up to greet me. While Levi always looked good, something about knowing he was exclusively mine for the night had me even more in tune with just how fine he was. The stubble on his chin was a little fuller, the tight curls at the top of his head looked freshly moisturized, and… *oh no.*

Not gray sweatpants.

How the hell am I supposed to focus all night?

I mean, sure we both needed to wear something comfortable if we planned to be monkeying around. But gray sweatpants were damn near a secret weapon, as if he needed anything to enhance what he was working with.

I tried to keep calm as he approached me. But the closer he got, the quicker he realized, "Jules, you jacked my t-shirt?"

"It looks better on me. Am I right?" I asked, running a hand from the V-neck collar to the knot I tied near my belly, turning the oversized tee into more of a crop top.

And while it was clear Levi appreciated the look, that didn't stop him from scolding, "That's not the point, Jules. How'd you even get it?"

"You left it in my room. So I washed it, and… *voila.* But, fine. I'll go change," I pouted, turning back towards the door, already thinking about what other shirts I could pair with my baseball cap, leggings, and retro Jordans I had on.

But Levi caught me by the arm before I could get too

far, turning me back around as he said, "Oh, no you won't. I love it. And I'm kind of jealous we don't wear the same size shoes."

I couldn't help but laugh, imagining how all-around wrong that would be as I insisted, "Levi, you'd look like a damn clown with feet as little as mine."

"Man, I remember calling every sneaker store in town to get a pair of those Jordans in my size. I even went online ready to pay triple the retail price, but nobody had them," he replied as he bent down to take a closer look at the shoes, even pushing down on my toes as if he was a shoe store worker checking to make sure I had the right size.

I looked down at him, crossing my arms over my chest as I asked, "Are we gonna talk kicks all night? Or are we actually going to get out of here?"

My question prompted Levi to stand up, quickly reminding me of my height disadvantage when he looked down at me with his lips pulled into a grin. "Nah, pretty girl. Leave all that attitude right here at the door. It's all positivity once we step outside. Deal?"

I shook my head, accepting the pinky he had extended my way and locking it with my own as I agreed. "Deal. Now come on."

The non-traditional nature of our situation made me giggle as he opened the front door of our apartment, letting me step out before he followed and locked the door behind us. Then he draped an arm around my shoulder, keeping it there until we made it to his car where he pulled the passenger door open for me.

"Wow. You're pulling out all the stops, huh?" I teased as I slipped inside, taking a full inhale of the Black Ice air freshener he had obviously just replaced considering its potency.

And as he waited for me to settle in, Levi answered,

"Getting your door is the bare minimum, Jules."

"Doesn't mean it always happens," I told him just as he was closing the door behind me.

But once he made it to his side of the car, he was sure to continue the conversation by asking, "So you're tellin' me Charlie never got your door for you?"

I rolled my eyes, irritation prickling my skin from the mere mention of his name, let alone his lack of basic gentleman skills. "*Ugh*. Can we not talk about him? I mean, unless you're trying to disclose something about your past relationships too."

Levi immediately shook his head as he pulled out of his parking spot. "Nah, let's not ruin our good time with irrelevant shit."

"Touché," I added as we dipped off into the light traffic.

For a moment, we rode in mostly silence, the only sounds being the light R&B coming from the radio station that had already transitioned into the Quiet Storm segment of the night. And as I took a closer listen, I realized they were playing one of my favorite songs.

"Ooh! Turn this up."

"Jules, what you know about *thee* Joe Thomas?" Levi asked teasingly as he turned the knob to increase the volume.

And I couldn't help but laugh as I replied, "I've never heard anybody call him by his full name. I mean, he was always just Joe to us."

"Who's us?"

"Elizabeth and I. We used to love his baldheaded, chocolatey ass back in the day," I answered thinking about the few times I was allowed to spend the night at her house during our teenage years before my father deemed her a bad influence and cut off all communication between us.

185

Well... *attempted* to cut off all communication between us. And it certainly didn't help that Elizabeth's family had decided to move out here around the same time, making it even easier for us to become disconnected. But somehow we still managed to keep in touch over the years, using the internet as our main line of contact until I could save up enough money for a ticket out of town right around my nineteenth birthday.

Even though I was busy taking a trip down memory lane in my head, Levi was completely present as he said, "That nigga Joe is a simp. Always trying to sing the panties off of someone else's girl. Just listen to this."

He turned the song up even louder as if I had never heard it before, allowing me to hum along as we both listened to him sing about all the things your man wouldn't do. And while it was clear Levi was bothered by the lyrics, I couldn't help but smile when I suggested, "Well... maybe ya'll shouldn't make it so easy for him to do."

"Nope. He ain't singing the panties off my girl," Levi muttered as he pressed the button to change the station.

"Levi! I wanted to listen to that," I whined with a smile as I reached for the button to turn it back.

But Levi blocked me as he said, "Now this is more like it." Before continuing on to sing the lyrics to the new song out loud.

"*From the first time, I saw your face. Girl, I knew I had to have you...*"

"Oh my God. *Stop*," I said, hardly able to hold in my laughs as he began to serenade me with another old school R&B song, *Let's Chill* by Guy. His vocals surprisingly weren't half bad. And by the time he hit the chorus, I couldn't help myself in joining in.

"*Let's chill. Let's settle down. That's what I wanna do. Just me and you...*" we sang in unison as Levi kept one hand on the steering wheel and used his free hand to snap to the beat.

"Just me and you, pretty girl?" he shouted over the music as the group went to the next verse.

"At least for tonight," I answered a little more eagerly than expected.

Levi was still vibing to the music as he said, "*See.* Real music is supposed to bring folks together, not pull folks apart. I'm about to get a whole ass girlfriend out of this one track."

I burst with laughter, shoving him in the arm as I told him, "Boy, be quiet."

And he joined in on my laugh, peeking over at me before he said, "Happiness is a good look on you, Jules. A *real* good look. I like this you even more than the other you."

I blushed, turning to face out the window even though it was dark enough that he wouldn't be able to tell anyway. But I felt… giddy - *excited* - even when I told him, "I want you to like both me's. Cause they're… both me. I'm not simple, Levi."

"I said I like this one *more*. Not I didn't like both. And trust me, I learned you weren't simple a long time ago. But that doesn't mean I don't want to piece your crazy ass together. Even if it takes a little while."

"Well you have a few more months to do so," I reminded him, suddenly rushed with mixed feelings that so much time had already passed meaning we were technically on the downhill slope.

But before I could succumb to the emotions, Levi reached across the center console and grabbed my hand, bringing it to his mouth for a kiss as he agreed, "You're right. And I'm about to take advantage of every second I can. Starting tonight."

&

"Get that shit out of here!"

I was hyped - *and tired as hell* - as I bounced down onto my butt after blocking Levi's shot, sending it halfway across the trampoline while also depleting the last of my energy reserve. We hadn't even been jumping for a full hour, but I was completely exhausted, especially after being challenged to a game of mostly airborne one-on-one basketball. And while guarding Levi was a tall order, I was proud to say I hadn't lost *that* bad, though I was sure he allowed me some points just to save my ego.

Of course he did.

He was a professional. This was his element even if we weren't on the hardwood he was used to. But I suppose he knew me well enough to know I would've been a poor sport if he didn't give me a chance to score. And since this was supposed to be a good, fun experience for the both of us, he had also allowed me to block his shot.

"Jules, you gotta chill. There are kids in here," he said with a laugh as he fell onto his back, the coils beneath us causing the surface to shake from his impact.

"It's past their bedtime anyway. If they wanna stay up with the adults, then they're going to hear adult words," I reasoned, peeking over to the kids who were hardly paying us any mind as they engaged in a game of trampoline dodgeball. In fact, that had been our first order of business; spending fifteen minutes playing dodgeball with the group of kids who were all fawning over Levi the second we arrived.

By now, he was old news.

"You really think you're all that cause you blocked my shot, huh?"

"*Twice*. I blocked your shot twice," I corrected, using my fingers as a visual.

"And I blocked yours how many times?" he asked, putting a hand behind his ear as he waited for the response that made my two blocks sound like zero.

So instead I answered, "Doesn't matter! You're like eight feet tall. And a professional basketball player. You're supposed to do that. I'm not."

Again he laughed, brushing me off as he sat up and replied, "Yeah, whatever. I'll let you have this one."

"Nope. I worked hard for it. So hard I feel like I need an inhaler," I told him, putting a hand over my heart only to find it still pounding way harder and faster than usual.

"*Damn, maybe I am as lazy as Hope said I was…*" I thought to myself as Levi asked, "*An inhaler*? Jules, I didn't know you had asthma."

"I don't. It just seems necessary."

Levi shook his head with a grin, taking a peek at the wall clock before he said, "I think our time is about up anyway."

"But it's so fun here," I whined, catching a second wind as I got back on my feet so I could bounce around a little more. And instead of joining me, Levi moved over just enough to catch me by the legs and pull me down on top of him.

"Levi, there's kids in here," I mocked teasingly as he fell onto his back, the coils ricocheting once again, causing us to jiggle.

And instead of being fazed by my reminder of our audience, Levi rolled me onto my back, hovering over me as he replied, "If they wanna stay up with the adults, then they're going to see some adult activities."

I dodged his attempts for a kiss, laughing and

squirming my way out of his hold as he tried to tickle me. And I suppose my competitive edge was still in full effect as I found extra strength to actually get away, even though I didn't really want to be away.

But I *did* want to jump around just a little more, and this time Levi decided to join me as he asked, "You having fun?"

"Can't you tell?" I fired back, doing a double bounce into a front flip that I just barely landed.

"*Impressive*," Levi said with a grin before asking, "You hungry?"

"Is that even a question?" I asked as I bounced up into a toe touch, living out the cheerleader dreams I never got a chance to fulfill.

And once again, Levi looked pleased when he said, "I'll have to make a mental note of all that flexibility you're showing off."

"Oh whatever. Are you ready to go home? I mean, we have food there," I insisted as I tried another front flip, this time falling short and landing flat on my butt.

But I bounced right back up just in time to hear Levi say, "Jules, we're supposed to be on a date. Are you gonna let me do right by you or nah?"

I smiled, the countdown clock on our time slot buzzing throughout, signaling it was time for us to go. "Alright, alright. Well what do you want to eat?"

"Nah, you can't ask me that. When you ask me that, I don't think of food," Levi replied with a smirk as he wrapped an arm around my shoulder and led us towards the row of lockers to retrieve our shoes.

I sat on the bench as Levi dug into the locker we shared, passing my shoes back before grabbing his own and plopping down next to me. And as I shoved my feet inside each, I was sure to clarify, "Well what *food* do you want to eat, Mr. Graham?"

"I think they have a taco truck a block or two from here. Is that cool with you?" he asked as he laced up his shoes then stood up, extending a hand to help me stand. And I nodded in response, accepting his hand and finding myself in the crook of his armpit once again as we strolled towards the exit.

I usually wasn't into public displays of affection, but something about Levi's actions felt too natural, too comforting for me to combat. So I didn't, instead slipping a little deeper into his embrace as we made our way down the street, passing an assortment of businesses that were closed for the night. In fact, all of them were closed for the night, except for the tattoo shop decked in neon lights.

"I've always wanted a tattoo," I muttered more to myself than him, thinking about all of the times I had almost talked myself into getting one.

But it was clear he had heard me as he stopped right in front of the window pane, turning my way to say, "Let's go get some. I've been itching for some new ink anyway."

"You're serious? I mean, what are you even going to get?" I asked, curious to see what kind of design he had in mind considering how elaborate and well thought out *most* of his artwork seemed to be. I was just sure he had a number of sketches in his head, or at least saved on his phone for whenever the time was right.

But to my surprise, he only shrugged when he answered, "I don't know. I'll figure it out after you get yours."

He was already pulling me by the hand towards the door of the shop, and I did my best log impression, forcing him to use extra strength to even make it a couple of steps. I mean, there were definitely more reasons than one that I hadn't gotten one up to this point, mainly my fear of needles and the excruciating pain that came with them.

But since I didn't want to look like a *complete* punk, I attempted another out route as I told him, "You gotta go first. Then I'll go. I just need some time to... get in the zone."

"Nah, Jules. You're going to chicken out if we do it that way. I already know."

"I'm not going to chicken out," I pleaded, though the ringing of the bell on top of the door once Levi pulled it open forced me to gulp before I actually stepped inside.

"Well what are you getting then?" he asked as he stepped towards the counter as if he had been there a million times, grabbing a book I quickly realized was filled with designs.

But I didn't need a book to know my answer, my only idea being one that had sat heavy on my heart for far too long. "A cross."

"*A cross*? Where at?"

This time, it was me shrugging when I answered, "I was thinking behind my ear. Or maybe I should put it somewhere I can actually see it. Like my wrist, or my finger."

"Whatever floats your boat, pretty girl. But once it's done, ain't no turning back. So you gotta make it count," Levi coached as if I didn't already know his words to be true; another reason on my list of reasons why I hadn't already gotten it done.

A tattoo was a lifetime commitment, unless I somehow became rich enough for laser treatments later down the road. And even if it was church-related, I could only imagine the look of horror on my father's face if he were to ever see it.

He wouldn't see it. He wouldn't see *me*. If we were to ever cross paths again, it would be by chance; not by choice. And since there was no way in hell I was getting caught in that wormhole of thoughts, I turned my attention to Levi and asked, "If you're supposed to make them all count, what the hell happened to your neck?"

He moved his hand to the exact spot I was talking about, running it against what looked like a spiderweb as he groaned, "*Eh…* I forget about that one."

"Its the most visible one, Levi!"

"Yeah. *I was…* that was a bad night. I was on my Allen Iverson shit. But everything else is solid though," he said with assurance as he closed one book and moved onto the next.

"So what are you getting then? Gotta tat my name on you if it's real," I teased as I decided to flip through the book of different fonts while we waited, reconsidering my idea as I imagined some powerful, life-changing word written in one of the options instead.

"Tat your name if it's real, huh? Yeah, aight. I got you," he replied as he abandoned his book to stand behind me, his arms straddling my body as I continued my search under his hovering gaze.

"I'm just joking. That's stupid. Don't do that," I told him with a laugh as I continued to flip through the pages just as Levi leaned in a little closer, his cheek nearly smashed against mine.

And while his close proximity gave me warm tingles, it was his words that set everything on fire when he replied, "Nope. It's happening. Find me a font."

I turned his way, pulling my head back so that I could actually see his eyes when I scolded, "Levi, don't! I'm serious."

Sure it might've been flattering, but it was also… *nuts*.

Beyond nuts.

Though Levi didn't seem to care either way as he said, "Alright, alright. I'll just get your initials."

"Levi!"

"Man, are you getting tatted or not?" he asked, reminding me of why we were here in the first place just as the tattoo artist emerged from the backroom with an obviously satisfied customer. The guy didn't look to be in too much pain, didn't look like he already regretted his decision. In fact, he looked thrilled about his new ink work that was already wrapped in a plastic bandage for healing as he shook hands with the artist.

Maybe this wouldn't be so mad.

I closed my eyes and released a deep breath, feeling a little more confident when I finally answered, "Okay, let's do this. I'm ready."

"You sure you're ready?"

"Yeah. *I'm...* I'm not ready," I squealed just as the artist approached us.

Since it was clear I wasn't as sure as I needed to be, Levi made himself busy dapping up the artist before turning back to me to say, "Fine. I'll go first."

He was already taking off towards the backroom, but I caught him by the forearm to remind him, "You don't even know what you're getting yet."

"I already told you. J.G.," he tossed over his shoulder.

And while I knew the whole *tat-my-name* thing was a joke, I couldn't help myself in correcting, "But my last name is Tyler." The least he could do was get it right for the sake of teasing.

At least I thought he was teasing until he finally turned back my way with a smirk to clarify, "Jules Graham."

The reflex of a punch flew faster than I could've imagined, landing right against his shoulder and eliciting a laugh before he continued, "I'm just messin' with you, girl. *Relax.* My mother's name was Jennifer. Jennifer Graham. J.G. I know she's always with me, but... I guess

I wanna make it real."

I honestly felt a little bad for being so self-absorbed, assuming he had really been talking about me the whole time. But since he wasn't, along with the story behind it, I could only smile.

"That's beautiful, Levi," I said as he settled into the large leather chair while the artist worked to exchange his used equipment for fresh, sanitized stuff.

That was another thing that had kept me away from the tattoo parlor; the idea of catching something because some lazy ass tattoo artist didn't use proper customer safety and health protocol. It would be just my luck that I'd be leaving with bleeding, bubbled over skin and an incurable disease.

"Yep. I definitely can't do this…" I thought to myself just as Levi asked, "What's with the cross though?"

I let out another heavy sigh, attempting to formulate my reasoning in my head before speaking it out loud. "I guess I… I believe in God. I follow His word in the best way I know how. But the way my father twisted His word to control me *was*… it was damaging. I need a fresh start in my personal relationship with God. *I*… I always want him with me."

"So make it real then, baby," Levi insisted as if it was suddenly a no-brainer, taking me by the hand and flipping it over before running his thumb along the skin of my left wrist as if he was giving me an expert suggestion for location.

I could only hope it was also the least painful.

Levi

Within the first ten minutes of Jules getting her tattoo, it was clear being super dramatic was really her thing. She was squirming, and screeching, and squeezing my hand so tightly you would've thought she was on the thirty-fifth hour of labor.

But, nope.

She was only on minute eleven of her tiny cross of ink.

"Jules, relax. It's not that bad," I told her in an attempt to keep her calm, though there was hardly any use. I suppose I was just trying to help the tattoo artist who was growing more and more annoyed with her antics, having to start and stop to ensure he wouldn't ruin her design.

But Jules still had tight eyes and tighter lips as she hissed, "I can't… *breathe*."

"You're almost done, pretty girl. Hang in there," I insisted as I peeked at her tattoo, the shading almost complete which meant her misery was thankfully almost over.

But closing in on the finish line obviously meant nothing to Jules as she croaked, "I'm… gonna... *die*."

The numbing buzz of the needle came to a halt as the guy gave her a little pat to the arm and said, "All done, mamas." Turning around in his rolling stool to grab the bottle of ointment to cover her tattoo. And as he rubbed it into her skin, I wiped the single tear that had seeped out of Jules's eye.

"Aww look at you. That's so cute," I teased, taking another peek at her now glossy ink.

Her eyes turned to darts as she shot them my way and spewed, "Shut the fuck up, Levi. I can't believe you tricked me into this shit. Sat there looking all cool and collected during your shit had me thinking this was a piece of cake."

"It looks good though, Jules. Fresh start, right? Maybe you should pray on it," I teased again, reminding her of the purpose of this whole thing; a purpose I honestly admired as the artist wrapped Jules's wrist in a plastic bandage.

While it would've been easy for Jules to hold ill-will towards God, confusing her faith with her relationship with her father, she was taking the first step in recreating the connection we all needed to succeed. And even if it was just a subtle reminder, the symbol represented so much more as it pertained to her future.

"You really think you're funny, don't you?" Jules asked with a roll of her eyes as she peeled herself from the chair.

And I could only smile as I told her, "Sometimes. You did good though. The wrist is a tough spot to get tatted."

"Is there anything that's not a tough spot?"

"Wherever you have more meat, really."

"So basically I should get your lips tatted on my ass next time?"

"As long as we get to do a few practice runs for accuracy first," I answered teasingly as we headed back towards the front to pay.

While I hadn't exactly budgeted for a tattoo coming into it, I also wasn't so broke that I couldn't afford it, even after paying Jules my half of the rent and utilities. I'd definitely be bringing my own lunch from home for at least the rest of the week though. And Jules was already busy pulling out her wallet until the artist stopped her to say, "Nah, mamas. It's on the house. Just let me snap some pics of ya'll for social media. Not every day we get a celebrity and his beautiful girlfriend in here."

I damn near choked at his words, but Jules wasted no time snapping, "I'm not his … *girlfriend*. And he doesn't deserve any special treatment. I'll pay. You did the work. I owe you money. And he does too. Don't let him have anything for free."

I immediately pulled her to the side, keeping my voice low as I told her, "Jules, the man said he wants pictures. Save your coins and give him what he wants."

Thankfully, she agreed even though she snatched away from me when she replied, "Well you better at least give him a tip, cheapie. And you still owe me tacos. *Plus* a drink."

"I got you, girlfriend," I teased before turning my attention back to the guy to ask, "Where do you want us to stand, bruh? Should I unwrap my ink to show off your handiwork?"

But apparently he had already had enough of us as he passed me his card and answered, "Nah, it's all good. Just tag the shop in a pic once it's all healed up."

I accepted the card, sticking it in my pocket before I pulled out my wallet to leave a tip as Jules suggested. "Well I… *we* appreciate you, man. I'll be sure to send a few of my boys your way."

"Thank you, sir. You did great," Jules added as she reached to stuff a handful of her own cash in his tip jar right after me.

And that seemed to brighten his spirits as he replied, "You're welcome, mamas. Maybe next time won't be so bad for you."

"Oh, no. This is *definitely* a one-and-done situation. But I see you also do piercings. Maybe I'll come talk to you about that another time," she told him with a wink that made him nod approvingly, though it was obvious I had missed the memo.

"Jules, your ears are already pierced in three different places," I told her as we stepped out of the shop onto the pavement.

And before I could wrap my arm around her shoulder, she fired back, "Who said I was talking about my ears?"

"Well damn. I'll pay good money for that right now if you're serious," I told her, refusing to walk until I heard her response.

But instead of taking me seriously, Jules only laughed as she practically started skipping down the block, tossing over her shoulder, "Come on! I'm hungry!"

It only took a few strides for me to catch up to her, shoving my hands in my pockets as we approached our original destination of the taco truck. And while I looked at the menu plastered against the side of the truck trying to decide what to order, Jules let out a subtle, "*Wow...*" right next to me.

"*What*? What happened?" I asked, peeking over to see what had her attention.

And as Jules continued scrolling through her phone at whatever she was looking at, she answered, "Elizabeth just sent me this link, and well… I hate to say I told you so."

Her words were enough to gain my full attention as she handed her phone over for me to see what she was talking about. And the second I saw the header - *Layna's Logic* - I already knew it was trouble. But I certainly wasn't expecting it to be trouble in the form of a fabricated story about the short stint of time we had spent together.

While she hadn't used full names, it was clear she was talking about me as I skimmed the article full of only partially-true details focused on her finding out Jules was my roommate. But the way Layna painted it made it seem like I was just some lowlife, live-in bum using Jules for a place to stay.

"Man, this bi… *woman* is lying," I hissed as I scrolled down to the comments that were filled with things far worse than what was included in the article. Some people were even taking guesses at who she was talking about though Layna only replied, *"I don't kiss and tell. Not too much at least. ;)"*

"What's the truth when the lie is so much more entertaining? I mean, at least she only used your initials," Jules added a lot more calmly than I expected her to be as she focused on the menu the same way I had.

"Yeah, with pretty direct descriptors. Anybody with a brain and internet can figure out who she's talking about," I replied as she stepped up to the window to place her order. And I followed up by doing the same, paying for the tacos and beer I owed her before we found a seat at the picnic table nearby.

Jules cracked open her can of *Tecate*, taking a long sip and swallowing hard. "Well… what's your move, L.G.?"

I thought long and hard, long enough to go pick our food up from the window and make it back to the table as I came up with a plan. And while I wasn't sure if it would even do more good than harm, that didn't stop me from telling Jules, "Come take a picture with me."

"What?" she asked, grease already running down her hand from her first bite.

And as she sopped it up with a napkin, I repeated, "Take a picture. Capture the moment. Remind me how much fun we're having."

Jules smirked, shaking her head as she crawled from her side of the table to join me on mine while I pulled my phone from my pocket. And the second I opened the camera, she used it as a mirror to make a few quick adjustments before suggesting, "We have to do something cute."

"So do something cute then," I told her teasingly just as she wrapped her arms around my neck, leaning in to give me a kiss on the cheek that caught me offguard. Thankfully I had also remembered to press the button to actually catch it.

She was still over my shoulder when she gushed, "That's super cute. Take one more."

This time, I took charge, grabbing her by chin with the hand that wasn't holding the phone and giving her a kiss on the cheek, the camera catching the perfect mix of bliss and annoyance she felt towards me. But it looked... *cute*. Relationship goals worthy. And definitely enough for me to use for my plan.

"What are you gonna do with that?" she asked as she returned to her tacos.

And I was already playing with the different filters when I answered, "I'm about to put this shit on the 'Gram."

Jules seemed tickled, taking another big bite of her taco and covering her mouth as she spoke. "You're crazy. It's really not that deep. The article will pass. Hell, I'm sure she's already scoping out her next prospect as we speak."

"Nah, I don't like that shit. So if she wanna play hard, I gotta let her know what's up."

"By using me? Thanks, Levi. It's *so* appreciated," Jules said sarcastically with a roll of her eyes that honestly had me worried, thinking maybe this wasn't a good idea after all.

Still, I tried to reason, "I'm not using you, Jules. I'm just... you don't like her either."

"You're right. I don't. Post that shit. And make sure

you tag me in it so she knows it's me," she replied, before taking another sip of her beer.

My fingers hovered over the screen as I typed and deleted a bunch of sayings before deciding to ask, "What should I put as my caption?"

Jules shrugged. "I don't know. Something shady without saying her name. The last thing you need to be doing is starting some real beef. Though I've been itching for a reason to lay hands on her."

Since the last thing *I* really needed was Jules catching a damn assault charge, I told her, "I got it. I got it. I'm gonna put, *"Little baby got 'em big mad"*. What's today?"

"It's Wednesday," she answered as she licked the combination of salsa and sour cream from her fingertips.

"Perfect," I told her before typing out loud, "*Hashtag W-C-W.*"

Jules burst with laughter, wiping her hands on her napkin as she squealed, "*Oh my God.* You are so damn corny."

"What? You don't wanna be my Woman Crush Wednesday?" I asked even though it was already too late considering I had just pressed the button to post it. Even if I were to go in and edit the caption, I was sure it had already been screenshotted for sharing.

But that was the least of Jules's concerns as she put a hand to her chest, and gave a sarcastic, "What an honor. Do I get a trophy too?"

I laughed, putting my phone back in the pocket of my hoodie as I answered, "Nah. You get tacos."

"Tacos are better than a trophy if we're being honest," she insisted as she started in on her second one while I inhaled my first.

And after wiping my face free of the condiments that had slipped out from my first couple of bites, I couldn't help myself in telling her, "Well you're better than tacos."

Jules blushed instantly, peeking up at me with soft eyes and boring into mine as if she was trying to read into my soul. And I wondered what she came up with, wondered if she finally saw the me beyond her original assumptions, the me that was trying so hard to come up in every aspect of my life, the me that was becoming more and more fascinated with her by the day.

"We should've done this sooner. What took us so long?" she asked, keeping her eyes on mine as if she was trying to read a reaction instead of hear one.

But that didn't mean I was going to give her one as I joked, "Couldn't get you out of the bed long enough."

"Oh, shut up," she said with a little laugh of her own, going back to what was left of her taco.

And I did the same, damn near chomping off my fingers with the bite before chewing through my words. "You're right though. We should've done this sooner. I enjoyed it. I enjoyed you."

"I enjoyed you too," she said with an innocent smirk that was soon covered up by her napkin.

"Maybe we can do it again some time. If you're free."

Even though I knew I couldn't get into anything serious with Jules, her company acted as a balancing act for everything else going on in my world. Whether she was chewing me out for leaving my basketball shoes in the middle of the living room floor or laughing at my corny jokes, spending any amount of time with her seemed to give me the boost of energy I needed to keep pushing towards my goals.

Being able to do the same for her was purely a bonus.

"If I'm free? You mean, if *you're* free? You're busier than me," she insisted as she gathered her trash in a pile.

And as I followed her lead, doing the same and pushing it to the side to clear the space between us, I told her, "Not really. I just happen to be busy during the times that you're not."

"Well, you make time for what you want, Levi."

"Jules, you already know what I want," I told her, knowing my intentions hadn't changed since the first day I met her.

Still, she acted unsure as she leaned into the table, licking her lips before asking, "What's that?"

"I want to get back into the league."

For a second she froze, looking surprised - *almost irritated even* - as she fell back from the table. "Right. The league. The faster you can get back in, the faster you can get back to your old life."

She was already climbing from the table when I stood up to catch her by the hand. "Hey. What's the matter with you?"

"Nothing," she answered, though the way she snatched her hand away completely contradicted her response.

"Jules, don't lie to me. What's wrong?"

"I said nothing, Levi. Come on. Let's go home," she replied as she grabbed her trash and headed towards the garbage can, confusing me even more.

And while I wasn't interested in causing a scene, I still grabbed my trash and caught up to her so that I could ask, "*Go home*? But I thought we were having fun."

She nodded, avoiding my eyes as she replied,

"We did. And now we're done. So I'm ready to go."

There was no way I was going to hold her against her will no matter how much her sudden change of attitude puzzled me. In fact, her attitude flip served as the perfect reminder that I shouldn't have had any real expectations for what was happening, couldn't rely on Jules to be consistent in her feelings towards me.

But for some reason I couldn't help myself in asking,

"Did I do something wrong?"

"No. This was my fault. I shouldn't have been so… *hopeful*," she answered, practically speed-walking down the block towards my car.

And as I worked to keep up with her, I pushed, "Hopeful? Hopeful for what?"

She shrugged, slowing down just slightly but still on a clear pursuit. "I don't even know to be honest. This is just… it's nice, you know. And when you experience something nice, you don't want it to be temporary, or used as a way to just pass the time. You want it to be real. You want it to be substantial. But again, my fault."

"Nah, it's not your fault. And you're not wrong. It's just… I can't guarantee you anything beyond right now. I don't know what my life is going to be like over the next couple of months. Hell, I could get the call tomorrow from my agent and be shipped clear across the country, even overseas, within a week. I don't want to do that to you; *to us*. I don't want to put you through that. I just wanna… do this."

"Because going on dates and fucking each other like rabbits can't possibly be the way to a woman's heart..." she muttered, surely rolling her eyes as she stopped just short of the car door.

But instead of unlocking it or pulling it open for her, I grabbed her at the wrist so that I could turn her around and tell her face-to-face, "You're right. We should probably put this shit on ice while we still have the option, huh?"

"Should've listened to me when I told you this was a bad idea," she replied, gnawing at the corner of her lip as she waited for me to agree.

And I did agree, no matter how distracted I was by her cleavage spilling out of *my* t-shirt. In fact, I couldn't help myself in running a hand from the crook of her neck down the crease she had unknowingly created as I told her, "I should've."

"I mean... what were we... *even thinking*?" she asked, her voice fading and her eyelids slipping lower and lower as I continued to graze her skin with my fingertips.

And they had already made it to the nape of her neck by time I said, "I know, right? *Trippin'....*"

Since we didn't have much of an audience, the streets dead with it being a weeknight, I didn't feel at all inclined to hold back on what I wanted to do to her, what I wanted to communicate even if both of our words were saying the opposite. But before I could actually bring my lips to hers for a kiss, her little whisper stopped me.

"*Levi?*"

"Yeah?" I asked, my face hovering hers as I waited for what I assumed to be permission.

But leave it to Jules to trounce any and all expectations as her eyes tightened when she snapped, "Do us both a favor and leave me alone."

Jules

I couldn't have timed the trip better myself.

Well, technically I *had* timed the trip myself. But when I planned the Las Vegas Bachelorette excursion for Elizabeth, I certainly didn't think my own love life would be in such a jumble that I needed to escape it.

To be honest, it was a stretch to even call it my love life since Levi and I weren't exactly pursuing anything *love*-related. We were just… doing the exact same stuff people did when they were which made it really, really easy to confuse the two.

And boy was I confused.

I didn't even tell him goodbye. I slept in my own bed two nights straight for the first time in weeks, and jetted out before sunrise to avoid running into him heading to his morning workout session, even if that meant being at the airport a whole hour early. But the last thing I wanted to do was see Levi, which meant being attracted to Levi, which also meant being reminded that Levi and I could never be.

He had his world and I had mine. And no matter how much us crossing paths for these few months said otherwise, that fact remained unchanged. I'd end up doing whatever I was supposed to be doing with my life, and he'd end up doing exactly what he had always planned; being the superstar basketball player - *albeit, controversial* - with plenty of money and women at his disposal.

The plane ride was numbingly quiet. No babies crying, nobody playing music out loud as if headphones didn't exist, no jokes from the flight attendants over the intercom. It was as if the world knew to just leave me alone the same way I had asked Levi to do, even though I really didn't want him to actually do it. But I knew it was for the best considering more time spent in that gray space equaled deeper heartbreak later; the last thing I needed to be adding to my long list of life's misfortunes.

I released a heavy sigh as I lifted the window shade so that I could search the clouds for some sort of clarity. But the slightest whisper of, "*Excuse me,*" interrupted my gazing before it could really begin.

I turned my head just as the woman pulled her headphones from her ears and continued, "*Hi.* I was wondering if I could borrow your black girl magic for a second. I'm reading through this script my agent sent over for a show I've been asked to produce, but something about it seems... off to me."

"You're a television producer?" I asked, my eyes wide as if she was an angel sent from heaven.

She really did have an angelic glow about her, her mocha skin perfectly highlighted and her diamond earrings popping, not to mention the rock glistening on her wedding finger. And it made perfect sense once she turned in her seat and answered, "Just a producer who accepted her first television opportunity." Then she extended her hand to introduce herself. "Alexis. Alexis Martin-Ross."

"Jules Tyler. Pleasure to meet you," I told her with a nod while also racking my brain for why her hyphenated last name sounded so familiar.

But before I could get lost in my internal search, she spoke again. "Now tell me. Does this really sound like a group of *millennial* black women talking to you? Cause to me, they sound like black girls written by goofy ass, middle-aged white men."

She turned her laptop my way as I leaned in to

read the screen line for line. And while I could definitely see the direction the writers were taking - *even found myself excited about the show's potential* -, the deeper I got, the more I realized how valid her point was. But considering she had already been tapped to produce the show, I tried to give a neutral response when I told her, "*Eh*… I mean, the jokes are kind of funny. If you have a dry sense of humor."

"*Dry*. Exactly. I mean, I would never say this kind of stuff to my friends," she replied with a laugh as she scrolled through the document, stopping to read, "*Girl, your outfit is so fleeky*," and tossing her head back with another laugh.

And I couldn't help but join in as I told her, "Me neither. It would be more like, "*Bitch, whose man are you trying to take in that dress though?*""

"Yes! Me too! See, I knew I wasn't trippin'. Thank you so much," she replied with a pleasant smile before turning to her computer to make a note. Then she turned back my way, her face pulled into a curious gaze as she said, "Hey. You wouldn't happen to be a writer, would you?"

For whatever reason, a bout of nerves rushed over me as I shook my head. "Uh… *no*. I mean, I never have. I just know how scripts work."

"Because you're an…"

"Actress. I guess," I answered, feeling more and more uneasy now that I had said it out loud.

Even though Alexis was a complete stranger who I would never see again, her confidence about what she was doing with her life was palpable while mine was still… under construction, making me feel lesser than though I knew it wasn't on purpose. In fact, she was far more worried about…, "You guess? What do you mean, you guess?"

This time I shrugged. "I want to be an actress. Just haven't caught a break yet."

"Yeah? Well, what's the issue? I mean, are you any good?" she asked as she closed her laptop, giving me her full attention which honestly made me even more nervous about the conversation.

And my voice was just above a whisper when I answered, "So I've been told."

"Have you been auditioning?"

I shrugged again, looking down at my lap and gnawing on my lip as I replied, "Probably not as much as I should be if I expect to actually win."

While Levi had been on my ass trying to get me to go to more and more casting calls, his push hadn't amounted to anything more than a few, "Thanks for your interest" emails and automated phone calls; two to be exact.

Still, his extra interest and my lack of real effort thankfully didn't stop Alexis from asking, "If I gave you an opportunity to win, would you take it?"

"In a heartbeat," I answered more quickly than expected, as if the hunger for success came from a place I hadn't been able to tap into until she asked. And while I wasn't even sure what she meant, I found comfort in the way she smiled as she dug in her purse for a pen before snagging the napkin from under her cup to hand to me.

"Here. Write your information down. I'm sure we'll be holding auditions soon, and I'd love to give you a shot at one of these parts if you're serious."

"As a heart attack," I told her, feeling myself on the verge of having one as I scribbled down my information before handing the napkin back to her.

She took a peek at it, making sure she could actually read my handwriting, before slipping it into her purse. "Cool. Once we get things set, I'll be sure to shoot you the information. You have to be ready though, Jules. I can only provide you the opportunity. It's up to you to make something of it."

"I'll be ready. I promise."

"Bitch, you're about to be famous!"

"And you're about to be married!" I squealed as Elizabeth pulled me into a hug so tight I thought I would burst. But I needed it - *all of it* - especially after the interesting series of events that had played out in my life, allowing me to add, "God, I've missed you so much. I can't believe you left me out there to fend for myself."

"You're not *exactly* alone," she gushed as she let me go, heading towards the in-suite bar she had clearly already raided without me.

And as I tossed my bag to the side in the room we would call home for the weekend, I was sure to remind her, "Oh, I'm definitely alone. And Levi was sure to remind me of that with his, "*I'll fuck the shit out of you until the lease is up, but that's about it*" speech."

I plopped down on the couch, replaying the moment outside of his car in my head as I thought about the different ways I could've reacted. Maybe I should've just kissed him; taken him up on the arrangement he was offering even if it meant disaster later. Or maybe it wouldn't be a disaster; maybe it would just fade to black like a movie, never to be picked up or explored again.

No matter how confused I was about it, that didn't stop Elizabeth from shoving a drink in my hand as she suggested, "That is not what he said, Jules."

"Might as well have," I muttered as I took a long

sip, quickly realizing I would've been better off making it myself considering how strong it was. And it was clear Elizabeth had made the drink to her taste as she took a sip from her own, hardly even blinking as she plopped down on the couch next to me.

"Well… at least he kept it real with you. I mean, he could've just dribbled your heart like a basketball until he was ready to slam dunk it in the trash can."

"That might've felt better actually. A clean break is much easier to heal than a partial one," I insisted as I took another, longer sip knowing the more I drank, the better it would taste.

"I'm not sure if there's any real science behind that, but I'll let you hoop," she replied with a smirk.

A smirk that only annoyed me even more as I told her, "*Oh my God.* Will you stop with the basketball zingers? I'm here to celebrate you, not be reminded of the shit show I'll be returning home to."

"Levi doesn't seem like a shit show, Jules. He actually seems like a nice guy. And that little picture he posted on Instagram of the two of you was so adorable. *Little baby.*"

I shrugged, holding my glass in front of me as I explained, "It was just a tagteam petty stunt."

"Tagteam petty stunt?"

"He was all upset because of that article Layna wrote. So to get back at her, he used me to make her *big mad*," I emphasized, thinking about how the picture had quickly shown up on her blog with the tag, *"New Couple Alert"* as if she wasn't the one trying to go at Levi in the first place. But I suppose her throwing her support behind us - *whatever us was* - was her way of waving the white flag since Levi had been one of the few to actually fight back.

Still, regardless of what I knew the picture to be, that didn't stop Elizabeth from suggesting, "You looked happy, Jules. Like, genuinely happy."

"Because pettiness brings me great joy, Liz. If anybody knows that, it's you."

"Nah, that was a different kind of happy. I mean, you said you guys were having a good time together before things went left," she reminded, causing a mix of emotions to run over me as I gave myself another highlight reel version in my head before peeking down to the tattoo on my wrist. And while it would've been easy to play it off, easy to brush off as nothing, I knew it was useless to hold back since she already knew the details.

So instead, I was completely honest when I told her, "That was the most fun I've had on a date in… *ever*. But it doesn't mean anything now."

She grabbed my free hand, squeezing it as she said, "Yes it *does*, Jules. You can still enjoy his company. Just have to ween yourself off of his peen."

"That's impossible. I'm already going through withdrawals," I told her as I pulled my hand away and started scratching at the back of my neck, making Elizabeth laugh as she smacked a hand against my thigh before standing up to head back to the bar.

"Girl, you better have Nori give you the hook-up with some of those toys from *Pleasures-R-Us* and call it a day," she yelled over her shoulder, clearly amused as she refilled her drink. And her mention of *Pleasures-R-Us* gave me the opportunity to match her amusement as I reached for my suitcase, digging past my clothes to find the first of many wedding gifts.

I pulled it from my bag just as she turned around, her eyes going wide the second she realized what it was. "Jules, this is…"

"Huge, right? Don't use it too much though, or Marcus might think you cheated on him. I mean, I'm sure he'd fall right in trying to follow that up," I told her with a laugh as I tossed the oversized dildo at her.

And she was quick to dodge it like it was the real thing, letting it fall to the ground as she replied, "I'm marrying him for a reason, Jules."

I stood up, heading towards the bar and almost tripping over the damn thing on my way as I assured her, "Well tonight, we're going to party like you don't even know that nigga."

I was already refilling my glass as she replied, "Now that's what I'm talking about." Then she held her glass up for a cheers; a cheers that I met even though I was getting ready to kill her vibe.

I swallowed the sip I had made to perfection, moistening my lips before I delivered the news. "*Actually*, Marcus's sister isn't really about that life. And neither are your sorors. So we're gonna... eat our cute little meal, have one non-carbonated beverage, and go to that snoozefest of a piano bar they recommended," I told her with a slow roll of my eyes, already dreading the stuffiness.

And it was clear Elizabeth was just as frustrated as I was when they suggested it in the first place as she asked, "You're kidding me, right? You actually agreed to that?"

"It's what they said you wanted," I reasoned, quickly pulling my glass to my lips so that I wouldn't have to say anymore.

But Elizabeth's face was already twisted with annoyance as she pleaded, "Jules, you know me better than any of them. And you know I don't want to do... *that*."

I nodded to agree. "I *do* know that. Which is why I… also came up with other plans; backup plans. I mean, I would've gone with it if you were game, but I also know you which means you wouldn't have been game.

So we *are* going to dinner. But then we will be

properly escorted to the party bus for the best night of your life, even if it's just the two of us and a couple of strangers off the street."

While I knew I'd be excusing myself from the dinner table to actually make the plans I had already spoke up, there was no way in hell I was going to ruin my best friend's weekend. And even though the expenses of it all would be cutting severely into my weave budget for the month, it was all worth it once Elizabeth smiled to say, "I knew I picked you as my Maid of Honor for a reason."

"Wearing my natural hair for a week won't be so bad. I can just… watch a bunch of YouTube tutorials," I thought to myself just as my phone began to buzz on the couch nearby. And the second I read the screen to see who it was, I was quick to excuse myself, though I was sure it only made things look even more suspicious as I slipped into one of the bedrooms just as the FaceTime call was connecting.

I couldn't help myself in licking my lips the second it did before I acknowledged, "Levi. *Hey.* Is something wrong with the apartment?"

I hated the way my body reacted to his heavy gaze as if we were even in the same room; even in the same city. And I was reminded of that fact when he finally spoke, "I haven't seen you. Haven't talked to you. I guess I was just making sure you were still alive."

Regardless of our current predicament, his concern was flattering, eliciting a smile as I told him, "I'm alive. I'm… in Vegas."

"*Vegas*? What are you doing in Vegas?" he asked as he sat up, keeping the phone in front of him as he showed off just how distractingly naked his chest was.

And no matter how tempting it was to come up with some elaborate story - *lie* - just to get under all the skin he was showing off, I decided to avoid adding any more controversy by answering shortly, "Liz's Bachelorette Party."

He nodded, running a thumb across his lip with a smirk. "Oh, I thought you were on the run or somethin'. Avoiding me on purpose."

"It's not that serious, Levi," I told him with a smirk of my own.

"Of course not," he muttered before picking up his voice to add, "Well… I'm glad you're alright. Have fun. Tell Liz I said what's up."

"I will," I told him with a half-hearted smile, feeling regretful that we had turned into this; had become worthy of only a surface level check-in. And by the look on Levi's face, it seemed like he felt the same way, forcing me to ask, "Is there… something else?"

"You look good, Jules. Don't hurt 'em too bad out there," he said, giving me the full smile I had fallen in… lust with.

And while I knew I was playing with fire, tiptoeing back into a place I didn't belong, I couldn't help myself in flirting, "If that's not the goal, you're doing Vegas wrong."

"You're right. I guess I'm just being selfish as usual," he said, giving me another one of those gazes that made my heart flutter.

But before I could get fully sucked back in, I told him, "Whatever, Mr. Graham. I gotta go." Though I wasn't exactly ready to hang up, wasn't ready to stop... looking at him.

I suppose this was why I had avoided him in the first place, so that I wouldn't find myself in this exact position. And I knew the small crack of vulnerability was officially under attack once Levi said, "I miss you, Jules."

"No you don't," I told him with a giggle as I shook my head, trying to maintain at least an ounce of control no matter how crazy the butterflies were going in my belly.

And it didn't help that Levi doubled-down when he said, "I'm serious. It's all quiet around here. And it doesn't smell as good."

"Try a shower. That usually helps," I teased, jokes and miles being the perfect buffer to separate myself from the situation.

But of course, Levi was quick to remind me that the distance was only a temporary thing when he replied, "Be good out there, Mean Ass. I'll see you when you get back."

"Yeah… see you then," I whispered as the call ended.

And while I expected to have a moment of silence to get myself together, to digest my thoughts and feelings about the conversation, Elizabeth line-jumped it all when she shouted, "Bitch, ya'll go together!"

"We do not!" I shouted back, feeling defensive as I stepped out of the room and found her leaning against the wall right outside of the door.

Of course her ass was eavesdropping.

"*I miss you, baby. Come home, baby. It's not the same without you,*" she mocked teasingly as she made her way back to the bar.

And once again, I found myself on the defense as I followed her while replying, "That's not what he said."

"That's what it translates to," she fired back as she handed me one of the shots she had already poured.

Even though my nerve endings were beginning to tingle from all of the alcohol we had already consumed in the less than an hour we had been together, the conversation with Levi gave me plenty needing to be washed down as I clinked glasses with Liz before tossing it back with ease.

I honestly wasn't even sure what to expect when I

made it back home. Were we supposed to be buddy-buddy acting like nothing ever happened between us? Or were we supposed to be cutty-buddy, acting like *everything* happened between us and we were desperate for more?

Girl, are you already drunk?

He said he doesn't want more.

"Are you ready to go?" I asked as I wiped my mouth with the back of my hand, knowing dinner was even more crucial if I expected to stop thinking about it all, let alone be able to survive the night.

And I was saved by the knock on the door, signaling the rest of our group's arrival as Elizabeth replied, "I guess I don't have much of a choice now."

Levi

I was desperate for a way to fill my time so my thoughts wouldn't be completely consumed by Jules. She had technically only been gone for two days, but it felt like a lifetime considering we weren't exactly on the best of terms when she left. And now that we seemed to be at least heading in the right direction after our phone call, I found myself trying to do everything I could to make the time go faster until she would make it back.

Playing basketball, watching film, and lifting weights was enough for me to exhaust myself to the point of needing a hot shower and a solid nap. But now that I was awake with most of the afternoon still remaining, I decided to skip over to Lily's crib for what was sure to be an equally exhausting experience with my niece and nephews.

The second I pulled up, I was bum-rushed by Adrian and Andre who were both anxious to update me on their lives as I made my way from the car towards the apartment. In fact, I hardly caught a word they said as they shouted over one another, both desperate to get their point out before the other could. But once I actually stepped inside, it was little Anastasia who toddled her way right into my arms, practically stealing the show.

"Man, I can't believe how big she's getting," I shouted to Lily as I picked her up and slung her against my hip just as her mother was emerging from the kitchen.

And as she wiped her hands on the dish towel she was carrying, she replied, "*You*? Imagine how I feel trying to carry her big behind around like she's still a baby."

"She *is* a baby, Lily. And she'll always be one with

those two guard dogs as her big brothers," I told her just as the two of them slipped off to their bedroom, already engaged in a new argument over what action figures they were going to play with.

I admired their connection, along with the way they loved on and protected their baby sister. But that wasn't enough to stop Lily from suggesting, "You know good and well you're way more protective than they'll ever be, Uncle Levi."

I snuck a kiss on Anastasia's cheek, causing her to giggle as she tried to push my face away with her grubby little fingers. "Just returning the favor since you've protected me all of these years, sis."

"Aww look at you. Jules is clearly softening that ass up," Lily gushed as if I hadn't always shown her and the kids mad love.

But since I knew she was just taking any opportunity she could to tease me about it, I was sure to do the same when I told her, "Yeah, softening my ass up by throwing that ass back."

"Levi!" she screeched, snapping the dish towel at my legs.

And I couldn't help but laugh, bouncing Anastasia in my arms as I replied, "I'm just messing with you, Lily. We haven't even been fuckin' around like that."

"Thanks for the update. So greatly appreciated," Lily said with a roll of her eyes just as my phone began to buzz in my pocket. Since I couldn't reach it with Ana in my arms, I sat her down on the ground before I pulled it out. And all it took was one quick glance at the screen for Lily to snap, "See. He's the exact reason I have to be so protective of you. What is that nigga doing calling you?"

"*Chill*. He's still my agent, sis. If he's calling, he must have some good news," I explained just as I tapped the screen to answer the call on speakerphone.

"Yeah, he better," was all she muttered in response, forcing me to shake my head as I said, "Damien, what's the word?"

"Levi Graham, it's good to hear your voice," he replied, his voice thick with satisfaction which instantly made me hopeful.

But I didn't get a chance to bask in it for too long as Lily shouted from nearby, "Get to the point, Damien!"

"Hello to you too, beautiful," he quickly added, obviously amused by my sister's disdain for him.

In fact, she was still rolling her eyes when I brought the conversation back to its original topic. "So what's up, Damien? What you got for me?"

He released a sigh that wasn't exactly heavy but also not as cheery as I would've liked when he finally replied, "Nothing set in stone just yet, but we do have a few things potentially brewing."

"Things as in contracts?"

"Things as in possible tryouts. Unfortunately, you're still considered damaged goods, Levi. So you'll have to prove yourself before anybody is willing to take a chance on you."

I tried to keep my composure, but the phrase "damaged goods" had my blood boiling as I thought about how hard I had worked over the years. Hell, how hard I had worked my whole life. Sure, I had suffered a few injuries, had ran into a few setbacks, but there was nothing *damaged* about me. So I had no problem defending, "Man, they know my game is tight. It's always been tight."

Again, Damien sighed before he added, "Your game has also been sitting dormant which means there's no telling what you can still do. Now I'm going to see if I can get the clearance I need to get them all set-up. But in the meantime, I need you to stay on your A-game."

I nodded as if he could see me, knowing if nothing else, that was something I could actually control. "I got you, bro. Thank you."

"You're welcome, Levi. I want the best for you. I want you to win. Don't ever forget that."

Once again I nodded. "Yeah, I hear you. But hey, while I have your ear. Do you happen to know any talent agents?"

"I know a few, why? Are you trying to broaden your portfolio?"

I peeked up at Lily and found her eyes boring into mine as she cocked her head to the side waiting to hear my response. But since I knew my answer would warrant even more of a reaction, I looked elsewhere when I told Damien, "Nah, not for me. For my gir… my roommate. She's a really good actress, but she doesn't have anybody to represent her."

"I'll make some calls. See what I can do."

"Bet. I appreciate that," I said as I peeked up to Lily once again, this time finding a smirk plastered on her face as I halfway listened to Damien respond.

"No problem. But remember, Levi. *A-game*. And stay your ass at home so you're not getting into any trouble. The last thing we need is another headline."

"You have nothing to worry about, man. I'm a homebody like a mothafucka these days," I told him with a chuckle that Lily silently mocked.

And while I rolled my eyes at her, I heard Damien say, "Yeah, alright Mr. Homebody. I'll get up with you soon." Before ending the call.

I was hardly surprised when the first thing out of Lily's mouth was, "Your gir… roommate, huh?"

The only thing I could fire back without completely outing myself was, "Shut up, Lily."

But that wasn't enough to stop Lily from continuing

on her teasing streak as she practically sang to Anastasia, "Your Uncle Levi is a homebody because he's whipped," before turning to me to ask, "Where is Jules anyway?"

I shrugged. "She's in Vegas. Gets back tomorrow afternoon."

"*Oh*, so *that's* why you're here. Your little gir… roommate is out of town so you're trying to pass the time. How sweet," she gushed in only a way she could.

"Man, whatever," I replied with a wave of my hand just as my phone began to buzz again.

Lily smacked her teeth as she picked Anastasia up from the ground before asking, "Geez, what does he want now?"

"Nah, it's Wes," I told her just as I pressed to accept the call and asked, "Wes, what's up?"

His heavy panting was enough to make me nervous when he replied, "Levi, can you meet me at the hospital? Chloe just went into labor!"

I flew up from the couch, surely doing nothing to help his anxiety as I shouted, "Oh shit! Hell yeah, I'll be there as soon as I can. Ya'll need anything?"

"Just support so I don't… pass the... fuck out," he stammered as Chloe let out a scream of pain in the background.

And as he coached her through with a, "*We're almost there, Chloe.*" I was sure to tell him, "I got you, bro," before I ended the call.

I was already on my way towards the door when I told Lily, "I gotta go, sis. Baby Girl Wes is making an early entry."

Her concern was evident when she replied, "A *really* early entry. Is everything okay?"

"Man, I sure hope so. Gotta get there and see though," I answered as I leaned in to give her a quick hug before I dipped out of the apartment, jogging to my car and taking off out of the parking lot with the speed of a racecar driver.

I was nervous as hell as I thought about something going wrong with the baby; thought about my closest friend going through the rollercoaster of emotions that came along with bringing a new life into the world. But since I knew there wasn't much I could do to control either, I was going to do for Wes what he had done for me from day one.

Have his back.

The moment of clarity came as I watched Wes stare lovingly at his family; his brand new baby girl resting in the incubator with an assortment of different cords attached, and her mother who was also fast asleep after surviving a scary eight hours of labor.

It wasn't that I suddenly wanted a child of my own. In fact, it really didn't have anything to do with the baby. But the way Wes looked at Chloe in awe for safely bringing his daughter into the world, the way he became enraptured by her presence after being traumatized by the thought of losing her, brought Jules to the forefront of my thoughts.

Sure, we hadn't been in some on-again, off-again relationship like Wes and Chloe, and we certainly didn't have a child on the way prematurely. But we *had* experienced our share of ups and downs, along with the middle ground we currently found ourselves sitting in; a middle ground that I was no longer interested in.

I didn't just want Jules in my life. I *needed* her. Her support, her energy, her… *insults*. She challenged me in a way that no one else had because she knew me in a way that no one else did. There were people who knew me solely for basketball, people who knew me from the shit in the media, and then people like Lily who knew me from the second I entered the world which created a totally different perspective. But the fact that Jules knew the complete me, flaws and all, and found a way to still admittedly like me was something I couldn't just let go to waste for selfish reasons.

Of course I knew there was a lot of risk in getting involved in something serious without any certainty of my next step in life. And I knew we had already agreed to let whatever was brewing between us simmer down. But after watching Wes and Chloe, and gaining a new understanding of how important it was to uphold valuable relationships in our lives, I knew it was time for a change of plans.

I was in the middle of straightening up the living room when the locks clicked with Jules arrival, making me anxious as I considered what her reaction would be. And while I hoped her feelings for me wouldn't have dissolved that fast, I also had to keep in mind who I was dealing with.

So I tried to remain neutral as I told her, "Welcome back, pretty girl."

"Hey," was all she offered in response as she closed the door behind her, dropping her bag right next to it before kicking off her sneakers.

While I could tell the little vacation had obviously gotten the best of her according to the sunglasses and baseball cap she had on, paired with her joggers and t-shirt, it still felt like the appropriate thing to ask, "How was your trip?"

227

Instead of answering my question right away, she made her way to the kitchen, pulling her stool from under the kitchen sink and using it to access the medicine cabinet so she could grab the bottle of Advil. And after opening the bottle and tapping two pills into her hand, she finally replied, "What happens in Vegas stays in Vegas."

I nodded to agree. "Good answer. I'm glad your back though. It's good to see you."

With the pills in her hand, she climbed down and headed for the fridge to grab a bottle of water to wash them down with. And as she twisted the cap off she said, "Levi, you act like life just suddenly came to a halt because I was gone."

"It did."

Instead of accepting my confession, she shook her head in disbelief, shoving the pills in her mouth and swallowing hard with a gulp of water before suggesting, "Your flattery really isn't necessary."

"I can't help it. I just... I want you, Jules."

I wasn't even sure why the words came out right then, let alone came out so strongly. But now that they were gone, released into the world and directed towards the person who needed to hear them, I knew there was no turning back. And I could tell Jules was just as surprised as I was when she pulled her sunglasses off, her voice low when she asked, "What does that even mean?"

"I can't go cold turkey like this. Shit doesn't even feel right," I explained as I took a step closer to her.

Though my step only prompted her to take a step away as she crossed her arms over her chest and tossed over her shoulder, "Doing stuff we have no business doing doesn't feel right either."

"It doesn't?" I asked as I closed the space between us once again, this time wrapping an arm low against her waist to remind her just how well we fit together; just how well we meshed.

And I could tell the memories were just as vivid for her as they were for me as she sank into my hold, releasing a heavy sigh before she replied, "I mean, it does. It *did*. It felt great. It just wasn't... smart. I can't operate under those uncertain conditions. I can't operate in that gray area knowing you're going to be one foot in and one foot out. But I respect what you're doing. I respect your dreams. I respect your goals. Which is why I'm saying no more. You can give all of your attention where it belongs. In the gym."

While I could appreciate the stance she was taking, the truth was..., "Jules, I've been playing basketball all my life. I can shoot free throws with my eyes closed, I can dribble in my sleep. Hell, I can probably cross somebody up with my feet tied together. But the fact of the matter is, I'm not really in control of how that all plays out. I can do the work, I can put in the extra effort, but at the end of the day, it's not in my hands. But you wanna know what is in my hands? *This*. You and me. *This* is something I can control. And I'll be damned if I drop the ball."

Jules peeled herself from my hold, turning around to see my face when she asked, "So what are you saying then?"

"I guess I'm trying to say... what's that life if I don't have anyone real to experience it with? To take the journey with me? To enjoy the process with? In all honesty, I think that's where I went wrong the first time. Surrounded myself with all of those fake ass niggas as if that was going to help my situation when it only made it worse," I told her before continuing, "Now I've worked my ass off to right my wrongs when it comes to my career, and I have faith that it'll all work out however it's supposed to be. But there's not as much value in that if I don't have my little baby rockin' with me too."

I had already learned early on to expect the unexpected when it came to Jules. But I still wasn't prepared for her to ask, "Did you rehearse that?"

"*What?*"

"That little spill. Did you rehearse that?" she repeated, her tight lips slowly turning into a teasing grin as she waited for me to answer.

And even though I wasn't sure where she was going with it, I still kept it real when I licked my lips to reply, "I thought about it long and hard while you were gone, but it came from the heart."

Her little grin turned into a full-on smile, making me feel hopeful as she started, "Look, Levi. I know I'll probably never be as important to you as basketball. Basketball is your life. It's your world. It's always *been* your world. And I know if I had something as important, *something as sacred*, I'd want someone to have my back too."

"I'll always have your back, pretty girl. You're like... *I don't know*. Like the best friend I never had," I told her, eliciting a laugh as she smacked a hand against my chest in disbelief. And while I was glad to see her back in good graces, I couldn't help myself in pulling her back in so that I could continue, "I'm serious though. You just... you get me, Jules. You challenge me. You teach me shit and allow me to do the same for you. You do cool shit so effortless that I'm forced to level up if I really wanna stand a chance with you."

"I'm really not that great," she muttered with a roll of her eyes as she rested her head against my chest.

And I put my chin on top of her head as I teased, "Maybe not, but still."

"Levi!" she screeched, pulling away to slug me in the

arm.

And I could only laugh as I reasoned, "You're the one who said it."

"See. You play too much," she insisted as she took another gulp of her water bottle, reminding me of her trip which also reminded me of something I had done while she was gone.

I knew I was in store for yet another unpredictable response, but I had a feeling this one would be even more positive than the last when I told her, "I have a surprise for you."

"Flowers and sea-salted caramels?" she asked, her eyes lighting up in the process.

But I shook my head no as I replied, "*Better*. I... I talked to my agent."

"And..." she trailed with confusion, waiting for a full explanation.

"And he talked to some of his talent agent homies..." I added, building the suspense of it all as Jules grew more and more confused.

In fact, she was so confused she could only press on with another, "And..."

"And... *we*.... found somebody to represent you," I spilled, bracing myself for whatever was to come.

But to my surprise, Jules was completely calm as she repeated, "*Represent me?*"

"Yeah. Those actress streets are rough, but having somebody to plug you will make it a whole lot easier," I explained in the same way Damien had explained to me during our latest check-in. While he only had potentially good news regarding my career, I was grateful that he had went the extra mile to pull some strings for Jules.

Still, she seemed stunned as she leaned against the kitchen counter before stammering, "But I... I can't afford that."

"You don't have to pay them anything upfront. It's a risky business, but agents know what they're doing which is why they're so picky about what clients they accept. And I mean, the quicker they get you a gig, the quicker they get paid. So it's really a win for the both of you."

"Well can I tell you a secret?" she asked, already gnawing at her lip as she waited for me to respond. And the second I gave her a nod, she continued, "I might have a gig. Like, a real one."

"Word? You got a call back?"

She shook her head. "No. I ran into this producer on the plane and we exchanged info."

My eyes rolled instantly as I caught myself growing angry when I told her, "Man, he was probably just some bitch ass nigga tryna get you to take your clothes off on camera."

But Jules was quick to throw water on my growing fire when she brushed me off to explain, "It was a woman, Levi. And she's legit. I looked her up. Alexis Martin-Ross?"

"*Alexis*? Like, Jaden's girl?"

"His wife now according to her Wikipedia. But you know them like that?" she asked, her eyes wide with interest as if the ideas were already churning in her head.

And I tried my best to explain, "Nah. I just know *of* them. Alexis, *uh*... she used to talk to Bryson Harris back in the day. Bryson and Wes played on the same team before Wes got traded so I got to know him a little bit through Wes. And he... he mentioned her a time or two."

Mentioned her seemed small scale considering how enamored with the girl Bryson seemed to be even though it was clear Alexis had her sights set on Jaden from the jump. But Bryson had always been convinced that she and Jaden were just some temporary thing until he was ready to make his move. A move that never actually got made since Jaden and Alexis had obviously stuck it out, and Bryson had thankfully found someone of his own.

Well… *sort of.*

Either way, none of that seemed to matter to Jules as she muttered, "*Ugh. He is so damn fine.*" Earning herself a stiff side eye as I brought the original topic back to the forefront of the conversation.

"That's what's up though, pretty girl. I hope it all works out for you. But I'm proud of you regardless."

Her smile was filled with pride when she replied, "Thank you, Levi. And thanks for talking to your agent. You really didn't have to do that, but I'm so glad you did."

"I'm just trying to put some good vibes out into the world, you know? And maybe they'll make their way back to me someday," I told her with a smile of my own, knowing even if they didn't, I was still glad to be able to lend a helping hand that didn't involve me handing over a check.

But Jules seemed to appreciate this kind of help more than anything as she stood on her tippy toes to pinch my cheek when she insisted, "I'm sure they will. You deserve it."

"You really mean that? I'm not just some basketball asswipe to you anymore?"

While I knew the dynamics between Jules and I were steadily changing, it was still a solid stroke for my ego to hear her answer, "No. You're actually halfway decent."

"Only halfway?"

She shrugged, falling back to flat feet as she ran a hand along my chest. "Depends of if you're trying to whip up some more of that spaghetti. I need some carbs to soak up all of this alcohol with."

"Yeah, I can still smell it on your breath," I teased, quickly dodging her attempt to slug me once again.

And I was already laughing by the time she said, "Shut up. No you can't."

"It's practically oozing out of your pores, Jules. Let me see if I can taste it too," I told her as I pulled her into a hug, trying to get a little sample of the lips I had been eying since she first walked in.

This time, it was her dodging me as she whined, "Levi, stop. That's not what best friends do."

"That's what I do with *my* best friend," I clarified as I took a plunge, only catching her at the cheek.

But I still wasn't giving up. And I could tell she was struggling not to give in to my pursuit, though she still found the power to tease, "I knew you and Wes were a little too close."

I shook my head as I gave her the leeway to break free. But she didn't budge, letting me know she was actually enjoying our little tussle, actually enjoying being this close to me. But since continuing to battle it out wouldn't necessarily get me what I wanted, I decided to flat-out ask, "Can you just give me a kiss already? I really missed you, pretty girl."

"If you *really* missed me, you would want to do more than just kiss me," she said with a sneaky little grin as she finally pulled herself away from me.

"Well *damn*. I didn't know that was an option," I called after her as she took off towards her bedroom.

And over her shoulder, she was sure to let me know, "You're right. It's not."

"*Wait*. That doesn't mean it can't be though," I insisted as I stepped out of the kitchen to find Jules leaning against the frame of her bedroom door with her arms crossed, reminding me of just how happy I really was to have her back.

Even if we still had some figuring out to do, and even if none of it was for certain, I was more than ready for whatever was to come. And if whatever was to come was somehow correlated with the invitation she was currently giving me with her eyes, I knew I was in for a treat.

Jules

There was nothing - *and I mean, nothing* - that could've knocked the smile off of my face as I strolled into work earlier than normal. After spending most of the week getting reacquainted with my roommate, sleeping in his arms and waking up to his annoyingly adorable ass kissing my face, I felt like a weight had been lifted off of my shoulders and instead moved to my heart where it belonged from the get go.

Well… maybe it didn't belong there. Maybe I was making a mistake in allowing Levi to infiltrate my being. But it felt like a mistake worth making as I considered the potential, not to mention how good things were already panning out.

The Max was still relatively quiet, only a few strays left from Happy Hour as the crew prepared for the night shift. And I wasted no time jumping in, humming as I filled the shelves with the freshly-sanitized glasses from the dishwasher.

"There's the Jules I know. What's up with you?" Kelvin asked as he joined me behind the bar, checking the bottles to make sure we had everything we needed in stock.

And as I continued to replace the glasses I fired back a question of my own. "A girl can't be happy for the hell of it?"

He smiled, nodding to agree as he replied, "I'm glad you are. We're expecting a big crowd tonight."

"Nothing I can't handle, boss man," I told him with a wink just as my phone began to ring in my pocket. It was too loud and obvious to ignore, even under the scolding eye of Kelvin who preferred we kept our phones locked away so that the customers always had our complete attention.

But once I checked the screen to see who the call was coming from - a number that wasn't saved in my phone with a local area code meaning it could've been just about anybody - I couldn't help myself in asking, "Can I... take this? *Please*?"

Kelvin released a heavy sigh, shaking his head as he answered, "Jules, you know you're not supposed to have your phone on the floor."

"*Please,* Kelvin. It might be someone important," I begged as the phone continued to chime in my hand.

And while Kelvin once again shook his head, this time it was paired with his permission to…, "Go ahead. My office door is open."

I damn near took off sprinting from behind the bar towards the stairs which lead to his office. But apparently I wasn't fast enough considering once I hit the staircase, the phone stopped ringing.

Shit.

I climbed the stairs two-by-two as I pressed the button to call the number right back. And after a few short rings, a familiar voice picked up to say, "Jules. Hey. I was just leaving you a message on the other line. It's Alexis. Alexis Martin-Ross."

"Hey! *Hi.* How are you?" I asked, my heart already pounding as I tried to stay calm long enough to hear what she actually had to say.

But it was clear my nerves were oozing through the phone as she chuckled when she replied, "I'm fine. How are you? I hope I didn't catch you at a bad time."

I shook my head as if she could see me, working to keep my breathing steady as I stammered, "No, no. You're fine. And I'm fine. It's all fine."

Jesus, help me.

Again, she chuckled. "Well I'm sitting here with the casting director, and we were discussing when and where we wanted to hold auditions which made me think of you. I showed him some of your work on YouTube, and we agreed that we wanted to make sure you got the first crack at things before we opened it up to the public."

"Oh my God. *That's...* that's amazing. I appreciate you thinking of me," I replied with the last thread of composure I had left. It would be just my luck that my excitement would boil over before I could contain it and scare the woman away.

But it seemed like she didn't care either way, her main focus being, "Well you know how important it is for us to look out for each other. But anyway, we're looking at a week from today. Say 8 PM?"

"That would be perfect," I answered with another unseen nod, making a mental note to take an off day from work.

"*Awesome*. I'll have my assistant shoot you all of the details. We're really looking forward to seeing what you're made of."

My cheeks were beginning to ache from smiling so hard as I told her, "I'm looking forward to it too. Thanks again, Mrs. Martin-Ross."

"Girl, call me Alexis," she corrected with another little chuckle.

"I'm so sorry. Thanks again, *Alexis*," I repeated with extra inflection to prove I was a good listener.

"Much better. You have a good night, okay?"

"Thank you. You too. See you next week."

I watched the phone closely to make sure the call was actually ended, waiting until it flashed back over to my home screen to let out the loudest scream I could produce. It was a scream I had been holding onto for years, waiting to be unleashed whenever I got the call that I had officially been booked for a part of this caliber. And even though the scream was a little premature considering this call was only for an audition, it felt good to finally release.

Though it also resulted in a concerned Kelvin busting into his office to ask, "Yo, are you alright? Why are you screaming like that?"

"I got a private audition!" I screeched, jumping up and down with a second wind of excitement.

"I knew your ass was all happy go-lucky for a reason. Congratulations, girl," he replied with a proud smile as he pulled me into a quick hug.

"Thank you, boss man. And thanks for letting me take that," I told him, holding up the phone that had been the ticket to it all, even though it had almost been the ticket to getting me in trouble.

But now that he knew it was actually worth the trouble, Kelvin replied, "I told you before, Jules. We don't want ya'll here forever. Just long enough to get shit figured out."

"Well I'm about to get it all figured out. Right after I work this shift."

While I had a strong feeling the good news would help my night at work go even better, Kelvin tried to one-up me by suggesting, "Why don't you go ahead and take the night off to celebrate? This is a big deal, Jules."

He was right.

It was a big deal. A *very* big deal. But it wasn't attached to any money quite yet which meant..., "You know good and well I can't afford to take the night off. Especially after that trip ended up costing me double what I expected it to."

Giving Elizabeth the time of her life had almost cost me mine, literally and figuratively. Drinking well past my limit and barely getting any sleep had easily been the worst combination ever created, not to mention spending hoards of cash like bills never existed. Thankfully, I had Levi around to nurse me back to good health *and* loan me some gas money to get to work.

Kelvin and I were already heading back down to the lounge floor when he insisted, "Well at least treat yourself to a drink or two. Just make sure you spread them out during the night, lightweight."

"Have one with me?" I asked as I slipped behind the bar while Kelvin made himself comfortable on the bar stool across from me.

Then he nodded as he answered, "Sure. We gotta make it quick though. You know Maxwell will be trippin' if he catches us."

"I'll just be sure to tell him the good news. That should be enough to yank the stick out of his ass," I joked as I poured a few of my favorites into a shaker with ice, giving it a stiff toss over my shoulder before distributing it evenly into two glasses.

And while I grabbed a few garnishes to top it off with, I listened in as Kelvin replied, "Only if Nori hasn't already shelved it for good. Hell, she might've just exchanged it for one of her little toys."

"Ew! I don't wanna think about… *anyway*. Come on. Let's cheers," I settled on as I slid his glass across the bar top.

And he held it in the air almost as proudly as I did when he said, "To your new career."

"To, what I hope to be, my new career."

I stumbled into the apartment, still grinning from ear-to-ear as I thought about all the good that had been thrown my way in the last week. Spending time with my best friend even if it almost ended in real ass death, the call I had been looking forward to since the plans were made to one day receive it, and then getting the blessing from my boss to celebrate on the clock, giving me the opportunity to drink while also making the money I needed to stay afloat.

Oh, and of course reconciling with the fine ass basketball player who I just so happened to share an address with.

In fact, he was the only thing on my mind as I tiptoed through the eerily quiet apartment towards his room, planning to share the news and continue my night of celebration with my knees pinned somewhere near my ears. But after a few short knocks on his door, and then a self-served invitation to step inside, I found it just as quiet as the rest of the place.

"*Maybe he went out with Wes*," I thought to myself, trying to maintain my excitement as I snagged one of his t-shirts before I headed towards my room to change out of my clothes into his. But after doing that, and twirling my thumbs, and scrolling through his social media for any clues of his whereabouts, I decided to do what should've been the first choice; give him a call.

He picked up after only two rings, his voice mellow when he said, "Hey Jules."

"Levi. *Hey*. Where uh… where are you?" I asked, trying not to sound too needy as I tugged at the hem of his t-shirt that hit me right above the knees.

But tugging quickly turned into fisting when he answered, "Just landed in cold ass Milwaukee."

"*Milwaukee*? What are you doing in Milwaukee?" I asked, my buzz officially blown now that I knew I'd be

242

spending the night alone.

And things seemed to be taking a slow turn for the worst as I listened to Levi explain, "My agent finally got all of my meetings and tryouts lined up. So I have one here first thing in the morning, then I'll take the short flight over to Chicago for another one in the evening. The day after that I'm headed to New York to do two. Then I'm shooting back over to Phoenix to wrap things up."

While I did the quick calculations in my head for how many days he would actually be gone - *at least three* -, I also tried my best to be excited for him. "Oh wow. *That's…* that's great. Congratulations."

"Thanks, pretty girl. What's up with you though? How was work?"

I yanked at the collar of his shirt, taking a deep inhale of its scent to calm me before I answered, "Uh… it was good. But I wasn't calling to talk about work. I was calling to… well I wanted to tell you to your face, but since you aren't here I guess this will have to do."

"What's going on?" he asked, his voice holding an undertone of concern as he waited for me to respond.

But for whatever reason, it no longer felt as exhilarating to share, "I got the call. My audition is next week."

My monotone didn't stop Levi from being excited for me when he replied, "That's dope, baby! I knew it would all work out for you."

"Yeah. I'm excited too," I replied, a half-hearted smile he couldn't even see being my best attempt at matching his enthusiasm.

I wasn't even sure why I was so suddenly… over it. Couldn't put my finger on why Levi's absence bothered me so much. But that didn't stop him from picking up on it as he said, "You don't seem too excited."

I shrugged, gnawing at my lip as I tried to find the

words to explain. "*I just…* I don't know. I guess I wish I could've told you here. At home."

"Yeah, I wish I was there too. But fortunately and unfortunately, duty calls," he reminded me as if it wasn't already being thrown in my face.

In fact, that's when it all really seemed to hit me. That this, *whatever this was*, would be the norm if we chose to move forward. Lonely nights at home while Levi chased his dream. Celebrating alone, *sleeping alone*, while Levi focused on himself and his career. And while I knew we had both made an effort to save ourselves from this exact predicament, I could only nod as I held the phone close and replied, "Right. I understand."

"Let me get all settled in here and I'll give you a call back. Bet?"

I would've loved to talk to Levi until I fell asleep the same way I did when he was here, but I knew a call back only meant prolonging the inevitable. And since that conversation wasn't exactly phone appropriate, I simply told him, "Don't worry about it. You probably need your rest."

"You sure?"

Again, I nodded. "Yeah, I'm sure. Good luck tomorrow. And the next day. *And* the next day."

He chuckled, clearly not taking things as deeply as I was when he said, "I appreciate it, Jules. Miss you already."

"I… I miss you too. Goodnight, Levi."

"Sweet dreams, pretty girl," was all he replied before ending the call. And then I just sat there, trying to evaluate my options though only one made real sense. The same one that had always seemed to make sense to Levi. Though I, for whatever reason, had never really accepted it.

Well, I tried to accept it, tried to keep him at a

distance. But I was also just as easily sucked back in by his charm, sucked in by the idea of being necessary for his success; being an integral part of his world. But the truth was, he never really wanted this. It was convenient for him, but he could do without it if he had to. It was me who had become completely attached, me who was holding onto the idea of being in an actual relationship with someone who had made his intentions clear from the get-go. Hell, it was obvious in the way he had skipped town without a fair warning, without even leaving a note when we were on the best of terms.

But everything about this was temporary for him; his current lifestyle and career, the balance in his bank account, along with the arrangements his sister had made for him to become my roommate in the first place. And now it was clear that the one thing I had foolishly thought of as permanent - *me* - was also going to be added to that list.

Levi

I couldn't wait to see her. In fact, I had decided to come to her the second I made it back in town instead of waiting for her to get off of work, way too anxious to reunite after a long four days without her.

It was crazy to me how used to being around Jules I had become, how much I craved her presence while I was away, not to mention the butterflies I got as I strolled into *The Max* knowing I'd finally be able to make good on all of the feelings that had stirred up during our time apart. But it also felt good to know I had something - *someone* - so special, worthy of the foreign mix of emotions. The emotions that went into overdrive once I laid eyes on her at the bar, using a quick hand to squeeze a lemon wedge before dropping it into a glass and sliding it to the customer.

I tried to keep a low profile as I slipped through the crowd, making a beeline to her station. And it didn't take long for her to notice I was there, though the reaction I had in mind wasn't the one she gave as she quickly masked the initial tight-eyed, tight-lipped face she gave with a smile before turning to take the order of another customer.

It was almost as if I had imagined the whole thing. But then again, this was Jules. I had to expect the unexpected. So I waited patiently as she served another two customers before finally making her way to me. And when she did, it was only to say, "What can I get you?"

"Well that's not the warm welcome back I was hoping for," I told her teasingly, trying to ease whatever tension she was obviously carrying from her day.

But apparently I hadn't eased enough of it as she quickly fired back, "I'm not exactly sure why you expected anything different. You came to a bar. People usually do that when they want something to drink."

I shrugged, giving her the smirk I knew she couldn't resist when I replied, "Well I guess I don't consider myself any ol' person."

She finally gave me a smile, though it was obviously laced with a layer of sarcasm once I heard her agree, "You're right. You're Levi Graham. *Superstar*. Welcome back to your old life. I bet you want a free drink, huh? Free section? Let me get my boss. I'm sure he'll take care of you the way you're used to."

She turned to walk away, but I reached over the bar top to catch her by the arm and ask, "Jules, what's the matter with you? Why are you being like this?"

"I have customers to take care of," was all she answered as she snatched her arm away, heading back towards the far end of the bar. And I could only sit there stunned, trying to figure out what could've possibly gone wrong in the short couple of days I was away.

I mean, we were good. We were happy. We... missed each other. At least that's what I thought, though it completely contradicted the way Jules was acting towards me.

And to make matters even worse, I felt a body squeeze onto the bar stool next to mine, the flowery smell of her perfume along with her chipper little voice being the first indicator of who it belonged to. "*Well, well, well.* Looks like there must be a little trouble in paradise, huh?"

"We're good. Not that that's any of your business anyway," I told her with a roll of my eyes while I kept my attention on Jules who was busy mixing another drink.

"Relationships *are* my business, Levi. And yours is clearly on the rocks. I guess little baby is big mad at you now, huh?" she asked mockingly, practically forcing me to turn her way in annoyance.

"Man, take that shit elsewhere, Layna. You're just mad cause I ain't wanna fuck with your wack ass like that. And I'm so glad I didn't."

Instead of being offended the way I expected her to be, she actually chuckled when she agreed, "I'm so glad you didn't too. I got a crazy amount of views on my blog from that post without having to waste my time trying to get you hard. Win-win for me."

"Fuck you, Layna," was the only thing I could reply without really going off.

But it was clear she was actually proud of herself for all the bullshit she had strung together, oozing with arrogance when she challenged, "You wanted to, Levi. Admit it."

"And catch whatever it was that required that penicillin shot Wes saw you getting at the hospital the other day? Nah, I'm good."

That seemed to get under her skin as she tensed up before replying through clenched teeth, "I had strep throat, asshole."

And this time, it was me feeling arrogant when I shrugged, smirking as I told her, "Never knew strep throat and syphilis were interchangeable."

But the smirk was knocked right off of my face once Jules approached us wearing a scowl of disapproval for obvious reasons. Reasons that Layna quickly doubled down on when she said, "There's little baby now. Jules, be a doll and get us a round of shots to celebrate."

Jules and I were equally confused when she asked, "Celebrate what?"

And I was pretty sure my heart skipped a beat when

Layna licked her lips before insisting, "Your breakup, of course. One woman's trash is another's treasure."

"*Bitch…*" was the only word I heard Jules grumble as she launched at Layna from over the bar top, knocking a few glasses to the ground when she grabbed a handful of her hair in one hand and landed blows to her face with the other all while balancing on her stomach as her feet hung in the air.

My body was frozen in shock though I was mentally cheering my girl on as her boss came out of nowhere to pull her away. "Jules! Jules, stop. Let her go!" he shouted as he pried her hand from Layna's hair until she finally let go, falling to her feet behind the bar then taking a glance at her hand.

And Layna was already putting a hand to her jaw, checking the damage as she spewed, "Oh bitch, you've fucked with the wrong one. I'm gonna bury your ass in so many headlines, you'll never get another job in this city!" Then she turned to her savior and demanded, "Kelvin, fire her."

"*Fire her*? I'm not gonna fire her just because you got your ass beat, Layna," he replied with a short laugh, turning to Jules to ask if she was alright.

And that seemed to piss Layna off even more as she screamed, "Are you kidding me?! Your bartender just attacked me and you're not gonna fire her?"

He shook his head, clearly amused when he answered, "Nah. *I…* Jules, how about you just… go home for the night? Until we can get everything all sorted out around here."

"*Go home*? But I need this money, Kelvin," Jules whined as if it was even possible for her to just go back to work like nothing ever happened, as if all of the eyes in the lounge weren't now focused on us.

In fact, some people even had their phones in their

hand as if they were just waiting for more action to break out so they could record it. And Layna certainly didn't help her cause when she muttered, "Poor ass bitch," Causing Jules to break out of Kelvin's protection when she climbed from behind the bar.

And now it was me stopping the fight as I stepped between them just as Jules said, "Oh, I got your bitch."

Luckily I caught her just as she tried to slip under my arm. "Jules! Come on. Let's go home."

"That's right, Jules. Go home with that moochin' ass mothafucka!" Layna shouted over my shoulder as if I was on her side and there was any truth to her statement.

I almost let Jules go tag her ass once more, but instead chose to do the responsible thing of escorting her to the back to get her stuff while Kelvin worked to get the crowd back to regularly scheduled programming. But no matter how removed we were from the scene, Jules's focus was still, "I'm gonna kill her. I *have to* kill her," as she snatched her jacket, purse, and a change of shoes from her locker before she started taking off her jewelry.

And I could only shake my head as I reasoned, "Jules, she's not worth it. Let's just get out of here while you still have your damn job."

Her anger in general suddenly became directed at me as she stabbed a finger in my chest. "You shouldn't have been entertaining that raggedy ass bitch to begin with. Shots to our break-up, right?"

While I knew what Layna said was a little fucked up, not to mention completely off base, I couldn't help myself in defending, "Man, I can't control what comes out of her mouth."

"But you can control this, right? Control what happens between me and you? Well, guess what? There *is* no me and you."

"Jules, you're buggin'. I didn't even do anything.

Where is all of this coming from?" I asked, unable to figure out how we had even gotten to this point. How things had gone from me surprising her at work, to me escorting her from a damn fist fight, to her now picking a fight with me.

But apparently it was *me* who was the problem as she groaned, "You're right. You *didn't* do anything. You just sat there, so worried about your own ego that you couldn't see yourself out of the situation. But you'll gladly use those around you to do your dirty work just like Lily said."

"So now it's my fault you wanted to go all Fight Club with Layna cause she got slick at the mouth?"

Before Jules could answer, our argument was cut short by Kelvin coming in the room. "Jules. Please tell me you had a good reason to cause such a scene out there. I mean, the DJ had to play three bangers in a row just to get shit back to normal," he said as he grabbed a hand towel to wipe his sweaty forehead with.

And angry Jules had quickly been replaced with a remorseful one as she replied, "I'm sorry, Kelvin. But it was long overdue."

"Well look. I'm not gonna fire you cause to be real, Tiana has been wanting to do that since before we even got engaged. But you're lucky Maxwell wasn't here, though you know he's going to hear about it from a few different people."

Jules nodded regretfully, her eyes directed toward the ground. "I know. And if that's what it has to be, I'll understand."

Lucky for her, her boss wasn't nearly as troubled when he replied, "You know I'll vouch for you, girl. Don't even trip. Now get your Floyd Mayweather ass out of here before Layna calls the cops. And take the back way."

Jules grabbed her things, sticking most of it in a jumble under her arm as she said, "Thank you, Kelvin. I appreciate it more than you know." Then she peeked up at me with eyes that shot darts straight at my heart before she slipped out of the room.

I was getting ready to follow her, but Kelvin stopped me in my tracks with a hand to my chest. "Say, bruh. Hold up a minute."

"What's up?" I asked, knowing I only had a few seconds if I really expected to catch up to Jules. But it hardly seemed possible once I watched Kelvin settle in against the wall, meaning he planned on holding me up for longer than I expected.

"First, I wanted to thank you for stepping in out there. I knew Jules had some fire to her, but I never would've imagined all that."

"I can't really say that I'm as surprised as you are," I replied as I thought about the hothead I had been dealing with since the day I moved into the apartment.

But it was clear Kelvin wasn't aware of those details when he asked, "So you and Jules are pretty close, huh?"

I shrugged. "You could say that."

"Well listen, my staff is like family to me and I want the best for all of them. So I'm gonna ask you again, are you and Jules pretty close?"

"Man, where are you going with this?" I asked as I felt myself growing angry.

It was already enough for me to still be on the spot in the first place. And while I could appreciate Kelvin being protective considering Jules didn't have her real family to look out for her, I was far more interested in working things out with Jules instead of getting the third degree from her damn boss who looked to be around the same age that I was.

But that didn't stop him from making his point when

he replied, "Jules is a good girl. A good person. That's not someone you toy around with. That's not someone you have climbing across bar tops making a fool of herself. That's not..."

I held my hands up to stop his rant, being sure to stay cool as I told him, "Look. I respect you. I appreciate you letting Jules keep her job and all that. But this little man-to-man bullshit ain't even necessary. I got Jules taken care of. She's good. We're good."

Sure, *good* might've been a stretch, but I fully believed we would make it out of this situation okay. We *had* to make it out of this okay.

Still, no matter what I said, it was clear Kelvin wasn't as convinced when he asked, "Oh yeah? Well what was that little scuffle about? You're tellin' me it had nothing to do with you and Layna? Cause to me it seemed like you were so focused on proving a point to the enemy, so worried about your own shit that you couldn't even see the one you actually care about as she gave ya'll both a death stare in the middle of serving a customer."

"I…"

"You didn't know, right? We never know. And I'm not here to judge you. We've all been there. But I guess I'm just letting you know with my man-to-man bullshit."

I nodded, knowing there was a lot of truth, a lot of wisdom in his words. "I hear you, man. I got you."

"Now I know Jules has a big audition coming up so she doesn't need to be dealing with all of this extra-curricular shit. Make sure you get that shit all sewed up whenever you get a chance to talk to her."

"That's *if* I get a chance to talk to her," I corrected, knowing Jules would try her absolute best to avoid me at all costs, especially now that she had been able to escape the lounge without finishing our conversation.

"Good point. You might have to assert yourself with

this one. Make her listen to you," Kelvin advised, giving me a reassuring pat on the shoulder before he slipped past me towards the exit. But he stopped just short of the door to turn around and add, "Oh, and make sure you take the back way when you leave, bruh. I worked too hard to calm things down out there for you to reemerge now."

I let out a little chuckle, more than likely the last one I'd get for the night. Then I followed both sets of his directions; taking the back way out while also coming up with a plan to get Jules to talk to me.

She didn't come home.

I wasn't sure where she went, wasn't sure if she even had a place to go, and I knew the only money she had was whatever money she had made in tips over the last couple of days. But the fact that she would use her last just to avoid dealing with me spoke volumes to the state of our relationship.

Well... technically, we weren't even in a relationship. We hadn't set any terms, hadn't made anything official. But the general boxes were all checked off for what a relationship would look like, which I could assume made Jules even more upset. She had been fully committed to whatever was happening between us, and *I was...* I was selfishly committed to myself while also taking whatever I could get from her.

"*I really fucked this up*," I thought to myself as I rested against the headboard, trying to figure out my next move.

Hell, maybe it was time for me to really leave her alone like she asked me to. Go on about our separate lives the way we had planned to all along. But that hardly seemed possible, especially considering the way my heart damn near leaped out of my chest at the sound of her keys jingling at the front door.

I climbed off of the bed and stepped in the living room just in time to catch her taking her shoes off. But the second she realized I was there, she rolled her eyes, grabbing the one heel she had already gotten off and carrying it in her hand while limping towards her room with the other still on.

"Jules. Jules, wait up," I called after her, easily being able to catch up since her one heel slowed her down.

But that didn't mean she was going to stop trying to get away as she tossed over her shoulder, "No, Levi. I'm not waiting up. I don't want to hear anything you have to say right now. Or ever for that matter."

"Jules, I'm sorry," I offered as what felt like a last resort though it probably should've been the first. And for a second I thought it worked considering Jules actually stopped just short of her bedroom door to turn around and face me.

But my hopes were immediately ripped to shreds once I heard her reply, "You're damn right you're sorry. A sorry excuse for a man."

"Jules, just chill out for a second. Let's be adults about this," I reasoned, brushing her insult right off of my shoulder.

And again, Jules got my hopes up with a smile, just to shoot them back down when she paired it with,

"Yes. Let's. Rent is due on the 1st. You can leave your half in an envelope on the counter." Then she turned back towards her room, taking off once again and attempting to shut the door in my face.

But luckily my reflexes allowed me to shove my foot in the crack just in time to stop it as I admitted, "Jules, I know I fucked up. Just hear me out for a second." And I didn't wait for her to actually agree to my request when I continued, "I don't give a fuck about Layna. I've never given a fuck about her. I just… my pride got in the way, she got under my skin, and… that's not an excuse. I didn't have to say anything to her. I could've been the bigger person and stepped away before shit got out of hand. But you know what? This shit isn't all on me. You're the one who punched the girl."

To my surprise, that fact was the one that got the door to come back open as Jules got right in my face to say, "I've always dealt with Layna since working at *The Max*. And somehow I never had a reason to punch her until I got involved with you! I was so on your side, so focused on setting her ass straight and defending us without thinking twice. But it took me calming down to realize, this was never about defending us because there really isn't an us. This was about defending *you*. All of this has always been about *you*."

"*Jules…*" was all I could get out before she continued on.

"I'm acting out of character. My emotions are in shambles. I could've lost my fucking job, the only thing I really have going for myself, over this. And you're steady putting up this front like you're really all in, steady acting like this is just some normal, everyday conflict that we can simply talk out and work past. But it's not normal, Levi. This isn't okay. And I don't know if it will ever be okay."

I reached out to touch her cheek, but she immediately yanked away letting me know just how bad things were. And I had no problem admitting that when I told her, "Jules, I know this shit is all fucked up right now. *I'm* a fuck-up. I get it. But my feelings for you have always been real. *I just…* I need you, pretty girl. And I don't care what I have to do to get shit back right between us. I know how I feel about you, how we feel about each other, and I'm determined to make it work."

She peeked up at me with glossed-over eyes that pierced right through my heart long before she even spoke because I knew they were all my fault regardless of if the tears were ever shed. And when she actually did speak, the piercing turned into more of a bullet as her face pulled into a scowl when she replied, "Well it's unfortunate that we couldn't have reached that place at the same time because I'm no longer interested."

Jules

I was bombing my audition.

I knew it, Alexis knew it, and the ultra-flamboyant casting director Tony especially knew it as he smacked a hand against his forehead when I messed up the line for what felt like the hundredth time even though it was really only the third. I wasn't even sure how it was possible for me to mess up a line that I was basically reading straight from the paper, but I also knew anything was possible considering the unfocused attitude I walked into the audition with.

I hadn't gotten a good night's sleep since the night of the fight - *the night of the fights, plural* - and that lack of sleep was clearly catching up to me as I shook my head and apologized. "I'm sorry. I don't know what's gotten into me. Can I try it one more time?"

"*Actually*, can I… speak with you for a minute? Outside?"

Again, I shook my head as Alexis stood up from the table and headed for the door with me right on her heels. And once we hit the hallway, she turned my way to whisper "Jules, this isn't you. I know this isn't you. What's the matter?"

I shrugged, the anxiety building as I whined, "I don't know. I think I'm just… *nervous*."

Alexis immediately shook her head to disagree, crossing her arms over her chest as she whispered, "I know nerves. I've seen nerves plenty of times. This is something different."

I released a heavy sigh, trying to find the words that didn't scream "man-problems" considering that wasn't really a valid reason to do a shitty job. And eventually I settled on, "There's just a lot going on outside of this. But I know that's not an excuse. You're giving me an opportunity and it's my job to kill it regardless."

This time, her nod was more empathetic when she replied, "I understand. We're all human. Things happen. But you're right. You have to kill it regardless if this is really what you want."

"I want it so bad," I admitted, feeling myself on the verge of tears as I thought about missing out on such a perfect opportunity.

But I was thankful that Alexis wasn't giving up on me quite yet, offering me a reassuring pat to the shoulder as she suggested, "So you know what you have to do then. Shake it off. Get a drink of water. Do whatever it takes to get back in here ready to show us why we should book you."

"Yes ma'am," I told her with another nod as she slipped back into the room, leaving me to get my shit together. And it only took a few deep, Levi-thought relieving breaths along with a good shake of my hands and a quick prayer for me to feel ready as I followed her tracks inside just as she was settling in at the table.

"I'm… so sorry about that. Time is our most valuable asset and…"

I couldn't even finish before Tony interrupted me to say, "Jules, you're only wasting more of it doing all of this talking."

I let out an awkwardly relaxing laugh when I told him, "Right. *Whew*. Okay. Here we go." And then I attacked the script, feeling like a brand new person - *Jamila to be exact* - as I flawlessly read line after line with the skills my mother had blessed me with. I even imagined her watching over me with the proudest smirk on her face as I made an effort to honor her legacy.

And by the time I was finished, Tony burst into cheers, standing up from his seat at the table to shout, "Now that's what I'm talking about!" While Alexis remained sitting with an expression of, "*I told you so.*"

I approached the table, leaving the script and extending my hand to tell them, "Thank you guys for the opportunity. I hope to hear back from you soon."

But Tony practically squeezed the life out of my hand when he said, "Oh, girl. You're going to hear from us right now. I mean, you're *clearly* our Jamila. That's if you want the part."

"Of course! I mean, if you're offering," I replied, trying to scale back my excitement so I didn't seem like too much of an amateur.

But that didn't seem to matter to them either way as Alexis stood up to say, "Our people will be in touch with your people to get it on paper. But verbally, it's all yours."

"*I...* wow. *Wow. Wow. Wow,*" was the only thing I could produce without completely going crazy.

Well, that was until Tony insisted, "Go ahead and let it out, boo." Prompting me to jump and down the same way I had done when I first got the call of the audition, pairing it with a scream that forced them both to cover their ears.

I held a hand over my mouth as I told them, "I'm sorry. This is just... words can't explain how much this means to me."

"I know you'll make us proud. Maybe even earn us some nominations one day. Then we'll get on *SuperSoul Sunday* and tell Oprah all about you funking up the beginning of your audition," Tony said with one of his exaggerated laughs that I couldn't help but join in on before he continued, "Now go on home and tell all of your little friends the good news."

I stiffened from both the words *home* and *friends*, knowing those two in combination literally equated to Levi. But we weren't even friends. We weren't… *anything*, even if he had been the one to encourage me to pick acting back up in the first place. In fact, it was him who had reminded me of my purpose for being out here, him who reminded me of my obligation to my mother's legacy, him who… believed I could actually do it, even going as far as attending class with me to make sure I wasn't bullshitting. He had been my main supporter through and through, pushing me to seek out auditions and casting calls that I wouldn't have otherwise.

Truth be told, I owed it to him to at least share the exciting news even if it was the last thing I ever said to him. But I also wasn't sure if I really wanted it to be the last thing I ever said to him. I was still angry, not to mention my damn hand was still throbbing at the knuckles from firing off on Layna's ass days ago. But besides that unpredictable fiasco, one I might've enjoyed a little too much, Levi had been more than a friend. He had been a confidante, completely generous, an incredible lover while also being more patient than most in regards to my attitude.

Was I really ready to do away with him? Do away with all we had built? Was I ready to struggle through the less than two months we had left together, knowing I could possibly be pushing away the one who was made for me?

The thoughts overwhelmed me as I shook hands with Tony and Alexis once more before taking the long way home in an effort to come to some sort of conclusion. But once I made it back to the apartment and found a stack of moving boxes sitting in the living room, I realized the conclusion had been made for me.

My heart was already racing, but I tried to stay calm

as I stepped past them on my way to Levi's room where he was busy ripping his clothes from the rack in the closet and stuffing them in a box. And while the view brought on a brutal mix of emotions, not to mention a boatload of confusion, I was mostly captivated by how happy he looked as he bobbed his head to whatever song was playing in his headphones.

Well… how happy he looked until he noticed me and all excitement was lost as he pulled one headphone bud from his ear to say, "Can I help you with something?"

"Uh… what's going on? What's all this?" I asked, struggling to keep my breathing steady as I answered my own question in my head.

But his version was a lot colder than I expected when he shrugged, offering a very short, very obvious, "My stuff."

"I mean, I know that. But… why are you packing? Where are you going?"

Again he shrugged, releasing a heavy sigh before he answered, "I got the call. Phoenix wants me. I don't have my first practice until Monday, but I figured I'd get there early so I could get all settled into my new spot."

"So that's it? You're moving? Just like that?" I asked, trying not to sound as frantic as I felt inside. But everything was happening so fast, seemed so sudden, seemed so… unreal.

But I knew it was real once he abandoned his closet and headed over to his dresser, picking up an envelope and handing it over to me as he replied, "Here's a check for the rest of the rent I would owe you so you don't have to worry about finding another replacement."

My hands went hot as I stared at what should've felt like a gift, but truly felt like a dagger. It was everything I needed while also being the last thing I expected to receive. "I… I don't know what to say. I mean, congratulations of course."

He gave me a half-hearted smile, far from the exuberant one I was used to when he said, "Thank you." Before quickly adding, "Is there anything else?"

"Um… no. Nothing else," I answered, swallowing hard as I turned to get away before I could burst into tears.

And it certainly didn't help when Levi offered, "It's for the best, Jules. So I'm not tempted to cause any more damage around here. I've clearly done enough wrong to you."

His words stopped me dead in my tracks as I quietly told him, "You did some right too. I… I got the part."

"No shit?"

I nodded, turning around to face him when I answered, "Yeah. Offered it to me on the spot. Well, verbally until they can get the contract stuff all sorted out which shouldn't be an issue thanks to that agent you hooked me up with."

His smile grew a little as he stepped up to me to say, "That's what's up. I'm happy for you. For real."

"I'm happy for you too," I told him as I attempted to match his smile, though it was hardly any use considering the blur of tears I knew were coming in my near future.

But for the moment, my eyes were locked on his as he stared down at me with a look of admiration. A look of passion. A look of… *love*. And it didn't take long for me to get lost in his gaze to the point where I hadn't even realized his face was moving closer and closer to mine until our lips were a few mere inches apart. Instinctively, I closed my eyes as he softly pressed his lips to mine, letting them linger for a few seconds before he pulled away and apologized. "I'm sorry. I just had to know what they tasted like. One last time."

Instead of accepting his apology, I wrapped my hand

around the back of his neck, pulling him in for another kiss. But this time, it was me in control as I slipped my tongue past the threshold of his lips, doing a dance we had both become familiar with. A dance we had both grown to love, though now I'd have to cherish it as only a memory.

The thought alone was enough for me to pull away, releasing my hold and using the same hand to wipe my lips as I told him, "Me too."

And he followed my lead, brushing a thumb across his lips when he asked, "Jules?"

"Hm?"

I watched intently as he pulled the single headphone bud from his ear, setting them aside before he asked, "Just one more? A tiebreaker?"

My body reacted long before my mind did as I jumped into his arms, wrapping my legs around his waist and my arms around his neck as I found his mouth for another kiss; this one being much more aggressive than the last. It felt as if I was releasing everything that had been bottled up over the last couple of months; every ounce of passion I had stored, every ounce of anger I still felt, every ounce of love I held in my heart for someone who had grown so close to me in such a short amount of time.

And no matter how wrong it might've been, it felt so right as he carried me over to his bed, keeping his lips locked on mine as he gently laid me onto the mattress. Then he moved from my lips to my neck, taking advantage of everything he had learned about my body during the nights we had shared as he licked and nibbled while pushing my shirt up over my breasts which suddenly felt desperate for attention. In fact, my whole body felt desperate for attention as each part waited to be tended to, anxious for the opportunity to commit the way it felt to be touched by Levi to memory as he landed short pecks down my stomach until he landed at my waistline. I lifted just enough for him to remove the jeans and panties I was wearing, shimmying them down my legs in record time before he stood up to remove his own.

That's when I knew I was in trouble.

I could get over kisses. Kisses were replaceable. But there was no forgetting the way it felt to have Levi inside of me. There was no forgetting the many nights we had shared tangled in positions we had no business trying. There was no erasing the memories of fucking each other's life up and then teasing one another about it later.

And it was clear I wasn't the only one thinking long and hard about it all as Levi hovered over me, his dick scraping against my belly when he whispered, "How did I mess this up so badly?"

"Doesn't matter now," was the only thing I could reply without getting even more emotional. And I was grateful that he didn't press me on it, instead using his position to spread my legs even wider before aligning his body with mine to finish off what we had started; to finish off what we had created over his time spent as my roommate.

I knew this was it. He knew this was it. And he took full ownership of that fact when he delivered slow, deep strokes as if he was trying to savor the moment. And while it felt as if I was able to unleash my feelings through our initial kisses, it was him who used our current position to communicate as he looked directly into my eyes while giving me everything he had down below.

I struggled to keep mine open, struggled to look at him as the mountain of regret grew taller inside of me. But it wasn't that I regretted what we were doing. I regretted that we had put ourselves in a predicament for this to be the last time.

And again, I wasn't alone in my thoughts as Levi whispered, "I'm sorry, baby." Forcing me to snap my eyes shut so he wouldn't see the tears welling up.

But the second Levi drove even deeper inside of me, a few tears managed to slip out anyway as I suddenly realized what was really happening. He wasn't just savoring the moment. He wasn't determined to break me by giving me more inches than I could handle. He was making love to me, decidedly leaving memories much fonder than a casual fuck. Because I wasn't just a casual thing to him. I wasn't just chosen out of convenience. He had meant everything he said, everything he did, everything we shared.

It was all real.

My conclusion came with a climax so powerful I thought for sure I would burst into tiny little pieces. And I was hardly surprised to find Levi on the same wavelength when it only took a few more strokes for him to get his own, his dick still throbbing inside of me when he asked, "Why are you crying, baby? Did I hurt you?"

I shook my head, using my weakened limbs to wipe away my tears as I told him, "No. I just…"

Levi put a finger to my mouth to cut me off. "*Shhh….* Come here, pretty girl. Let me hold you."

He had already moved from above me to behind me, adjusting against the mattress by the time I replied, "No. I… I can't. *This is…* this is already too much."

"Just one last time, baby. *Please*," he begged, pulling me against his frame and quickly reminding me how perfectly we fit together.

It wasn't fair.

With his chin nuzzled in my hair and his arm draped comfortably over my body, I laid as still as I could, imitating sleep as I tried to remind myself why this was the end; remind myself why we really couldn't be.

But my thoughts became a nasty blur when I listened in as Levi whispered, "I'm gonna miss you so much, Jules. You're the best thing that ever happened to me. The best roommate ever. I hope we can still be friends someday. The best of friends. You're gonna be so dope on the big screen, pretty girl. I can't wait to brag to my folks about you. Can't wait to tell them all about the girl who stole my heart. *With your mean ass...*"

His little chuckle rumbled against my back as my breathing became even more calculated while I tried to digest his words without freaking out. I could pretty much assume he thought I was asleep which was why he was delivering such a heartfelt message. But I wondered how long he had been holding onto it, wondered if I would've ever received it if we hadn't gone so far, wondered if I had really stolen his heart the way he insisted.

Sleep didn't come easy, but when it did, it came hard. In fact, it came so hard that by the time I woke up, Levi was already gone. A set of keys, his mattress, and the small collection of his t-shirts I had permanently borrowed without him knowing were the only things left; the only things that proved he ever existed.

I hadn't even realized how much I relied on his company until I no longer had the option. Hadn't realized how much he contributed until I found myself in a bind, trying to put together some resemblance of a breakfast when it was usually Levi who made sure we had everything in stock. Hadn't realized how much I enjoyed nagging him about frivolous shit like leaving his basketball shoes in the middle of the living room floor until they were no longer there.

But this was the new reality. This was the next step. This was… for the best. And regardless of how either one of us felt about it, there was no turning back now.

It was time to move on.

Levi

"*Gotdamnit*, Graham. Are you really that damn rusty?"

I shook my head, more disappointed with myself than coach could ever be as I jogged to pick up the ball that I had bounced off the edge of my foot when I tried to make a quick move to the rim.

It was an elementary mistake. One I really couldn't afford to make considering I hadn't exactly been signed to an official contract. But it felt like I had no control with the way my brain seemed to be consumed with everything that had transpired over the last couple of days. From the fight at *The Max* that thankfully hadn't shown up on any headline, to the fight with Jules that ended things before they could really even start, to our share of equally good news - *news we had both been waiting to hear* - that we couldn't even celebrate because of the terms we were on, and then the goodbye sex that was beyond anything we had ever done before.

Basketball truly felt small scale compared to that crazy chain of events. But basketball was also my job. It was what I wanted. What I had worked so hard for. And there was no way I was going to let that all go to waste on account of my fucked up personal life.

Still, it didn't take long for the feelings surrounding my personal life to seep back into my professional one as I caught a pass from my new teammate and went up for a shot, only for it to be an airball.

Coach snapped immediately, blowing his whistle before he demanded, "Graham, out. Williams, in."

And again, I could only shake my head, mad at

myself for much more than just basketball. Though that didn't seem to matter to Damien who was wearing a tight scowl as he hung over the ledge of the section designated for agents trying to get my attention.

For a second, I considered ignoring him, knowing nothing he had to say would help my game. But since he had been more than helpful getting me this opportunity in the first place, it felt like I owed it to him to at least hear him out.

"Levi, I've worked too damn hard for you to blow this. What the hell is going on with you?" he asked the second I was close enough to actually hear him.

And I could only shrug as I told him, "I'm just... I'm a little off today. That's all."

My partial-truth wasn't enough to stop him from scolding, "Well today is not the day to be a little off. You know you can be cut at any given moment which means your ass is right back to the car lot. And if what my brother told me about your salesmanship is true, I doubt that's where you want to be."

I shook my head, wiping the sweat from my forehead with the hem of my practice jersey as I replied, "Not an option. I'll do better. I got this."

"Yeah, you better," was all he offered before sending me back to join the other players.

I stood on the sideline, trying my best to stay in the moment as I watched the team execute flawlessly without me, earning praises from Coach as he exclaimed, "That's the kind of offense that wins championships!"

It was the truth. Phoenix was an excellent team. They didn't need me. But I sure as hell needed them. And if there was anything I had learned from dealing with Jules, it was the importance of letting that be known early and often.

So I decided to play the part of the supportive

teammate, cheering the squad on until I got the opportunity to earn the same support from them. And when I did, even though Coach wasn't exactly thrilled to put me back in, I was sure to remind him why he decided to take a chance on me in the first place, busting my ass on every play until practice was over.

My body ached in places that it hadn't in months, my heart rate still hadn't gone back down, and there was already a stack of towels covered in my sweat. But I felt... *great*; felt like things were slowly coming back together, getting back to the normal that I had wished for all along. The only problem was, I was no longer interested in the old normal. I wanted the new normal that included Jules, included everything we had built together.

But unfortunately for me, that wasn't an option. We had ended things. We had said our goodbyes one way or another. I was no longer her roommate, was no longer her anything, no matter how much our last night together said there may actually be more to the story.

Once I made it to the locker room, I checked my phone out of instinct and found a notification from Jules. Well... more like a notification *of* Jules since my Instagram was set to alert me whenever she posted a new picture. But even that little bit of access gave me the opportunity to stay connected to her no matter how far we got offtrack.

I clicked on the notification which led me to the picture of Jules holding her script next to her face with the caption, "*New character. Who dis?*" And I couldn't help but smile knowing she was finally making her dreams come true, no matter how much it sucked that I couldn't share in the moment with her.

I clicked on her profile, scrolling through the pictures I had already looked at hundreds of times since moving out. And I was almost to one of my favorites - a picture of her wearing one of my old college t-shirts - when I heard someone behind me ask, "So that's what this is all about? That girl you left back in the city?"

I exited out of the app, dropping my phone into my duffle bag as I told Damien, "She was just my roommate."

But he wasn't convinced as he stepped in front of me to say, "Your gir... roommate, right? Lily told me all about her."

"Since when do you and Lily get along well enough to talk without me being around to break up the fight?" I asked, knowing how much my big sister despised him for reasons I would never understand.

Damien was hardly fazed by the details of my question when he answered, "I was curious. And I figured she had some insight. Told me you had fallen in love."

"Well she lied," I replied sternly as I exchanged my practice jersey with a fresh t-shirt, opting to shower whenever I made it back to the extended-stay I was calling home until Phoenix made an official decision of what they wanted to do with me.

"Let me give you some advice, Levi. If you're going to go that deep into her Instagram, you might as well just take a couple screenshots while you're at it. Saves you the trouble later," Damien teased as I threw my shoes into the locker that hadn't even been labeled with my name yet which meant the situation between Jules and I was the last thing I needed to be talking about with my agent.

We had bigger things to settle like..., "Man, do you have any real news? Or you just coming in here to get on my nerves?"

Damien's demeanor became a little tenser, a little more serious when he finally replied, "Coach said he has some concerns. Said you didn't seem to be all in like he wants you to be, like he needs you to be. But he's not giving up on you yet. He wants to try you on a 10-day contract. Maybe two so he can get a full evaluation."

My face scrunched instantly as I asked, "*10-day*? Man, that ain't no real contract."

"But it's a whole lot better than no contract. And it's almost double what you would make in comparison to them dropping you back down to the D-League, not to mention what you would make if your ass ends up back at the car lot. You just have to take what you can get until you prove you deserve more. That's the name of the game around here."

I nodded, knowing Damien was telling the truth no matter how much it felt like I was being dealt a shorthand. But since the only thing I was in control of was my skills on the court and my attitude about it all, I tried to see the bright side of things when I told him, "I'm grateful they're taking a chance. But I'm also hungry for more."

"Well that's up to you to show them. As soon as possible, preferably."

I chuckled, catching Damien's hint about the payday that was waiting for him if I were to get a full contract. In all honesty, it was long overdue.

"I got you, man. Tell Coach I said I appreciate it. And I won't let him down."

He gave me a pat to the shoulder as he said, "Go ahead and get home so you can get some rest. Your first game back is in two days and those lights have surely gotten a little brighter since you've been away."

"You really think he's going to play me?" I asked, knowing it was a stretch for me to see the court considering the all-star worthy line-up ahead of me.

But I felt a little more hopeful when Damien answered, "Ya'll are playing a team that has been last place in the conference for three years straight. And I mean, if you can't get clock against them, you must really suck."

I laughed again, tossing a dismissive hand his way. "Man, whatever. Thanks for everything though. I appreciate you."

"I got you covered, Levi," he replied with a nod just as his phone began to buzz in his hand, the picture on the screen catching my attention since it looked like the girl version of me.

"Yo, what is my sister doing calling you?" I asked, more confused than anything since I didn't even know she had his number.

And I became even more curious about their involvement when Damien stammered, "I called to uh... let her know about... the contract. She must just be returning my call. I'll holla at you later." Before he skipped out of the locker room, letting me know that was definitely something I needed to check Lily about later.

But for now, my focus was back to Jules as I pulled my phone out to look at the picture that had originally gotten my attention. The one of Jules doing exactly what she had set out to do while I found myself applying old habits to a new situation.

"*Not all in like he needs you to be*," were the words Damien came up with though I imagined Coach delivering them a lot less kindly. But it reminded me of the time Jules said something similar when describing what I was doing wrong. If I really expected to be with her, everything in my actions should've said that clearly, otherwise I was just wasting both of our time.

And it was exactly the same with basketball. If I expected a real contract, I had to be all the way here. I had to give it my all, give it my last. I couldn't just have my cake and eat it too because that was how things usually worked out for me. I had to contribute to the creation, make adjustments to the recipe, provide real value and recognize that it wasn't just about me. It was about being a good teammate, being a good partner.

I released a heavy sigh as I gathered my things before leaving the locker room, being sure to dap up a few of my teammates on the way out. And once I made it to my car, I decided to make an effort at righting my wrongs by giving Jules a call.

Of course she didn't answer.

I could imagine her avoiding me to protect herself; sitting on the couch we used to share and staring at her phone as it rang the same way she used to do when a bill collector called. Or maybe she was just busy. But no matter what tactic she was applying, I knew I wasn't giving up.

I had to make this work.

Jules

It wasn't the first time I had received flowers, but it was definitely the first time I had ever shed a tear over them. The arrangement was beautiful, an assortment of yellow roses and lilies with a few lavender carnations mixed in. But it wasn't the colors nor the types that had me emotional, it was the sender along with scroll of the message attached to them.

Jules,
I couldn't remember which ones were your favorites, but I promise I was always paying attention. And even if I managed to drop the ball, I'm so proud you didn't do the same. Congratulations on finally getting that script, pretty girl. No one deserves it more than you. Because you deserve the world. Just make sure you let me screen the nigga who gets the opportunity to give it to you first. Ex-best friend privileges.
- Love, The Basketball Asswipe who couldn't see how good he had it.
PS: We're still volunteering for the holidays. BeBe's Kids need toys.

I laughed quietly as I swiped at the tears, thinking back to the time I had drunk-cried over *Bebe's Kids* in the first place. When Levi and I had really taken the time out to get to know each other, and ended up falling in love. Because that was the only reason this all hurt so bad; I loved him. We just… couldn't figure it out in time to really do something about it. Couldn't possibly draw a conclusion we were both unconsciously trying to avoid no matter how much it had already taken over.

Sure, Levi hadn't been bright about handling Layna. And sure, he still might've been a little more self-absorbed than I would've liked. But he wasn't a bad person. In fact, he was a pretty amazing individual, one I could count on for just about anything - *from tampons to gas money* - even now that he was states away.

But that was the thing. He wasn't just on the other side of the apartment anymore. He was a good five hours by car, hour and a half by flight away which meant no matter how much my anger had subsided, the damage was already done. Levi was going on about his life, doing what he loved, and I was supposed to be doing the same.

Still, while my actions followed that protocol, my mind couldn't help but wonder what if. Wonder if maybe it was possible to… start over, start fresh, with our new circumstances.

"*Girl, you're trippin…*" I thought to myself as I abandoned the flowers in the kitchen and headed to the living room, hoping to find something distracting to watch on TV. But when I turned it on, the only thing I saw was Levi smiling as the correspondent interviewed him after what had to be his first game - *first win* - with his new team.

"*Twenty-five points in only fifteen minutes of playing time is almost unheard of. What message were you trying to send to the coaches along with the rest of the league?*"

"*I just wanted to come out here and do what I love. Whatever the coaches pull from that, I'll gladly accept. I'm just happy to have the opportunity to be back on the court.*"

"*Well it's obvious the game missed you, though we were all a little surprised that Phoenix took a chance on you considering your checkered past. What do you think convinced them to go out on a limb and sign you to a 10-*"

day contract?"

"At the end of the day, we both want the same thing and that's to win ball games. Sometimes all it takes is a chance. A second chance, that is. And I definitely learned my lesson the hard way. When you love something as much as I love ... this game, you have to take good care of it. I will no longer take this opportunity, or any opportunity, for granted. That's for sure."

"Final question, what number are you going to negotiate for now that you have a little leverage after your performance tonight?"

"That's up to my agent and the front office. I'm just here to play ball."

I paused the TV just as Levi gave the interviewer another one of his signature full smiles, making me smile as I thought about how far he had come. When I first met him, he was down on his luck, broke, not to mention completely misunderstood. But this Levi, the Levi on screen, had come into his own. He was happy, secure in himself and proud of his work without requiring the validation of others. It wasn't about the money, or the fame, or the glory, it was about doing what he loved to do.

And I was beyond proud of that.

Before I could change my mind, I snagged my phone from the coffee table, scrolling through my contacts until I landed on his name that I thankfully hadn't deleted. My finger hovered over the screen as I processed everything that could go wrong in calling. But once I peeked up at the screen - *peeked up at Levi* - I realized it wasn't likely that he'd actually answer which meant I could leave a message without really having to talk to him.

As the phone rang in my ear, my heart raced as I thought about what I would do if he really were to answer. And I was grateful when I had actually survived long enough to get his voicemail, though I wasn't exactly sure what I was going to say once I got the beep signaling it was my turn.

"Uh… *hey.* It's Jules. I… I didn't really want anything in particular. Just wanted to tell you thank you for the flowers. And congratulations on the game. I didn't watch it, but I caught your interview and you… you looked great. I'm so happy for you. And I'm… rambling now, so I'm gonna… *oh God. It's you,*" I muttered as my phone chimed with an incoming call on the other line.

And I tried to stay calm as I clicked over to say, "Hello?"

Levi sounded completely energized, as if it was normal for me to be calling when he replied, "Hey pretty girl. Sorry I missed your call. I was doing my postgame press conference. Forgot how hectic this shit was."

"I bet. I, *uh*… I left you a message, but I guess I can repeat my thank you. For the flowers. And the note," I told him as I peeked back towards the kitchen where the flowers were still sitting.

"You know I got you, Jules. So damn proud of you. Everything been going well with that?" he asked, his background filled with what I could assume was a mix of locker room banter and sports reporters.

And I nodded as if he could see me when I answered, "Yeah. Everything is good. *Busy.* But good."

"That's what's up."

There was an awkward silence between us as Levi's background went quiet, like he had switched rooms for the purpose of being able to hear me better; to prolong the conversation. But no matter how good it felt to talk to him, to hear his voice, I couldn't help myself in attempting a grand escape by telling him, "Well I'll… get out of your hair. Just wanted to say thanks. And congratulations on the game. Glad you're making good on that second chance."

"Glad I have one to make good on. Seems to work well for me," he replied, his voice holding an extra hint of sweetness as if he was trying to make a point.

"Uh… right. *Oh,* and you can delete the message I left. It's not important anymore."

"Which means I'll listen to it a few times over and then save it just in case I never get one of these phone calls again," he added with a little chuckle before stopping my heart when he continued, "I… I miss you, Jules. And you don't have to say it back or anything. I just wanted to get it off of my chest while I had your ear."

I wanted to say it back. Saying it back would've been admitting the truth. But saying it back also meant being sucked back into Levi's aura which was the last thing I was prepared to handle. So instead I told him, "I'm glad you're doing well, Levi."

"Damn, lettin' me down easy, huh?" he asked with another laugh, quickly adding, "I'm just messing with you. But hey, maybe you can come check out one of my games. We'll be in your neck of the woods for the start of our three game road trip."

I gnawed at my lip as I took another peek at the TV screen, imagining the hopeful gaze on Levi's face as he waited for an answer. But I had to be completely honest when I replied, "I don't know if that's really a good idea, Levi."

Seeing him in person meant being reminded of the good times, the good feelings, the good… *everything*. But it felt like I had already lost the fight once Levi begged, "Aww come on. It's just a basketball game. And if it makes you feel better, Lily and the kids will be there too."

"I… *okay*."

"Okay?"

I nodded. "Yeah, I'll come. When is the game?"

"Day after tomorrow."

"Oh wow. That's soon," I replied, processing how much I would have to get done in such a small amount of time. I mean, it wasn't nearly long enough to prepare myself emotionally, get a mani and pedi, let alone get my weave tightened up.

"Is that a problem? You already have plans? Too busy for an old friend?"

I closed my eyes, shaking my head as I answered, "Nah, it's not a problem. I'll be there."

"Bet. I'll leave you two tickets at Will Call just in case you have a new friend you want to bring."

I smacked my teeth instantly, knowing he was offering just to hear me reply, "I don't move that fast, Levi."

And he even had the nerve to give me another one of his little chuckles before he said, "I'm glad to hear it, pretty girl. Looking forward to seeing you."

"And I'm looking forward to seeing you get dunked on by the home team," I teased, peeking up at the screen once again and imagining Levi having the same smiling reaction to my words in person.

"Ahh, you got jokes, huh?"

I shrugged. "Maybe a couple."

"Well maybe we can... *I don't know*. Do dinner or something. After the game?"

Internally, I swooned. But outwardly, I knew it was in my best interest to pump the breaks when I answered, "Now you're pushing it."

"Can't blame a nigga for trying though," he offered, far from defeated as I originally expected him to be. But then again, this was Levi. He was the king of working harder, pushing through, finding a way; something I honestly admired about him especially now that it had all truly paid off.

So I couldn't help but smile when I replied, "You're right. I can't. You've always had a way of getting things to go in your favor."

"Well it sounds like I need to brush up on my skills."

I rolled my eyes, still grinning as I suggested, "You worry about basketball, and I'll see you in a couple of days."

"Can't wait, pretty girl," he said before he ended the call. And while I wanted to sit there basking in aura of light created from a simple conversation, I knew I had more important things to do.

Like finding something to wear.

I was nervous.

The game was tied, and Levi's team - *Levi* - had the ball as the clock ticked down to the last few seconds. It had been a tight one all game, the two teams trading the lead back and forth up until now where things were all even. But it was now or never as Levi took off towards the rim, stopping just short of the free throw line to take the final shot just as the buzzer went off.

All net.

Even though it was an away game, the crowd still went nuts in excitement as Levi's team rushed to celebrate with him on the court. And I didn't really have a choice but to join in the fun once Lily, who was also holding Anastasia, pulled me into a hug and screamed,

"That's my brother!" While Andre and Adrian did their own little celebration below us.

I watched intently as the courtside reporter slipped

through the crowd of players to pull Levi to the side for a quick postgame interview, completely enthralled as he gave a few short answers before the reporter sent him on his way. But he didn't get too far once he heard the twins screaming, "Uncle Levi! Uncle Levi!"

He turned our way with a smile, pulling the headband from his head and tossing it to the boys which they immediately began to fight over. Then he looked at me, and his smile seemed to grow even larger as he gave a little wink just as his coach wrapped an arm around his shoulder to escort him towards the locker room, though Levi was sure to shake a few hands and sign a few autographs along the way.

I tried to keep calm, act like I had imagined the whole thing until I heard Lily ask, "You know ya'll aren't slick, right?"

"I can't say I know what you're talking about," I replied, avoiding her eyes as I grabbed the bucket of popcorn I had been snacking on throughout the game, planning to throw it away on my way out.

But Lily wasn't letting me off that easy as she adjusted Anastasia on her hip before she said, "Jules, I saw the wink. I saw the way he looked at you. And I damn sure saw the way you looked at him."

I shrugged, adjusting the denim jacket I wore over my dress as I explained, "I'm happy for him. They won the game. He hit the gamewinner. He…"

"Is just as in love with you as you are with him. And I wish you guys would stop making it so damn complicated."

I released a heavy sigh, thinking about what kind of conversations Levi could've possibly had with his sister for her to have drawn such a conclusion. But regardless of its truth, fact of the matter was, "Lily, it's really not that simple. A lot has happened. A lot that can't be forgotten."

"So you decked Layna in the face. She's clearly moved on from that," she replied with a nod, forcing me to turn around to find Layna leaving the arena with the rest of the crowd, holding hands with her latest victim. And while I wanted to be annoyed, wanted to tell homeboy to steer clear, I couldn't say anything as Lily continued, "Now I know my brother isn't perfect. He's proven that on a national scale, on a national level. But you and I both know he's worth the trouble. He's a good person, Jules. And he really cares about you."

Again, I knew she was telling the truth. While Levi had always made it clear that he cared about himself and his career - *as he should* -, he had also done plenty to prove that I was just as important to him. Even now when he was so focused on solidifying his spot on the team, he made sure to take a little time out to show me love by sending flowers.

Still, I found myself making excuses like, "It's too late, Lily. He's in a different city now, and..."

She grabbed my shoulder, cutting me off to say, "You're here. You showed up. So that has to mean something, right?"

I shrugged, gnawing at my lip as I told her, "He asked and I didn't have anything in particular to do."

The little chuckle she let out in response reminded me of her brother's. "Girl, you're even more stubborn than I thought."

"So what am I supposed to do, Lily? Just... start over, act like none of it ever happened, be in a long distance relationship with the person I couldn't even be in a relationship with when he stayed right across the living room from me?"

It sounded even more foolish now that I had said it out loud, not to mention the fact that I was asking his sister of all people. And I was hardly surprised when she suggested, "When you want something, you make it work. You figure it out."

"Jesus Christ, was that written on the refrigerator when you guys were growing up or what?"

Again, Lily gave that oh-so-familiar chuckle. "The Grahams are a persistent bunch. Now come on so we can catch Levi after his postgame press conference."

I tensed up instantly. "*What*? That wasn't in the plans. I was just going to… go home. Maybe shoot him a text later."

Lily grabbed my hand with her free one, already making her way out of the seats we had watched the game from when she replied, "He wants to see you. And I know you want to see him."

My steps were a lot slower than hers, forcing her to practically drag me down the aisle when I whined, "But I don't even know what to say."

She stopped to turn my way just as she hit the stairs, giving me a genuine smile when she insisted, "Just tell him how you feel, Jules. Trust me, he's itching to do the same." Then she peeked past me, locking eyes with the twins to tell them, "Adrian and Andre stay close. Matter of fact, hold Jules's hand."

My eyes went wide as I felt a sticky hand slip into mine before being yanked away just as quickly. "I wanna hold that hand!" one of the boys shouted as he slid his equally sticky hand into mine.

And while I was already grossed out by the mystery adhesive, I knew the only way we could solve the problem was if I reminded them, "Uh… I have two hands, boys."

I stepped out of the row to let Adrian get in front of me so that he could take the hand his mother had originally been guiding me with. And with Andre on my other side, it felt like I had personal escorts as we made our way onto the court to wait for Levi which brought on a new bout of nerves.

I tried to distract myself with just about anything; the size of the now mostly-emptied arena from court view, the distance between the baskets, the two boys arguing at my sides, and... *oh snap, who is that?*

I didn't want to make my snooping obvious, but there was no ignoring the way Lily looked completely enamored with whoever the guy she was talking to. And I certainly couldn't blame her cause he was fine as hell, his suit perfectly tailored to his frame and paired with designer shoes I couldn't place a brand on from the distance.

But they were *definitely* designer.

I watched closely as he pinched Anastasia's cheek, obviously familiar with her considering the way she immediately giggled in response. And then he looked at her mother - I mean, he *looked* at her mother - giving her all types of panty-wetting mannerisms as he brushed his thumb against her cheek before leaning in for a kiss.

Until he wasn't.

And I didn't understand what had happened until I saw Levi emerge from the tunnel, freshly showered with a bag over his shoulder and headphones draped around his neck as he approached the pair that now looked completely frazzled; completely disconnected. He shook hands with the guy, exchanging a few words before turning his attention to Lily to give her and Anastasia a hug. And then his eyes were on me, and it felt like I stopped breathing for a second as he excused himself to head my way.

Well... head *our* way considering he also had two anxious nephews to greet. And they could hardly contain themselves as they let my hand go to dash his way, screaming, "Uncle Levi!"

He pulled them both into a hug, scrubbing their heads before telling them to go wait with their mom. And then it was back to me as I balanced on my heels, trying not to melt under his heavy gaze. The closer he got, the weaker I felt as I became immersed in his scent, a scent I had missed like crazy since he moved out, especially now that it was beginning to rub off of his t-shirts that I still slept in.

But it was now or never as I faced him straight up, trying to find the words and somehow coming up with, "That was a great game. You were… *amazing.*"

He smiled proudly, licking his lips to reply, "Yeah. I'm glad you showed up. Must be my good luck charm."

I tried not to blush, but it was practically inevitable considering Charmer Levi was in full effect. Still, I managed to at least avoid his eyes when I told him, "I don't know about all that, but I'll take it for now."

"Thank you for coming. *Seriously.* I know you have a lot going on right now and…"

I cut him off, peeking up to remind him, "You make time for what you want."

But it turned out that that simple eye contact was my biggest mistake considering the way Levi's eyes bored into mine, looking right past the friendly facade I was trying to put up and digging into the one he knew best as he took a step closer and said, "Jules, there's so much I wanna say to you, so much I *need* to say to you."

"So say it."

My heart was already pounding through my ears as the arena suddenly felt even more empty; only he and I as I waited for his response. And while I had a strong feeling I knew what his words would be, there was nothing that could've prepared me for actually hearing them out loud when he took my still sticky hand to say, "I love you, Jules. I've been in love with you. And being away from you has only made that fact even more clear for me. But I know things are different now. I know we're both in a different space, trying to get our solo shit figured out, and…"

"I love you too."

"You do?" he asked, almost as surprised as I was with how easily it had slipped off of my tongue. But it was the truth. It had always been the truth.

So I had no problem admitting for a second time, "I do."

"So what are we supposed to do about it, pretty girl?" he asked in a voice just above a whisper as he wrapped an arm around my lower back.

I smiled as I tilted my head back to meet his eyes. "Well… for starters, you can tell me about your new life in Phoenix so far, and I can update you on mine here. Maybe over a quick bite to eat since I'm sure you have a plane to catch. And when you land, you can FaceTime me until we fall asleep."

"What if I can't sleep? Shits been a struggle without your hot ass all over me," he said as he pulled me in tighter, landing a kiss on my forehead.

A kiss that I completely savored as I answered, "Then I guess we'll have to try something else to knock you out until you can come see me again. You know, get creative."

"I'll be on the first flight here after these last two games. I can promise you that," he said with a sneaky little smirk, letting me know exactly what was on his mind.

"Can you promise me something else?"

"What's that?" he asked, landing another quick kiss on my forehead.

And while his lips against my skin were quite the

distractor, I was sure to be clear when I answered, "Promise that you'll always have my back. No matter how tough things get."

"That's never changed."

"And promise that you'll break up with me before you even think about cheating because I don't play that shit."

His little chuckle warmed my skin when he replied, "Jules, I just got your ass back. Why would I already be thinking about messing it up?"

"I'm just saying. I've already delivered one fade behind your ass, and even that was too many."

"Well can you promise me something?" he asked, his expression hopeful as if he was going to make a serious request. But when I gave him a nod to continue, I could only laugh once I heard him add, "Promise you'll give all of my damn t-shirts back."

"Oh, whatever! You know you love when I wear your clothes."

"Yeah, until my ass is running around here naked cause I'm all out of stuff to wear," he replied, making me laugh even harder.

Though I had no problem telling him, "Guess you'll just have to buy new ones with the money you'll get off of this new contract."

If there was any truth to the numbers being thrown around on the various sports networks about how much money Levi could earn when Phoenix decided to extend his contract, he would be able to buy much more than just a few replacement t-shirts. But to my surprise he only shrugged when he replied, "The money will come when it comes. Right now, my focus is on you and playing ball. Everything else is a bonus."

"Wait a minute. Did I just come first on that list? Me *and then* basketball?" I asked teasingly, knowing it was surely just a coincidence.

But Levi's expression was completely serious when he looked down at me and answered, "That arrangement wasn't by accident. Just like our arrangement wasn't by accident. You knew exactly what you were doing when you approved me to be your roommate."

"Falling in love with you was *definitely* an accident," I admitted as I snuggled in a little closer, my heart full as he rested his chin in my hair.

Though I could only shake my head when I heard him reply, "I'm Levi Graham. What's not to love?"

"Oh God. Here you go..." I groaned, following it up with a laugh.

"I'm just messing with you, pretty girl. You changed me for the better and now I'm ready to move forward. You with me?"

I nodded. "Yeah. I'm with you."

"Even when it's tough and I'm getting on your nerves?" he asked as he let me go to wrap an arm around my shoulder, leading us towards where Lily, Damien, and the kids were still standing.

And this time, I rolled my eyes as I reminded him, "There's never been a time when you didn't get on my nerves."

"*See*. And you're still around, holdin' it down. How could I not love you?"

Again, I laughed. "You're crazy, Mr. Graham."

"Crazy about you, Ms. Tyler," he muttered just as we joined the rest of the group.

Of course Lily was all smiles when she said, "*See*. Aren't you glad you stayed, Jules?"

"Stayed to see the two of you? I sure am," I told her with a smile of my own, though I certainly wasn't expecting the rush of panic that ran across her face from my words.

But it made complete sense once Levi stepped away from me to ask, "The two of you? What is she talking about, Lily?"

"Uh… nothing," Lily stammered in response, turning the guy's way to continue, "Nothing. Right, Damien?"

But instead of agreeing, the guy only shrugged. "Lily, just tell him. He should know."

Lily released a heavy sigh, adjusting Anastasia on her hip as she turned Levi's way to say, "Damien and I are… seeing each other. Have been seeing each other. For a few weeks now."

"A few weeks?" Levi asked, obviously surprised by his sister's admission.

And she only added to it when she replied, "Maybe months…"

"All of this time I thought you two hated each other and ya'll were actually boning behind my back?"

"Hey man! There's kids around," Damien said as he made an attempt to cover the twins' ears, though they were already busy snickering to each other as if they knew what their uncle was talking about.

And it didn't seem as if Levi cared either way as he continued, "Well I'm sure the kids were around when it was happening too. That apartment isn't that damn big."

Thankfully, Lily stepped in, taking full control of the conversation when she said, "Anyway! We're both adults who can do what we want. Just like you and Jules are adults who can do what you want."

Damien nodded, wrapping an arm around Lily's shoulder to agree. "That's right. And this doesn't affect our business relationship by any means. I'm still your agent, still going to do right by you as my client."

"As long as you don't accidentally create a little conflict of interest with my sister. Her clan is already complete, bruh."

Lily brushed him off with a wave of her hand. "Oh shut up, Levi. You worry about you and Jules. Damien and I are just fine."

"So are we. Isn't that right, pretty girl?" he asked as he wrapped me in an embrace.

And even though it had been quite a ride, even though I wasn't exactly sure what would come of it, there was no doubt in my mind that we would make the best of wherever we found ourselves when I nodded my head and told him, "Absolutely."

Epilogue.
Christmas Eve.

Levi

Jules was the happiest I had ever seen her as she handed over a Barbie to a little girl who looked just like LaShawn from *Bebe's Kids*, giving her a big hug before inviting the next kid up to pick a gift. I was grateful to have all hands on deck - Lily and Damien, Wes and Chloe, Elizabeth and Marcus, along with a few others - for my first charity event under the Graham Family Foundation that I had put Lily in charge of. But my work wasn't done until I was able to give Jules her Christmas gift in the form of a new group of hands that had just arrived.

I was honestly a little nervous for what her reaction would be, nervous about if she would even recognize our special guests since she hadn't seen them in so long. But there was no turning back as I sent the youngest one - *Jacob* - to tap his big sister's shoulder.

It took a while for her to react. But when she did, she grabbed the attention of the whole building as she screamed, wrapping her arms around his neck before pulling away to take a better look at him while the other two - *Joseph and John* - snuck up behind her. And once he directed her to check them out, it elicited an even louder scream as she pulled them both into a hug so tight I was sure they would burst.

I watched from afar as she wiped the tears from her face, excusing herself from her post as she pulled her little brothers to the side, giving them another set of hugs while she asked them all an assortment of questions. And I could pretty much assume what question she had asked when they all pointed at me in response.

Her smile bloomed even larger as she left them to head my way, already rattling off, "How did you… where did you… when did you…?"

And I caught her in a hug as I told her, "You make time for what you want. And I wanted to give my girl the best Christmas ever."

"I can't thank you enough, Levi. I… I missed them so much," she whispered through her sniffles.

And I made myself busy wiping her tears away as I told her, "I know you did, baby. Which is exactly why they'll be out here for a week to spend time with you. My treat."

"*Wow*. That's… I don't know what to say."

"You can tell me how much you love me and stuff. That always works," I replied with a smirk as I pulled her even tighter.

She smacked her teeth, brushing a hand against my chest as she said, "You know I love you, crazy. But now my gift feels… *silly*."

"No such thing, pretty girl. What'd you get me? Lingerie?" I asked teasingly, taking a little pinch at her butt that was turned away from the crowd.

But she still jumped away in response, giggling as she dug in her pocket and pulled out a little box. "No. I got you this."

I wasted no time pulling the top off, though I was a little confused when I found…, "A key?"

She nodded, smiling as she clarified, "Your key. To our apartment. I renewed the lease."

"So I actually have a place to call home again?" I asked as I pulled her back into an embrace, giving her a quick kiss to thank her.

And as she rested her hands on my chest, she replied, "You've always had a place to call home, Levi. I mean, it's not like you didn't pay your half of the rent. You could've always came back if you had to."

While I knew she was telling the truth, I also knew my truth was a little different as I explained, "It's not about the rent, Jules. Home is wherever you are. And I'm glad you've welcomed me back."

"Well I'm glad you accepted my invitation."

"Why wouldn't I? You're Jules Tyler. Superstar in the making. Gotta hop on the bandwagon while there's still room," I told her teasingly as I gave her a little kiss on her forehead, just the way she liked it.

And as my lips lingered on her skin, she replied, "You're gonna mess around and make me get a big head like you did."

"And I'll be the first one to humble you just like you did me with your mean ass," I joked, making her laugh before I insisted, "Now get back to your brothers. They've been looking forward to seeing you."

Jules got on her tippy toes, getting as close as she could to my face when she said, "I love you so much, Levi."

"I love you too, baby. Merry Christmas."

She gave me a quick kiss before she skipped off back towards her brothers, leaving me to take in the scene in front of me.

I was surrounded by people who I knew all cared about me just as much as I cared about them, I had found the girl of my dreams in Jules, and I had my career back to the point where I was able to make a difference in the lives of others.

It was much more than I could've asked for, more than I could've even imagined just a few months ago. But it definitely proved one thing. When you work hard, push through, and do everything in your power to make it work, you can have anything you want.

The End.

Enjoyed this book?
Please leave a review on
Amazon or Goodreads!

To stay up-to-date with all
of Alexandra Warren's
happenings including samples
and excerpts, visit
actuallyitsalexandra.com or
like her Facebook page!

More Books by Alexandra Warren

Attractions & Distractions
Series
Getting The Edge
An Unconventional Love
The PreGame Ritual
Distracted
The Real Deal
A Rehearsal For Love
Love at First Spite
In Spite of it All

72056287R00168

Made in the USA
Columbia, SC
14 June 2017